*Two action-packed
novels of
the American West!*

SIGNET BRAND DOUBLE WESTERNS:

Rich Man's Range

and

Gun Code

D1231226

Other Westerns from SIGNET

Rich Man's Range

by
JOHN REESE

and

GUN CODE

by
PHILIP KETCHUM

A SIGNET BOOK
NEW AMERICAN LIBRARY
TIMES MIRROR

SIGNET TRADEMARK REG. U.S. PAT. OFF. AND FOREIGN COUNTRIES
REGISTERED TRADEMARK—MARCA REGISTRADA
HECHO EN CHICAGO, U.S.A.

SIGNET, SIGNET CLASSICS, MENTOR, PLUME AND MERIDIAN BOOKS
are published by The New American Library, Inc.,
1301 Avenue of the Americas, New York, New York 10019

First Printing (Double Western Edition), September, 1978

1 2 3 4 5 6 7 8 9

PRINTED IN THE UNITED STATES OF AMERICA

Rich Man's Range

by

JOHN REESE

For Paul G. Hunter

Chapter One

THE STAGE came into Strickland, Texas, at 2:30 P.M. on a day early in May, 1889. The four fine horses were running wildly. To judge by the sweat that soaked them, they had been on the gallop for miles. Behind the stage and tied to it, ran a horse with the stirrups tied over the saddle. It bore a Mexican brand.

George Merrit, seeing the changes in the town as the stage flew through it, wished he had felt up to riding on the box with the driver. But his wounded leg needed all the kindness he could give it. That business back at the creek, which had startled the four-horse team, had opened the wound again. It had a burning sensation that he did not like.

I wouldn't know the town, he thought. Eight years. Why, the whole shebang is new. . . .

The driver hauled in the spent team in front of the brand-new Empire Hotel. Across from the Empire, on its own block, stood the equally brand-new courthouse. Some new stores—most of them made of wood. Adobe had been favored when Merrit was here last.

There were four men in the coach besides Merrit. One, a plump man in a black suit, offered his hand as the stage door was opened. "Believe I speak for all of us when I thank you, sir," he said. "There could have been real trouble back there."

"Guess so," Merrit said. "The urge to chivaree the stagecoach comes over them cowboys now and then. It's a dull life they lead."

"You're just as well as dead when they mean it. Will you go first, sir?"

7

Merrit shook his head. "Thank you. I'm cherishing some saddle sores, if you don't mind."

The other four passengers got out. The spokesman said, "Ask the druggist for some astringent powder. Dust it on after a bath. A doctor would charge you two dollars for the prescription. I sell drugs. I know."

Merrit thanked him and got out carefully. He was pleased to discover that he could stand, and even walk, without betraying his wound. The stage driver had handed his lines to a hostler and was waiting for Merrit. "Thanks," he said. "You're George Merrit, ain't you? Didn't recognize you."

"It was eight years ago."

The driver cleared his throat. "If I'm not out of line, I'd like to return a favor. Like to pass the word on what happened there at the creek. If it's known you can handle a little thirty-eight like that, it might save you proving it."

"You take a lot of interest in me."

"You're a rich man now. All you have to do is collect it, and then live to enjoy it. Shall I have your valise took in?"

Merrit looked at the new Empire. "This looks pretty slick for me. Is the Speece House still running?"

"Well, it's not where you'd register your old maid aunt, if you know what I mean."

A smile flitted across Merrit's thin, dark face, which needed a shave badly. "I know what you mean. I'll go there anyway."

"I'll send your grip over and have your horse put up. Anything else I can do?"

"There's a lawyer, name of Newton Price. . . ."

"Yonder, facing the courthouse. This time of day he's generally home, toes up. He drinks a mite."

"I never worry about another man's vices."

"Right. But facts are facts. I owe you one. I never had passengers shot up yet."

They shook hands. Merrit started walking. He felt the moisture from the wound on his leg, and it worried him, but the movement eased the pain. He turned a corner, walked a block, and was on familiar ground—the old part of Strickland. The Speece House, a long, low building, had not visibly gone to seed, but there were now heavy curtains at all the windows and the shades were all drawn. There was no hitch rail in front of the building now; it had been moved to the alley behind.

But the Palace Bar, across the street, appeared unchanged. It was empty when Merrit walked in. Billy O'Shea came out of the back room, yawning. His yawn vanished, and he rumpled his white hair with the old, familiar gesture when he recognized Merrit.

"Finally!" O'Shea said with pleasure, offering his hand. "You were a hard man to find."

"I was to hell and gone, down in Sonora, mining on the Yaqui River."

"Do any good?"

"Wages. Maybe a little better."

"How'd you hear?"

"Saw an ad in a paper wrapped around a side of bacon. I wrote to this fellow Price. He said to come on."

"You're a rich man, Merrit. How does it feel?"

"Price said nothing about values in his letter. When I left here eight years ago, it was a poor man's range. I hear there's a railroad coming."

"You can believe it. They're grading on the Keller place —your place—now. Be here before snow flies."

Merrit pointed to a bottle. O'Shea set it out, and Merrit poured himself a drink. "There's always so much talk about railroads. That's all most of it is. Talk."

"This is not talk. Look, Merrit," O'Shea said earnestly, "this is what it means to the Twenty Plus. They can ship four thousand head this fall. Suppose we get one more good rain, and they can ship fat. Suppose they can drive to railhead without walking the fat off, what does it mean? Five dollars a head extra."

"Twenty thousand dollars!" Merrit whistled. "The Twenty Plus still owned by the British syndicate?"

"Yes, but it's got a new manager. Aaron Davidson."

"What's he like?"

"Why?"

"Billy, four boys on Twenty Plus horses tried to chivaree the stage today. It wasn't much. I shot one fellow's hat off. Nobody hurt. If that outfit's going to be my neighbor, I'd like to know if this is all their cowboys have got to do."

O'Shea rubbed his face thoughtfully. "Leave me out of it,

will you? I don't take sides. Of course, there's a lot of talk. . . ."

"What kind of talk, Billy?"

O'Shea said, "I'm not taking sides, Merrit. But Dick Keller's widow inherited half of the PK from him. The other half's yours now. People remember how he met her. She's still a widow. Naturally there's gossip."

"I had better not hear any of it."

O'Shea seemed to make up his mind. "When you left here, we were all one short jump from broke. We've had some wet years, and now the railroad. The Englishmen who own the Twenty Plus stuck it out through Indians and politics and drought. Now they mean to cash in. The railroad's going to be on the PK—your land. If you wanted to take ten or fifteen thousand for your undivided half interest in the PK, you probably could get it right now."

"That much!" Merrit caught his breath. "I don't see why. What's a few miles?"

"Leave me out of it, but it's easy to figure. I told you they could ship four thousand head this fall. If they had the PK land, they could ship seventy-five hundred next year."

"I see."

"They want the railroad on their land. Maybe you wouldn't fence them off from it. But I'm not saying they wouldn't fence you off if that line was resurveyed."

Merrit thought it over. "Do you know a fellow by the name of Harmon Griffin?"

"He's a good man, Merrit. Works for the Twenty Plus."

"I used to know him. In Chihuahua. Some years back. Fellow who laughs—you know, giggles—when he gets excited."

"That's the man. Why?"

"I think I recognized that giggle this afternoon. Those boys who tried to rough up the stage. The Harmon Griffin I remember liked his fun, but something like this proposition this afternoon would strike him as plain silly. What I wonder is —was he ordered to do it? And why?"

"Leave me out of it, but you could be right. They tell me Aaron Davidson has a percentage deal with the Britishers. What would you do if you were a raggedy-pants rider and somebody gave you a chance to make yourself fifteen or twenty thousand dollars in the next few years? You'd try anything, wouldn't you? Look, Dick Keller was shot——"

"In the back, I hear."

"That's what you'll hear, yes."

"Before or after it was known that the railroad was coming through?" O'Shea just shrugged. Merrit smiled and said, "That answers my question. Where'd it happen?"

O'Shea pointed. "Back of the Speece House."

"Well, well, well! Who runs it now?"

"Woman by the name of Albine Anderson. I hope I'm not going to get credited with any of this information you picked up in here," O'Shea said. "The Twenty Plus runs a big crew. A big one! Good customers, but they'd make bad enemies."

"Billy, you know me better than that, don't you?"

"I'd forgotten," Billy said.

Merrit crossed to the Speece House and opened the front door. The lobby looked the same. A slender woman, plain-faced yet somehow handsome, was sitting behind the low desk in a rocking chair, knitting. She nodded toward Merrit's valise, which was on the desk.

"I'm afraid we're full up," she said. "I told the boy not to leave your satchel, but he did anyway. Sorry."

Merrit smiled at her. "If my name was John Smith, would you have room for me?"

"Don't drag me into this!" she snapped.

"You just dragged yourself in. When you turn down a traveler, you're taking sides, ma'am." Merrit pulled the register to him and turned it around to read it. "Your last registration is two months old. You're careless about the inn-keeping laws."

He wrote "George F. Merrit" and the date. The woman put her knitting down. "For how long?" she asked wearily.

"That depends, mother."

She almost smiled. "Mother, your foot. Listen, Merrit, the Twenty Plus has forty hands. Do you want me to pick a fight with the biggest outfit here? My girls won't bother you, but don't go out of your way to be unpopular. Take number six."

He thanked her and carried his grip down the hall to number 6. He bolted the door behind him, dropped his pants and drawers, and removed the wet bandage from his wound.

The bullet hole was on the inside of his thigh, three inches below his groin. It was oozing slightly, but the exudate looked pink and watery, with no sign of pus.

Well, he told himself, that's a relief! She's going to heal clean, from the inside out. I hope the son-of-a-bitch that did it is smelling by now. . . .

. . . He came up from Sonora fast, in his pocket a greasy piece from a Texas weekly newspaper: "Anyone knowing the whereabouts of George Fallon Merrit will oblige him by notifying him to communicate with Newton Price, Atty., Strickland, Tex. He is legatee under the last will and testament of Grace M. Keller, deceased."

. . . Next to his skin was a money belt containing $3,200 in gold certificates that represented a year of the hardest kind of work in a desert hardrock gold mine. He had no idea what Ma Keller had left him. Not much, probably, but he had to find out. Her late husband had left half the ranch to her, half to their son Richard. He didn't know then—when he saw the paper—that Dick was dead. But he did know that the Kellers had been land-poor. That old woman would have sold her immortal soul to hold the PK together.

. . . Merrit's reasons for coming were dim, dark ones that he did not quite admit, even to himself. But in the back of his mind a refrain beat and pounded—the woman, the woman, the damned woman who had been his and then Dick Keller's. Where did she fit into this?

. . . He rode by way of Ballard's place, near Yuma, to collect the money Ballard had borrowed. When he rode out, he had had more than $4,400 in the money belt. Maybe others besides Ballard knew about it. Maybe! And maybe somebody just did not want to see him reach Strickland, Texas.

. . . Streams were scarce there, but he knew them all. He was lucky, hearing the ring of shod hoofs on the ford just as it came on daylight. He hauled back on his horse as a Mexican rider blundered out of the brush. The Mexican had not expected Merrit so soon. He was carrying a rifle in his right hand. He fired it like a pistol, too quickly—a high shot that squalled off through the brush. Merrit dug in his spurs. His horse slammed into the Mexican's bony little pony. Merrit got his hands on the rifle and swung it like a club.

. . . He thought the Mexican was going for a knife—until he heard the crack of a pistol and felt the burn in his leg. I'm a ruined man, he thought. He broke the rifle over the Mexican's head. The Mexican's wild horse broke loose. Merrit fired two shots after him with his .45 before he piled off his horse to see how badly he had been hurt. . . .

In number 6 at the Speece House, Merrit wrapped a fresh bandage around his leg, pinning a pad under it first.

Ballard put him up to it he thought. I'm sure it was the money they were after. But it's a rimfire cinch I'm far from welcome here. It would've been too damn lucky for somebody if I'd never showed up, if I'd been bushwhacked and buried where I got this wound. . . .

The Twenty Plus? What was the name of the fellow Billy said had a percentage deal, running the outfit for the British syndicate? Aaron Davidson. That was it.

Whoever he was, Davidson had this town of Strickland whip-broke and hobbled. But where did the woman—the woman who was now Dick Keller's widow—where did she fit in?

Something wild and directionless, like a tornado, went through Merrit as a face, which he thought he had forgotten, came sharp-etched into his mind. He had to know. All right, why not now? The day was young.

He put the .38 in his valise and took out his holstered .45. He pulled on a fresh shirt and went out. Number 8, the door next to his room, was open, and a woman, neither old nor young, was leaning against the frame. She smiled at him.

"Hello there," she said.

He smiled back. "Didn't Albine tell you? You're not supposed to bother me."

She nodded. "I'm not bothering you. You're Merrit, aren't you? I just don't like that son-of-a-bitch of an Aaron Davidson. You don't need to tell him I said that, but that's how it is. He is a mean man. Mad-dog mean, snake-mean, tarantula-mean."

"It takes all kinds," Merrit said. "If you mean, don't expect a fair fight——"

"That's it."

"I never do. If it'll comfort you, I can be mean, too. Fighting like a gentleman is all right, but if the other fellow don't take any stock in it, why neither do I. So don't worry about me. What's your name?"

"Bessie." She lay a hand on his arm. "Maybe you're as good as you think you are. I've wished to God I'd never seen this town many a time. Now all I wish is that I could get out with the little money I've saved. If it comes to where you have to run for it, Merrit, take me with you, will you? Just get me out of here!"

The woman was afraid to stay, still more afraid to go. "I'll remember that, Bessie," Merrit said, with only half his mind on his words. Life in the last few years had taught him to take it easy, slow down, and look around carefully before he started jumping to conclusions. There was time to study things out that way. But the other woman—the one whose face was now no longer so sharp-etched in his mind—was a disturbing fever in him.

He walked swiftly on down the hall. Bessie frowned at him, shaking her head. Just before he vanished into the lobby she called after him, "I doubt you're up to it, Merrit. You're just a cow-camp tough. It ain't enough." Merrit did not even hear her. The weakness she sensed in him—the other woman —had taken possession of him body and soul.

Chapter Two

THERE WAS lots of daylight left as he got his horse out of the town stable and cantered out of town. His wound was nothing more than a trifling sting.

Immediately he was on the Keller range, riding beside a strong barbwire fence across which he could see fat Keller critters. The brand—the backward P and upright K—he remembered as something from another life. Lord, how he had worked in those days! "My good right arm," Ma Keller used to call him.

Merrit smiled. Ma could turn the tears, the smiles, and the kisses off and on like a spigot in a keg. She was a brute under all that fat, though. She had to be, with her husband dead and her son a worthless brat. It took a battleax.

He let the horse run it out, and in less than two hours he saw the windmills and the cottonwood grove. The trees had grown, and their pale spring foliage made a homey picture against the darkening sky. Merrit felt a quickening of his nerves, as well as a wild desire, as old memories ate into his guts. He cursed himself silently, saying, The hell with Bonnie. I'm over her. . . .

Not a soul was to be seen on the place. He tied his horse up under one of the cottonwoods, went through a wooden gate, crossed a bare but well-raked yard, and stepped up onto a long, low roofed galerie with a tile floor. Ma's plants still grew in their rows of clay pots along the edge, where they could catch the morning sun. The place had been kept up, he decided. The main difference was the quiet. Ma Keller had been a noisy woman, and she had attracted noise.

A Mexican girl answered his knock. He spoke to her in Spanish, which came as easily to his tongue as English: "Is Señora Keller here? Say that it is Merrit."

She repeated his name to make sure she had it, then closed the door in his face. But a moment later she reappeared and invited him inside gravely. He refused a chair and remained standing, holding his hat.

He could not tell in what way this big room was different. Same furniture. Standing in the same places. Maybe it was the neatness. The big fireplace had been swept. He couldn't picture anyone mending a saddle here, or. . . .

"George!"

He turned carefully, saying, "Hello there, Bonnie."

It took all his self-control. She was as white-skinned as ever, with the same towhead-blond hair and the same wide-set almond-shaped blue eyes. She looked no older than when he had first seen her as a white-trash kid of sixteen, trying wildly to break out of the family poverty and the mover's wagons that symbolized it. The riffraff she was born into called themselves horse-traders, but anything they had that was worth trading was stolen. Their men were deadbeats, thieves, so lazy they stank. Their women were tramps.

He had rescued this woman from that, but he had never gotten around to marrying her. Dick Keller beat him to that.

"All right, you've seen me," Bonnie said. "What are you waiting for? Say it!"

He recoiled from something in her tone. "Say what? What have I done to you?"

"You've got a nerve to ask that!"

He shook his head. "I mean it, Bonnie. What did I do?"

"You sold out! Sold the PK to those dirty thieves at the Twenty Plus! There's no name low enough for you. Will you get out? Or shall I have you run out?"

He said, "I doubt if you've got men enough to do it. I hear I own half of this, Bonnie. My days of giving up what's mine ended eight years ago. And you know what I mean!"

She came across the room and swung to slap him. He caught first one then the other hand in his and held her off. Her movement and presence struck so deep that his arms felt weak. Partly it was her clean, soapy smell and the clean hair that was so fanatically cared for—Bonnie had had dirt enough in her childhood. And it was more than that. There was something deeply, mystically moving about her—a wounded look in her eye, a pain she had never stopped feeling, and that he always used to feel with her.

They struggled silently. He had to hurt her arms to subdue her. He clung to her hands, and made her face him and listen. "You've lost your mind, Bonnie. I haven't sold anything to anybody."

She stopped resisting, but she still panted. "I don't believe you!"

"But you'll believe anything anybody else tells you. You're a fool!"

"You really didn't sell? But Aaron Davidson said——"

"I never heard that name in my life until today."

"But . . . but you . . . but he told me he sent you the papers. He said as soon as they got back——"

"And you fell for it!"

She crumpled suddenly, began crying, and fell against him. Her thin strong arms caught his at his sides and pinioned them. He winced as her weight came down on his bad leg. He dropped his hat and shifted to spare the leg.

Otherwise he did not move, because the feel of her sent him too close to total surrender.

He saved himself by thinking coldly, This little tramp, this movers' brat . . . white-trash . . . cheating little bum . . . never again can she make a fool of me. . . .

She seemed to feel his impassive resentment. She let go of him, stepped back, and looked up at him. With the backs of her hands she wiped away the tears, a childish act he also remembered well. "I—I had no way of knowing, George," she said.

"You do now."

"Oh, why didn't Newt Price tell me you were coming?"

"He didn't know. I had no way myself of knowing when I'd get here. I haven't seen him yet. I understand this is his time of day to be drunk. I don't know what I'm here for, Bonnie, except that Price told me I'm heir to Ma Keller's undivided half interest."

She withdrew a step from him. It seemed to him that her mind and her heart moved back half a world at the same time. "Yes, an undivided half. To split it, we have to agree to a fair division. Until then, Newt says, we're partners."

"I see. We were partners once before."

"Don't throw that up to me!" she flared.

"What's to throw up to you? I didn't get around to marrying you. Dick did."

"Let's get it straight, George," she said calmly. "Marrying me wouldn't have helped. You made fifteen dollars a month. We'd have been trash together. We *were* trash."

"So what? You don't try to lie out of it."

"You never heard me lie out of anything! But don't blame me for believing you'd sold out. You owed me nothing. I know that."

"I owed Ma Keller something."

She laughed scornfully. "What? She used you. Not that I blame her! A woman with her back to the wall has the right to use any man, any way she can. But that's what she did, George. She used you."

"What I remember is that she took you and me in. What I know of the cow business, she taught me. She paid me for it."

"Fifteen dollars a month!" She squinted at him. "But I forgot what you were like, I guess."

"What I'm like?"

"You're not scared inside."

"Scared of what?"

"Of being a tramp. I'm a rich tramp now. I'm the Widow Keller, not Bonnie Travis. I'm the only one who knows that deep inside I'm still trash."

I'm a damn fool, he thought, but she means this and I can't stand it. . . . He put a hand on her shoulder. "You never were that, Bonnie," he said, "and who knows it better than me?"

"Oh George, George. . . ."

"Bonnie. Oh my God. . . ."

She was in his arms and reaching hungrily for his kiss. Her limber body still fitted his, her kiss still had that sweet taste, and she still gave him that exalted sensation of possessing something tiny and pitifully precious. Eight years vanished then.

She squirmed free, panting, "We've got to cut this out."

"Why?" He reached for her.

"No, stay away! Because you're not a forgiver. Sooner or later, Dick would come between us. Dead or alive, he's there, George."

"Bonnie. . . ."

She stepped nimbly out of his way. "Damn you, listen to me! If I had it to do over again, I don't know what I'd do. I *think* I did wrong to marry Dick. I *think* if I had lived up to you, it would have worked out some way. But I don't have the courage to do what I think is right. I've got that trashy streak in me."

She looked up at him. "You know that, deep in your heart. And you'd never forget that I doublecrossed you once. You see, I can blame life for what I am. I lived in the movers' wagons until I was sixteen, a woman grown. That's my excuse. But you—you'll always blame me. Not life, not yourself, not Ma Keller—me."

Just let me out of here, he was thinking. I got over this once. I can get over it again. . . .

"We are still partners," he said.

She nodded. "And we can split a hundred thousand dollars here someday, if we can hold out."

"Hold out?"

"I'm broke. I've got eleven men and I owe them for three months. I owe eight hundred or more in town. I haven't wasted it, George. Ma didn't leave any cash money, and I hate to sell a beef. It'll be worth so much more when the railroad gets here! There's good feed, George—there'll be plenty of hay to winter every head we own."

He remembered her avarice so well. It had been a pitiful thing when pennies and nickles meant so much. Get a grip on yourself, he thought. This is business, just business. . . .

"Can't you borrow?"

"Ha! Ma gave the town the land for the new courthouse. She left me a hundred shares of bank stock, and Dick owned a hundred. Can't you get it through your head that this is a Twenty Plus town now? I could sell—sure! But borrow? No."

"We'll come to money in a minute. I heard they shot Dick in the back. How did it happen?"

She said steadily, "Two years ago March. They announced that the railroad had sold its bonds and had its money the December before that. The second of January, Aaron Davidson offered Ma twenty thousand for her half of the place. You can imagine what she told him. Then. . . ." She hesitated.

"Go on, then what?" he said.

"You'll hear it anyway," she said unhappily. "Aaron started in on me then. Cornered me on the road, in town, anywhere he could. I should have horsewhipped him but I tried to—you know—act like a lady." She blinked away tears. "Can you see me acting like a lady?"

"Yes I can, Bonnie. What did Dick do?"

"What did he ever do? Nothing!"

"But he was still shot in the back."

"Behind the Speece House," she flared. "Do you think it was over me, when it happened there?"

"But why, Bonnie?"

"He was shot in the back," she said dully. "I was half-owner of the PK from that moment on. Wait till you know Aaron Davidson! He never did care about me—only about this place. He'd shoot me in the back, if that would help him get the PK."

Merrit paced the floor slowly, keeping his eyes away from her. Talking about Dick Keller had given him back his perspective, cooling the blood she had heated in him.

"Suppose I raise the money to pay your bills——"

"Oh George, could you?"

He could look at her now. He said irritably, "I wish you wouldn't look so happy when I mention money."

"Money's what we're talking about, isn't it? A hundred thousand dollars!"

He could remember when they had spent their last two dollars, a nickle at a time, making it last, covering the miles until—oh, to hell with it! "I want to see this lawyer, Price. I hear he's a good drunk. What else is he?"

"A good lawyer. A good man."

"Suppose I come out tomorrow and pay off your men. Suppose I pay off your bills in town. . . . Whose are they and how much?"

"Newton Price has the bills," she said eagerly.

"Then I guess seeing him is the first thing. Then I'll come out here and pay your men."

"Why don't you see Newt this evening? Why wait?" She came closer to him. "Go ahead and hate me, George. I hate myself. All my life I've been scared. I'll go on being scared until I've got the money from this place, until I'm so rich nothing can ever hurt me again! Money is all that matters, I know that now."

He walked toward the door. She followed him and offered her hand. "Please see Newt tonight. Please!"

He took hold of her hands. "You're too much for me, Bonnie," he said, smiling.

She smiled back. "I'm too much for myself. Only you and I know that deep down inside I'm nothing. That's why the money's so important. Without money I'm trash."

He had no hatred for her now, only a touch of impatient anger and a tenderness that enraged him. But he had himself under control. He leaned down and kissed her forehead lightly. He thought she trembled, but nothing moved him.

"All right, I'll see Price tonight."

"Can I tell the men they'll be paid tomorrow?"

"Sure, sure. Good night, Bonnie."

She caught his arm as he started out the door. "After you see Newt, are you coming back here?"

"No."

"If I need you, where'll I find you?"

"I'm at the Speece House," he said brusquely, and went out.

Chapter Three

"IF I DIE," said Merrit, "what then?"

"Depends on when you die," said Newton Price. "If you had died before Ma Keller—'predeceased' her is the legal term—the estate would have gone to the next of kin. She said she had no relatives, but everybody has relatives somewhere. However, if we found none, Bonnie would have inherited."

"Suppose I die now?"

"In the absence of your own will, the court would divide the estate among your parents and other natural heirs."

"It wouldn't go to Bonnie?"

"You can arrange that only by making a will."

"What if I don't make one?"

Price folded his hands together, to steady them, Merrit thought. The lawyer was not an old man, but he had a used-up look about him that was older than age. Tall, heavily-built, with a shock of long, heavy brown hair, he had once been a handsome man. It had taken a quart of whisky a day to wash the strength and looks out of him, but not all of those qualities had been eroded away.

"As far as the PK goes, I just told you, Merrit," he said. "Additionally, it could wreck the town. Suppose your natural heirs got into a court fight that held up the distribution of your estate? Suppose the railroad chose to stop construction rather than fight?"

"I thought they had their right-of-way."

"By grant deed, a gift, sold to them for a dollar, the nominal amount to make it binding. But suppose one of your heirs charges Mrs. Keller with having been of unsound mind when she made that deal? Suppose they asked an injunction?"

"And suppose the railroad moved the Twenty Plus range rather than fight it? I see what you mean!" Merrit smiled. "Then I need a will?"

"As much as any man alive needs one."

"Can I leave the estate to anybody I choose?"

"Within limitations. You must provide for your natural heirs unless they have disinherited themselves by their behavior, which is something for a court to decide. The easiest way is to leave them a dollar each, to prove you did not deprive them of their rights under natural law."

"All right, I've got four brothers and two sisters, if they're all living. You make me a will, Mr. Price, leaving three of the brothers and the two sisters a dollar each. The property I want to go to my brother Clint."

The lawyer had reached for a pen, but he paused to look at Merrit curiously. "May I ask why?"

"You figure it should go to Bonnie?"

"The old lady thought you'd keep the ranch intact. She was afraid Bonnie would sell, without you. Frankly, she told me she figured you two would make a match of it, and that you'd hold onto the PK."

"She ran my life once. She can't again. Mr. Price, I don't know what's going on here but I know this—it's not the kind of layout where you leave a woman like Bonnie all that property, with nobody to back her up. My brother is a pious old skinflint who fights for what's his—yes, and for what's yours too—if he can get away with it. Bonnie will need that kind of partner if anything happens to me."

The lawyer sighed and picked up his pen. "The names then."

"Clinton Enos, my oldest brother. Address is Rome, New York. He's the heir."

"The others, for a dollar each?"

"The girls are married. I don't know their names."

"First names will do, just so it identifies them."

"Well then . . . Justus Lemuel, then Ezekiel William, then Mary Sabetha, then Elizabeth Sarah, then James Isaac."

"You were the youngest?"

"Eight years younger than James Isaac. Clint took me in when Ma died, when I was four." Merrit smiled. "There was a time I'd have seen that skinflint hypocrite in hell before I'd have lent him a dime. But he's the kind of partner Bonnie will need."

"Your will will be ready to sign in the morning. I'll record the deed to the property as soon as the judge signs the distribution order tomorrow, too. Mr. Merrit, I get three dollars for drawing up a will. If it won't be an inconvenience, I can use it now."

Merrit put three dollars on the desk. "I might as well out with it, Mr. Price," he said. "Bonnie tells me she owes some money in town and that you have the bills. Can you pay them, or should I?"

"Can I be trusted with the money? Is that what you mean? So far I've never embezzled a dime, but you'd know better than I how far to trust a drinking man."

"Eight hundred dollars, about, she said." Merrit counted out the money on the desk and left.

Merrit went looking for a place to eat. He walked passed the Empire Hotel, caught himself, and turned back. He had over $3,500 in his money belt. He was on the deed as half-owner of a place that could be worth $100,000 in a few years! I'm a man of substance now, he told himself, as he mounted the steps of the Empire. . . .

He stopped in the bar for a drink. The place was too ornate for his taste and too quiet for its own good. But, he supposed, business would catch up with it when the rails got here. He shook his head when the bartender started to fill his glass again. "No thanks. One does me fine."

"You're Mr. Merrit?" the bartender said.

"That's right."

"Then if I may say so, good luck to you, sir!"

"Thank you, surely. But why?"

"I work for a living. I'm always on the side of the man who is fighting the propertied interests."

Merrit smiled. "When it comes to that, I'm a propertied interest myself."

"Not the same kind." The bartender shook his head. "The Twenty Plus boys don't come in here. Davidson's orders. I say to hell with a man who even tells his employees where to drink! You've still got to fight for yours, anyway."

"That's what I'm told. But nobody's proved it yet."

"They will. There was a lady in here asking about you earlier. I think she's in the dining room. Excuse me if I talk too much."

"It's a bad habit," Merrit said.

He crossed the lobby to the dining room, which seemed emptier than the bar. He stood waiting for someone to tell him where to sit.

"If you don't care about your good name," came a voice, "you can sit with me and have your back to the wall."

There in a corner sat Albine Anderson. Merrit knew instantly that she had been drinking and that she had been waiting impatiently to talk to him.

"Thanks," he said, sitting down. "I hope somebody will come up with something to eat though."

"You're early, Merrit. Strickland has gone fashionable. It's dinner now, not supper. Well, how do you like it? Where you find yourself, I mean."

"I've been in worse jams."

"I'd like to know when."

Merrit had never felt easy around such women. They could be good scouts, and he had heard of them chunking in their last chips for a friend. He had never seen it happen though, and until it did he was skeptical. He said, "How am I in such a terrible jam now?"

"Because you like it that way."

"That's where you're wrong. I want no trouble."

"You won't sell to the Twenty Plus, though, will you?"

"No. A man's got a right to——"

"Rights! How much is that property worth? Today, I mean. Twenty-five to thirty thousand, tops. Right? And then only if people feel free to bid on it. They don't. You've got one buyer. One!"

"Mother, when the rails get here——"

"I'm talking about now. Don't bet on the rails. *And don't call me 'Mother!'* What would it take to buy you out?"

"I don't make deals with a gun in my back."

"With twenty thousand you ride out in style, Merrit."

"Are you offering me that?"

"You could get it. A smart man would take it, but you're not smart. It's the lady that bothers you, isn't it?"

"Let's leave her out of it," Merrit growled.

"Why? You're not going to marry her, are you?" When he did not answer, she went on, "Of course you're not! But that's still why you came back here, and she's still a lot more important to you than the money. But she won't do you any more good than the money. And do you know why?"

"If you don't mind——"

"You don't want to talk about her to the likes of me, is that it? And you won't marry her either! Oh, you pious, hypocritical missionary. I hope she makes you sweat!"

He started to leave, but a waitress came with menus, and Albine Anderson pulled him back down again. The moment the girl left, the woman began again.

"I know your kind, Merrit. You're a troublemaker, that's all. One good deed, you high and mighty bastard, and you think it does you for the rest of your life!"

"One good deed?"

"You took her out of the wagons, I'll say that for you. Except for you and Grace Keller, she'd be working for somebody like me. And that makes you too good for her."

"She married another man."

"Why shouldn't she? *You* sure as hell didn't marry her! All you did was saddle up, and all she saw of you was the back of your neck. She was sixteen years old and she weighed ninety pounds, sopping wet. She could read and write a little. She could cook beans because beans was all she'd ever had to eat. How was she to make a living, if you got tired one day and rode off?"

He said, "I don't know how you know so much about my affairs, but they're still mine."

She opened her purse, pulled out a bottle, and took a quick drink.

"I'll tell you how I know," she said. "Dick Keller told me. You bought that girl from her father for twenty dollars. You had a lame horse and an old saddle. The first night out, you led the horse and she rode. You got a ride with a freight team then. You got a couple of days' work, haying. You ran out of money anyway and had to sell your horse."

"What's your point?"

"Maybe a man can forget times like those, but a woman can't."

He knew he shouldn't be talking with Albine about Bonnie, but he couldn't help it. "It seems to me she did," he said. "I believed Ma Keller when she said it scandalized her because we weren't married. She said she was taking Bonnie into the house to protect her good name. And Dick was my friend! You trust your friends, don't you?"

"Make me cry, why don't you?" Albine said, taunting him. "I'm on her side! And I'll tell you something else, Merrit. I'm on Aaron Davidson's side. I like winners, and he'll run over a narrow-minded missionary like you were a June bug!"

Their food came. "Maybe he will," Merrit said. "Maybe he will."

Eating calmed him. There was something about this woman and her interest in him that he did not understand. He watched her carefully for a moment.

"Another thing," he said, finally, "what's this about this fellow Davidson having a crush on Bonnie?"

She dropped her fork. "That's the silliest thing I ever heard of!" she exploded. "Where did you get that crazy idea?"

He finished eating as quickly as he could. With a smile Albine refused his offer to escort her back to the Speece House. "All you could do for me is draw fire," she said. "You're a troublemaker. You know it all! No thanks, Merrit. But I'll come to your funeral."

"I'll appreciate that."

His leg ached, and when he went outside the streets were suddenly full. He made his way slowly and carefully toward the Speece House, wanting no trouble this night. He did not like the looks of the men he saw. There were too many of them, and they were riffraff. The kind of men who worked only when there was no other way to get along, and the men who hired them were not thinking in terms of work.

Davidson's men? Twenty Plus men? Some of them looked him over carefully, as though they had been told "Merrit's in town!" Or was he imagining it?

No, he was not. A block from the Empire, he met two of the traveling men who had been passengers on the stage that afternoon. They nodded and smiled, but they did not stop to pass the time of day. They had already been in Strickland long enough to have heard all about him.

It seemed to buzz ahead of him like a whisper: *Merrit's in town, Merrit's in town.* His temper surged up in him as he saw the men look him over and stay out of his way. This is a hell of a town, he thought. I might as well have the small-pox. They can't all be Twenty Plus people! Or is that what I'm up against? *Are* they all against me. . . ?

There were a dozen horses tied in front of Billy O'Shea's place, but when he saw the Twenty Plus brands on them, he decided against stopping in. Why put Billy on the spot? And he was suddenly tired. Making up his mind quickly, he crossed the intersection and went into the Speece House.

The woman from number 8, the one who had spoken to him that afternoon, was behind the desk. The place was as quiet as a church. Albine believed in discretion, if nothing else. "Got your key?" the woman asked.

He nodded. "Good night, Bessie."

"Sweet dreams, Merrit."

He went back to his room and locked the door. Well, he told himself, I found out one thing—Albine figures this Davidson fellow as her man. How she did flare up when I said he had a crush on Bonnie! It's a mighty strange setup, whichever way. . . .

His bed had been turned down, and he would have bet his last dime that someone had gone through his valise. He smiled, hoping they had had fun. He undressed and again examined his wound, and was satisfied with the way it looked. To judge by the welcome this town was giving him, it could not heal any too soon.

He crawled into bed with his money belt and the .38 under his pillow. He had not realized how tired a man could get, favoring one leg all the time. He drifted off to sleep instantly.

Five minutes later he was wide awake, trying to shake off a dream that was more real than reality. He was a kid of nineteen again, and Bonnie was sixteen. It was the third night they had slept out in the open, that night in the oats field. His arms ached from swinging a scythe all day, but they had eaten well. Again he heard that cry of hers, so wild and strange and unexpected. *"Oh, you'll take care of me*

*always! Someone to take care of me! You won't let me go,
will you? Will you? Will you? Oh George, hold me, hold me!"*

He got up, made a cigarette, and smoked it sitting in
his underwear on the edge of the bed. Little by little her
image faded, her voice died out, and for this loss of sleep
he could blame Albine Anderson's talk. He got up and walked,
smoking cigarette after cigarette. I was outbid by Ma Keller
and Dick, that was all. Bonnie took the better offer. What do
I owe her?

And now I've got to take care of her again. . . .

Chapter Four

MERRIT LAY AWAKE so long before he slept that it was
late when he woke up. He had a slight headache, like a hangover, only not so bad. Still worse was his angry depression and
the disgust he felt at himself. Somehow he had come off second best twice yesterday. He had meant to keep his distance
with Bonnie, but not to hurt her. Then that Albine woman
had baited him into talking about things that were none of
her business.

He shaved carefully. While he was shaving, the girl in
number 8 pounded on his door and told him there was hot
water if he wanted a bath. He thanked her and said yes, it
was a good idea. He carried his money belt down the hall to
the bathroom and left it where he could watch it while he
soaked.

He dressed in his best clothes, taking all but $400 out of
his money belt and stuffing it in his pocket. There was a
good Mexican restaurant near the Speece House, but he went
to the Empire for breakfast. By the time he had finished,
Newton Price was in his law office. The lawyer was shaking
badly, but the will he had drawn for Merrit was in a clear,
even hand.

"That won't get you through the pearly gates, Mr. Merrit, but it will take care of your problems up to that point," he said.

"Fine! Now what do I do with it?" Merrit said.

"You keep it in a safe place or you have someone keep it for you. The principal heir can usually be counted on to preserve it. Or the bank's a good place."

Merrit grinned. "Believe I'll take the bank."

"One thing. Are you sure your brother is still alive?" Merrit shook his head. Price went on, "The way the will is drawn, his children would inherit after him. Is that what you want?"

"I don't know. A man can't think of everything. That'll do until I change my mind."

Price is thinking of Bonnie, Merrit told himself angrily as he left the office. He'd like to get her on that will somehow.

. . .

The Strickland State Bank was in the same place, but it was not the building he remembered. The old building had been of native stone, this one was of terra-cotta brick with arched windows. He went inside, and as he hesitated, a short, bald man rose behind a walnut partition and leaned over to offer his hand.

"You must be Mr. Merrit," he said.

"I am," Merrit said, shaking hands.

The banker smiled. "Don't look surprised, sir. Everyone knows you're here. The name is Champion, Walter C. Champion. I'm sort of the president here."

"You've got guts, Mr. Champion," Merrit said. "I haven't found myself very popular around here so far."

Champion opened a gate in the partition. "Come in and sit down. No, it's not guts, sir. That kind of talk has gone far enough. Grace Keller banked here. She left stock in this bank to the young Mrs. Keller. Aaron Davidson and the firm he represents bank here. So will you. What's this absurd talk about a range war?"

Merrit sat down. "You're a Yankee, I'll bet."

"Boston originally. But I was in St. Louis five years before I was offered this position."

You don't cheer me up a bit, Merrit thought. You mean

well now, but will you stand when it thunders. . . ? He said, "How long have you been here?"

"Right at six months, as you Texans say."

"Then you've got a lot to learn, sir, and I'll not make it any worse than I have to. First I want to leave a document in your care. It's my will."

"There is no charge for that."

"Then I'd like to open an account." Merrit put a wad of currency on the desk. "I want it so Bonnie Keller or I, either one, can draw on it."

"Easily done, and I thank you for the business."

"Yes, I bet you do," Merrit said. "I'd like to know why Mrs. Keller can put money in here, but she can't borrow any. The Kellers helped found this bank. There's only one outfit that has more money behind it than she does. That's the Twenty Plus. We have come to a hell of a point, Mr. Banker Champion, if a Keller can't raise money here to pay bills with."

The banker narrowed his eyes and drummed on the desk. "That is right," he said, "but I'm not responsible for it. I didn't promote this conflict between these two outfits! But I am responsible for the soundness of this bank, and if real trouble comes, it can wreck the town, the bank, and the county, for a generation."

"And so you're taking sides."

Champion shook his head. "No. So long as its credit is recklessly impaired by this trouble, the Twenty Plus can't borrow a dime here either."

And you are a plain damn fool, Merrit thought. He said, "They don't need to borrow. Bonnie Keller did. The rain falls on the just and the unjust, as a brother of mine used to say. Those sayings never did satisfy me. God help you, Mister Champion, if you disadvantage us with any more of your piety."

Champion kept on shaking his head. "I will run this bank until I'm relieved, and I'll run it my way. I will not lend money to either outfit until this trouble is settled." He shot to his feet and went on swiftly, "We're in luck, Mr. Merrit. You haven't met Aaron Davidson yet, have you? Here he comes. You are two sensible men. Why can't we settle this trouble now?"

Merrit stood up and swung to face the door. He heard Champion making the introduction. He shook hands and said he was pleased to meet Mr. Davidson. All the time he was thinking warily, This fool of a banker is wrong and Albine Anderson is right. Bessie is the rightest of all. I would sooner shake hands with a rattlesnake. . . .

About forty, Merrit judged, and not a big man at all. Bowlegged and workworn, his goatskin chaps had Montana written all over them. Homemade pants, with a .45 shoved into a pocket made big enough for it. Small, ruddy clean-shaven face, good white teeth in a thin mouth, gray eyes that popped a little.

It was his hair that grated. Aaron Davidson wore it shoulder-length and well brushed. It was hard to tell whether he was trying to look handsome with it, or like one of those old buffalo hunters.

"I just came from Newt Price's office," Davidson said. "He tells me you don't want to sell."

"You didn't expect me to, did you?" said Merrit.

"I'll go to fifteen thousand."

"No, Mr. Davidson. It's not for sale."

"Sixteen-five! It's a fair offer."

"I reckon I'll hang on, thanks the same."

Davidson smiled. "You'll take less before you're offered more," he said. "And turn that down, too, I guess. Well, I won't plague you again about it."

"Then we're friends?" Merrit said dryly.

"No reason we shouldn't be."

Champion burst out, "There's no difference that men of goodwill can't settle. I've been worried about——"

"Get your God-damned hands off me!"

The banker had put a hand on each man's shoulder. Davidson flung off the one on his, shrinking from Champion's touch with a violence that made his whole body quiver. The banker turned red with embarrassment.

"There was no call for that," Merrit said.

"I can't stand to be touched by people!"

"There was still no call for it."

"Are you going to tell me my business?"

He's crazy, Merrit thought, plain crazy! He wants to try me for size—well, why not? He said, "When I feel called upon, Mr. Davidson. You feel free to speak your mind to me, too. Any time you feel lucky."

Davidson licked in the saliva that had sputtered out around his lips. He had turned white at Champion's touch, and now some of the color came back into his face. He had to look up to meet Merrit's eyes, but his cold gaze did not falter.

He said swiftly, running the words together, "I speak your language—you speak mine. Listen! Five years ago, I was running an outfit no smaller than the Twenty Plus for fifty dollars a month. Fifty dollars! Do you think I want to go back to that? Do you think I *will* go back to it? Do you know the stake I have here? Ten percent!" He almost screamed it. "*Ten percent!* Do you think I'm going to let a saddle bum like you get in my way?"

"I would hate to be your British bosses," Merrit said softly, "and count on getting my ninety percent."

"You're a smart bastard!"

"Since you feel lucky this morning," Merrit said, and swung a long, low left.

It caught Davidson under the ribs and doubled him up with both hands over his body. His long brown hair swirled forward, over his face, as his hat fell off. Merrit kicked him in the leg. Davidson, choking for breath, turned and tried to ram Merrit with his head.

Merrit caught both hands in the long hair and jammed Davidson's face down on the corner of Champion's desk. He jerked forward and lifted the man erect by his hair. He waited until he was sure Davidson had his breath back, and then he held him by the hair with his left hand and hit him over the temple with his right.

Davidson's eyes rolled up. Merrit half pushed and half threw him through the gate in the railing. Not until that moment did he realize that he had not felt a single twinge of pain in his bad leg.

He saw three heads pass the arched windows at a run. He stepped quickly through the gate, hooked Davidson's .45 out of his pocket with the toe of his boot, and kicked it behind him. He stepped clear of Davidson and stood with his back against the railing as the three men came cautiously into the bank.

"Hello, Rob," Merrit said. "Keep your hands off your gun and I'll do the same."

The first man into the bank nodded. "Hello there, Merrit," he said. "What happened?"

"He called me a name."

"It was not the smartest thing he ever done, I reckon," the man called Rob said reflectively. "Or you either. I reckon you remember these two."

"Old Home Week!" Merrit said. "Hello, Jake. Hello, Harmon. I think you and I met yesterday."

Harmon Griffin laughed that raucous giggle of his. "We are in for some sudden times, 'pears like," he said.

"If we have trouble, you'll start it."

"That could be," Rob said.

Merrit grinned. "You'll have to carry your pretty-haired boss. Jake, you've got a strong back and a weak mind."

Jake, by far the biggest of the three men, stooped and swung Davidson up over his shoulder. "A job is a job, Merrit. I hired out to the man. Stay out from mine way," he said, slipping into a thick Dutch accent.

"Be seeing you, boys," Merrit said.

The three went out, big Jake carrying Davidson, who bled freely at the nose. The banker, Champion, slumped down in his chair and mopped his face with his sleeve. "Do you know those men?" he said, trembling.

"Sure! It's Rob—let's see—Rob McKesson. The Dutchman's name is Seeck. The other one is Harmon Griffin. We worked together a few years ago, down in Chihuahua."

"But if you are friends . . . I don't understand."

"As the Dutchman said, a job is a job. Ours was to steal cattle. One rich Mexican *ranchero* hired us to steal another outfit's cattle and run them across the line and sell them. He paid us two dollars a head. If you mean, why don't these fellows come over to me—why, they hired out. They're probably getting bonus pay. You don't take a man's money and switch sides on him."

"My God!"

Why did this fool's innocence irritate him so much? "There's little sentiment in the cattle business when prices are good, and even less when they're low," Merrit said.

"But Davidson's syndicate owns stock in this bank. Why

should he have to hire cattle thieves?—beg your pardon, Mr. Merrit, but it's—it's incomprehensible."

"Mr. Champion, you just said it. 'Syndicate.' What are people in Texas to the British investors who own the Twenty Plus? What's the PK to them? An empty place on the map, one they want to fill in. I've worked for outfits like the Twenty Plus myself. Sir, you're accustomed to thinking of the banker as being the big man in town. Do you know who's the big man in cattle country? The man with the land—and the guns to hold it."

"But we have laws. We have officers——"

"Elected by poor men. The poor men always have the votes. But poor men never stick together, and nobody knows it better than the man they elect—after they elect him. What's your sheriff like here? I can tell you. A good, decent, upright man. Wears a clean shirt. Goes to church often enough to be noticed. Pays his bills. Can you see him bucking a crew like Davidson's, law or no law? Hell, what's the use! You'll have to see for yourself."

The banker's hand trembled as he made out Merrit's passbook. He did not offer to shake hands, nor did Merrit. He went out of the bank and heard a small boy yelling something about a wagon train. By the time he had got his horse out of the town stable, he could see the train approach. He waited curiously.

"Where did they night?" he asked a loafer.

"Got a yard five miles west," the man said. "Too much trouble when they camp here. Bring a lot of business, but you know teamsters."

"Yes," said Merrit, thoughtfully. "Yes, I do. Railroad supplies?"

"And horses. Cheaper to ship the horses down by water and work them here from Corpus Christi than to ship by rail."

They would cross PK land then, en route north to the grading camp. Merrit walked his horse down to where he could size up the train as it passed. Ahead of it came the extra horseherd; he counted nearly ninety fine big horses and mules. They had been on the road long enough to need little herding, and two men handled them easily.

There were fifty-one wagons in the train, a few pulled by

four-horse teams, most by a single span. Nearly 230 head of work stock here—a small fortune, even to a railroad. The train boss appeared to be no more than a kid. He kept a good saddle horse in a lather, riding up and down the train.

"Move up there! Check in your leaders there, fella. If you can't handle four, say so. You! Remind me to have the pins tightened in those bolsters tonight. Move up, move up!" he kept shouting.

This was no time to talk to him. Let him get well out of town first. Merrit rode to the Speece House, tied his horse in the alley, and came around to the front door to enter. Albine Anderson was at her eternal knitting behind the counter.

"Morning, Merrit. Checking out?" she said.

"Not yet. Soon, maybe."

"Your things are packed."

He smiled. "You run an efficient establishment. Too bad you miss out on the teamster business."

"I don't."

"Oh? They went right on through."

"They'll stop on the way back. They leave the horses and wagons and go back by stage. They don't get paid, anyway, until they're unloaded. That way, they're fairly sure of getting there."

"I see. The train boss, what's he like?"

"A fool like you. Yourself, five years ago. Why?"

"Nothing. I met your friend Davidson this morning."

"How'd it come out?"

"He was carried out."

Albine did not ask for details. She said, "You've got to make trouble! There are two things fools like you will always fight for."

"Women and money?"

She laughed scornfully. "What does money mean to a fool? No, women and what you call 'honor.' I'll bet Aaron offered you money, didn't he?"

"Sixteen thousand five hundred."

"You could get twenty."

"Maybe once I could. Not now."

"Want me to try for you?"

"You're too thoughtful, mother," he said, leaning across the counter to tweak her cheek.

"You try that again, and I'll kill you!" she blazed.

"On second thought, maybe I will check out."

She controlled her temper and stood up to push his valise around the end of the counter with her foot. "There's no bill. Proud to have had you as a guest," she said, and suddenly she was laughing. She held out her hand. "You're still a damn fool, Merrit, but I always did like fools. Did you hurt Aaron bad?"

"I tried to. He hadn't woke up to report when I last saw him."

"Get out of here before I like you too much!"

Chapter Five

BILLY O'SHEA'S place was-open when Merrit came out of the Speece House. He did not want a drink, but he felt the need of someone steadfast, someone who believed in a few things and stood up for them. By the look on Billy's face, he knew that word of his fight with Davidson had already gotten around.

"You don't have to take sides, Billy," he said. "If my custom embarrasses you, I can swear off."

Billy roughed his white hair with both hands. "I wish you hadn't said that, Merrit. You're mighty cocksure. I don't worry about myself. I do about you."

Merrit thought it over. "Cocksure? Billy, I have no idea what I'm doing. I'm not going to look for trouble. I won't run from it, either. But I shouldn't be fighting this damn fight alone. Seems to me it's time for a few others to stand up and be counted."

"Who?"

"Not you. But this is Strickland's fight, not just mine."

"Believe me, you have many well-wishers!"

"Then why don't they say it out loud? Nobody's backbone

is showing. What'd they say if Bonnie and I did sell out to the Twenty Plus? It'd be Davidson's town then. In five years there wouldn't be another small outfit left within driving distance of the rails. Every cent made here would be shipped to England to pay the stockholders. Don't they think about those things?"

"Not if they can help it. Merrit, people are as good or as bad as they have to be. If somebody with a bigger stake will fight their fight for them, they'll let them. If you know what you're doing—and it appears to most people that you do—they'll say a little prayer for you and wish you luck behind your back. But it would be hard to smoke them out," Billy added earnestly.

Merrit drummed thoughtfully on the bar with impatient knuckles. "Maybe I do know what I'm doing, at that," he said. "Maybe it's time they were smoked out. If there are a few men here, let's see them get up on their hind legs."

He rode slowly out of town, following the dust of the wagon train. He approved of the way the PK fence had been stapled up again, after the wires had been dropped to let the wagons through. As he trotted his horse past the long file of teams and wagons, he waved and nodded and spoke to the drivers.

They barely nodded back. Teamsters were a clannish bunch. Everyone who did not drive a team was either a farmer or a dude. Merrit was a farmer and he knew it. All right, let them see that he was a friendly farmer.

The kid trainboss came pelting back on a lathered horse, and Merrit waved him down. In time this youngster would put on weight. Today his boyish wiriness merely made his hard, worried face look dissipated and strange.

"What d'you want?" he said, reining in impatiently at Merrit's wave.

"You're on my land. I like to know my guests."

"Then you're Merrit." The kid rode closer and put out his hand. "Will you be in charge now?"

"Why?"

The kid said stridently, "It's too long a haul on this lap. It'll shorten as the rails move south, but from where I have to bed down, beyond Strickland, to where the grading camp is now, is just too danged fur!"

"Bed down anywhere on PK range."

"The lady said no."

"Mrs. Keller? A lady alone mightn't want a wagon outfit so close to her house. But she's not alone now."

It just poured out of the kid. He was big enough for his job, all right, but sometimes he did not know it. "Say, that'll help, Mr. Merrit! We won't make trouble. I'd like to buy beef, too. There's a spring—I think it's called Willow Springs —with a good flow of water. There are some cottonwoods there I could drop to make a dam and a pond where I can water my horses."

"Go right to it. Don't kill any cow stock, and don't run 'em, and you can help yourself to beef."

The kid looked as though he wanted to cry. "By God, Merrit, that's plumb handsome! I'll pass the word to these bellyachers of mine. It'll cheer 'em up some. And listen, Merrit, my horse herd is scattered from hell to breakfast on up ahead. I'm shorthanded, and two men can't keep 'em bunched when we leave the road. I'm sorry, but——"

"No cause for sorrow. There's grass enough. Those big fellas take a sight of feed."

"They ain't horses," the kid said scornfully. "Them elephants ain't what you and I was brought up to say was horses. Them's homesteader stock."

"Well, there's no homestead land in Texas."

"That won't stop 'em. The sodbusters always follow the rails. My name's Phelps, Willie Phelps. You taken a hell of a load off'n me today, Mr. Merrit. Any time I can return the favor, send up your smoke."

They shook hands again, and the harried kid dashed off to change to a fresh horse. Merrit trotted on down the length of the train and as far as the scattered horse herd, the glimmering of an idea illuminating a corner of his mind. Phelps was right—homesteaders, grain-growers followed the rails. They would need workhorses.

A lot of these big, expensive horses would be used up on the grading gang and would not be worth shipping to another job. A lot of them would be mares. Maybe they couldn't buy their hay on a construction job anymore, but they could throw colts. Get him a couple of crossbred studs—out of native mustang mares and Percheron or Belgian sires—and in a few years he'd have himself a horse crop.

He rode almost to Willow Springs, where he had told Willie Phelps he could make camp, and he had seen all he had to see this day. He turned and put his horse into a fast, easy lope, and in two hours was back at the PK. Saddled horses were tied to the corral fence, but he could hear the men in the bunkhouse. Half the morning gone, he thought angrily. But then he forced a grin. I've waited for my wages in my time too, he thought. Payday. . . !

Bonnie heard his horse and came out to meet him at the hitching rail in front of the house. She noticed his valise tied on behind the saddle. "You plan to stay?" she said.

"This is where the work is," he said.

"You'll find it's a change from the Speece House."

"I hope so."

"Where do you plan to sleep?"

"Bunkhouse."

"No one will believe it, George," she said coolly.

"I'll swear it before a Notary Public and talk it up around town," he said, irritated not so much by the hint of antagonism in her manner, as by his own treacherous feeling of tenderness. "I guess the boys are waiting for their pay. Some of them I probably won't keep, Bonnie."

"You're taking charge, are you?"

"We have to work together, Bonnie, and this is my end of it."

"These men have stuck by me."

"But some of them won't stick by me. They won't admire me for the same reasons, and they won't have the same hopes, if you get what I mean. Another thing—I told the kid trainboss that he could build a camp and a dam for a pond at Willow Springs."

"He's a fresh one. And you know the trouble teamsters can cause."

"I do, and that's why I want them on our side. Bonnie, we're scratching for friends! I'll strike a deal with the devil himself to beat Aaron Davidson to him."

Merrit stayed in the saddle, looking down at her. If she had aged a day since sixteen, he couldn't see it now, with that frowning, faraway look on her face. Slowly, her blue eyes came up to meet his.

"Whatever you say, I guess," she said. "But it's hard to look men in the eye when you can't pay them and they stay and work for you anyway. I'd hate for you to let any of these fellows go. They stuck with me."

"I like people who stick. I just like to know why they stick. Let's get on with it."

He took the money out of his shirt and slid to the ground. He tied his horse, loosed his grip, and went to the bunkhouse with it. Bonnie followed. Someone must have been watching through a window, because as they neared the bunkhouse, the men filed out. He counted twelve. Bonnie had said eleven. The twelfth, then, would be the cook.

Behind Merrit, Bonnie started to say, "Boys, this is George Merrit and——"

Before she could take charge, Merrit said, "Bonnie says this is the best cow crew in Texas, and I'll have to say the place shows it. I may do things different than she does, and you may or may not like it. Those who want to leave are free to do so. The ones who stay are through working for nothing."

Every bunch had its leader. This leader was a short, broad-shouldered, gray-haired man with squinting eyes and a lip that stuck out as stubbornly as Lincoln's. He said, "I been satisfied with the way Bonnie runs things. I might not like your way."

"That's right, you might not. How are you called?"

"Lawler."

"I don't call a man by his last name and I never stood for being called by mine. You've got another name, don't you?"

"I'll explain it one more time," the old man said wearily. "My mammy and pappy was second cousins. Both named Lawler. My name is Lawler E. Lawler. That suit you?"

Bonnie again tried to interrupt. Merrit said, "Lawler, I hope you'll stay. You and I will never have any trouble. Now how much do we owe you?"

Bonnie was determined to have her say. "I've kept the books. Here's the tally, George."

He took the paper from her and called the names, counting

out the money from his stack of bills. Lacking silver, he rounded off odd amounts with an extra dollar or two. By the time they were all paid, he knew he had some good men here. And yet. . . .

You had to be a cowboy to understand them, and Bonnie never could. Being homelessly footloose, any place became "their" place if the pay and food were good and the bunks were clean. But most of them had a lonely man's bad judgment of women and fierce loyalty to them. They fell passionately in love with women like those who worked for Albine, and they would work for nothing for someone like Bonnie.

But if you had sat around enough cow-camp fires, and had heard enough stories of riders who hit it lucky and married a propertied widow, you learned to pick the men to whom this was the chief ingredient of loyalty. He picked three who he was sure had dreamed of marrying the PK.

"You three," he said. "Like to talk to you later, so stick around, will you?"

One said, "Why, I don't know as there's anything to talk about, Mr. Merrit. I'll take my time."

The others made up their minds as quickly. They went into the bunkhouse for their things while Lawler and the others untied their horses. Lawler walked his horse over to where Merrit was putting away the rest of his money.

"Three men quit," he said flatly.

"They're not like the rest of this bunch, Lawler."

"Well, no. But they'll just go to work for the Twenty Plus."

"They'd quit next week or next month and go to work there anyway. The more Davidson loads his payroll with deadheads, the better it suits me. I wish I could send him ten like them. Is there a harness team and a buggy? I'd like to ride up to the grading camp."

It took a little time to filter through Lawler's stubborn mind. "Never figured it thataway," he said at last. He smiled at Bonnie. "Don't you worry, Bonnie. The work'll get done. Them was the deadheads, all right." He turned and bawled to another rider, the only one older than himself. "Whitey! Hook up Buck and Mike to the top buggy for Mr. Merrit."

The three deadheads came out carrying their bedrolls. Merrit took his grip inside and threw it on one of the empty bunks. When he came out, the three were cantering off toward town.

"If you're going up to the grading camp, George, you can do with a cup of coffee first," Bonnie said.

He shook his head. "It'll just make talk. I mean to stay away from the big house."

She took his arm. He could not embarrass her in front of the crew. "There'll be talk anyway. Come on," she said.

She had learned some niceties of manners from Ma Keller, things a girl from the movers' wagons would never know. She let him open the gate and the front door. In the house, she called, "Maria! Coffee, please."

"You have learned to give orders, Bonnie."

"What did you expect? Sit down, George."

Two big wooden chairs with cowhide seats always stood beside the fireplace. She took one, he the other. A strange sort of embarrassment came over them, and it was her fault, not his.

"Out with it, whatever's on your mind," he said gently.

She swallowed. "You wouldn't marry me, would you?"

He winced. "Why?"

"That answers my question, I guess," she said in a low voice, dropping her eyes. "If you wanted to, you wouldn't ask why. Now I wonder if I've got the nerve to say the other."

"What other?"

"You wouldn't just move in?"

"With you?"

She said in a rush, "There'll be talk anyway. People expect it. It'll make me look cheap if you stay down there with the men. They'll know, but nobody else will, don't you see? I—I hate to be a laughingstock for anybody."

God, how he pitied her. "It wouldn't work, kid," he said gently. "I had a brother used to quote Scripture a lot. I don't remember the verse exactly, but it goes something like this: there's a time to reap, and a time to sow, a time for this and a time for that."

"I guess that puts me in my place." She picked up a corner of her apron, wiped her eyes, and tried to smile at him. "I guess I'm still only a step from the wagons, George. I—I keep forgetting people don't know me as well as I know myself. Laughter—I can stand anything but that!"

He said in a hard voice, "Just keep remembering you own half of the PK. Nothing is comical if you're rich."

She studied him. "George, what's wrong with you?"

"Wrong? Nothing's wrong with me."

"Then why do you want a buggy? You've been hurt. Or maybe you're just laid up?"

She said it maliciously, to embarrass him, and it worked. Cowboys who became diseased at places like Albine Anderson's, and who had to work at walking jobs for a few days, were said to be "laid up."

"I'm not laid up," he said. "I'm taking care of a small wound."

"I'm glad that's not why you don't want to move in."

The Mexican maid came in with a tray and saved him further embarrassment. He was even a little amused at the easy, queenly way Bonnie poured the coffee and served the cream and sugar. Ma Keller, he thought, must have drilled the living hell out of her on table manners, and I must say, it took. . . .

"*Por favor, Señor,*" the maid said.

"*Si? Digame,*" he replied absently.

The girl spoke swiftly. Bonnie's expression showed she had never learned Spanish. "What's she saying to you?" she snapped.

"She has a friend who needs a job, that's all."

"I know all about her friend. It's Emilio." Bonnie threw up her hands. "That Emilio is no good. Lawler says he's a fugitive."

"From where?"

"Who knows? Someplace in Mexico. Lawler says one wouldn't be so bad. But if you hire Emilio, he'll have every brother and cousin and uncle and brother-in-law here, and we'll get a bad name we'll never get rid of."

"He's right," Merrit said, "but Bonnie, we can use a bad name for a while." She wanted to argue, but he talked over her. "Maybe you couldn't handle a gang like that. Maybe Lawler can't. I can. Listen—I had a run-in with Aaron Davidson this morning. I know what we're up against."

She was shaking her head stubbornly. He tried to plead. "Bonnie, we mustn't quarrel over every little thing. I know what I'm doing and I mean to do it. You must go along with me.'

"Aren't I?" she cried hotly. "Do as you please, then. You will anyway."

"No. You tell the girl yourself. Start now to show people we're a team. Keep telling yourself how much money is at stake and you'll find it's easy."

Bonnie looked at the Mexican girl. "All right, Maria. *Hay trabajo para tu Emilio.*" She gave Merrit a cold look. "I know that much Spanish, damn you!"

Maria snatched up Bonnie's hand and kissed it before running out. Bonnie stood up. "Have you finished with your coffee? I'm going with you."

"No, you're not. I've got to make friends with the grading outfit. I'll do it best my own way, alone. A woman complicates things."

"You have become a talker. You never were before."

"We all change."

"But not in all ways." Somehow she suddenly had some sort of advantage over him that he did not understand. "Oh George, it's so strange to see the new in you, and so much of the old too. You forget that I am wiser, too. Don't make the mistake of thinking I'm still sixteen."

"I don't understand that, Bonnie."

"Because you don't understand women. How terribly unscrupulous we are! How singlemindedly we go after what we want. I'm as tough as Ma that way—and as dishonest."

"What are you getting at?"

She stood with her small hands on the back of the chair, looking into the dead fireplace. "Dick and I never once sat here. He hated this house. He hated everything and everyone but you, George, and he only admired you because you were a better, stronger man in every way. He didn't know you as I know you now, suddenly—how weak you are, in some ways."

"What ways?"

"You need love more than anything else in the world, yet you can't give love." Her eyes came slowly around to meet his. "If you could love me as I want you to—as you want to yourself, deep in your heart—oh, what love I could give you!"

Spurs clinked on the tiles of the galerie. "Team's hitched," Lawler called. "They don't stand worth a damn."

"Thanks, we're just coming," Bonnie answered him.

Merrit stood up. "Bonnie, let's agree never to speak Dick Keller's name again."

"I'll wait until you speak of him—all right?"

"I never will," he said violently.

She came up to him and put her fingertips against his cheek. "Poor, lonely George. You shaved this morning, didn't you? You know what we used to say when I was a kid? 'A shave without a kiss is a creek without a bridge.' "

Her hand dropped. She went to the door and stood waiting for him to open it.

Chapter Six

THE OLD MAN called Whitey was holding a pair of wildly fidgeting horses, a bay and a black. Lawler gave Bonnie his hand to help her into the buggy. Merrit got in with only a mild twinge from his bad leg.

"The bay is Buck, the other'n's Mike," Lawler said. "They're all right once they've had their run."

Bonnie said angrily, "Damn! There are better teams than this wild pair, Lawler."

"But none that will outrun them."

"You figure we might have to run?" Merrit said.

"The time will come. Mike gets sore-mouthed if he's handled rough, but he's only coming three, and he'll make a horse yet. These are both out of that half-Irish stud we had here. Mike's out of Ma Keller's own buggy mare. I never knowed her to make a mistake about a horse, a man, or a woman."

Whatever your meaning is, Merrit thought, I'm glad to have this team in front of me this morning. . . . He let the wild pair run, while Bonnie clung to the side of the buggy with one hand and to his arm with the other. When he snubbed the team in, a little at a time, they responded smartly. He liked them better and better.

"You always could handle horses," Bonnie said dreamily.

He did not reply. He drifted into memory without pain, seeing Ma Keller clearly again, and this time without resentment. In her way she had been more than a mother. She had, after all, taken him and Bonnie in when they were broke and hungry. She had seen that Merrit felt considerably less than a man, with a woman he couldn't support, and with no horse of his own. A man afoot was nobody.

A fellow by the name of Cartlidge was foreman of the PK then. "Ma says make a hand of you," he told Merrit one day. "Says give you a saddle and a string of horses. One thing, kid—nobody's overworked here, but nobody abuses a horse, either. So what you can't handle, don't ride."

"I can ride them," Merrit said.

And in two weeks, Cartlidge had him breaking both saddle and harness colts. A good hand drew twenty a month, a horsebreaker twice that. Merrit kept on making fifteen.

One night he came in and found Bonnie gone from their room in the kitchen storehouse. "I had no idea you two wasn't married," Ma said, in a shocked voice. "I won't put up with such a thing for one minute. I moved her into the house. She can work for me, learn a few things she never learned in no damn trashy movers' outfit."

"If I could draw my wages, we'd get married."

"Why . . . I'm short now, boy. But you're doin' real fine! I was thinkin', later I might put up a house for you. A steady married man on the place is allus a good thing. Only I'm tur'ble short of money now."

Fat, sweet-faced, the tears always on tap, and how she could cook. Back her into a corner and she flanked you by going to the range and messing around with the grub. Weeks went by. Every time he talked of drawing his money to marry Bonnie, that God-damned old woman was a little short.

And then one day: "Set down, Georgie. I got to tell you something and it breaks my heart because I was young once, too. Nobody can predict a woman's *heart*. It's useless to try to hold a woman against her *will*. You want her to be *happy*, don't you? That's what counts, ain't it—Bonnie's happiness?"

"Ma, what the hell are you talking about?"

She burst into tears. "Oh, I'd give *anything* if I didn't have to be the one to tell you this. But Dick and Bonnie went into town today to get married. You just got to be a *man* about it. . . ."

Merrit came awake suddenly. Bonnie was pointing at some new fences and saying something.

"How's that, Bonnie?"

"That's where most of the money went. What Ma didn't spend, I did. So far it's waste, but it won't always be. Look, George—did you ever see anything prettier?"

He remembered these marshy bottoms, and the bluestem grass that grew belly high here. There were thousands of acres of it, four or five or more sections. Now they were fenced, and on the high, bare spots stood rich haystacks—hundreds of them. On a low hilltop stood the mowing machines. He counted thirty of them.

"Whose idea was that?"

"Ma's," Bonnie said. "Only she was afraid to go whole hog. I wasn't. If you can winter your cattle, you're going to make money."

"You're a manager, Bonnie. Only trouble is, you've got all the hay in the county and only one buyer. . . ."

"The Twenty Plus."

"That's how I cipher it."

"It won't always be that way. You never saw a prettier sight than haying time. They put four horses on one of those mowers and go at a dead run. They stop at noon to change sickles and teams. Oh, it makes a roundup look like nothing!"

"You're not as helpless as you look. But it seems to me Davidson missed a bet, not burning your stacks."

She colored a little. "I asked him not to."

"You *asked* him not to?"

"In church." She threw back her head defiantly. "I told you, George, women are unscrupulous. I went every Sunday last fall. The Lutheran Church, a new one. I had Lawler drive me and wait. I knew what would happen, and it did."

"Aaron Davidson got religion, too."

She laughed with delight. "Pastor Schneider thought he had

Aaron converted. At least I got him to promise to leave me alone."

That long-haired man in church, thought Merrit. "I wish I could have heard it, Bonnie," he said. 'Praise the Lord, Brother Davidson, peace reigneth and thy land be blessed, only please don't burn my son-of-a-bitching haystacks.' "

"It wasn't that simple. He kept thinking they might be his haystacks someday."

"You flirted with him."

"Yes. You don't think much of that?"

He shrugged. "I reckon we each use the weapons at hand. But it makes a man wonder."

"Wonder what?"

"Who to believe—and when?"

"That'll never be your problem again, George," she said. "Just remember, if you ever feel like asking me to marry you, that I asked you first and you turned me down."

"I'll keep it in mind," he said bleakly.

They caught up with the wagon train. Willie Phelps had ridden on ahead to Willow Springs, but obviously he had passed the word that they would camp there. The teamsters this time did not wait for Merrit to speak. They raised their whips to him and their hats to Bonnie.

"What a bunch of gorillas," Bonnie murmured.

"But they're our gorillas now. Bonnie, you could spend a night in that camp, and they'd treat you like the Queen of England."

She looked at him thoughtfully. "I suppose you're right. But I wonder if I'll ever get over hating a wagon? Always going somewhere—nowhere. Suspicious of everybody, suspected by everybody. Land is what counts, George—your own land. And oh God, isn't this just perfect?"

A stillness, broken only by the musical jingle of harness and doubletrees, lay over an empty empire of grass. Merrit had never seen short-grass range look better. He had never seen fatter spring cattle. Buffalo peas were in bloom. The warm spring air was sweet. Merrit thought, Two months ago I was on the Yaqui River, broke except for what I could gopher out of the red rock. I know how Bonnie feels about this place. But can she ever understand how I feel about it, and about Ma Keller, and about Dick—and about herself. . . ?

The ring of axes beckoned them to Willow Springs. Two of the cottonwoods had already been felled across the trickle, and two men were shoveling dirt over them to make a dam. Two other axmen had another cottonwood ready to drop whenever Willie Phelps gave the word. The kid trainboss had hung his guns on a sapling, taken off his boots, and was down in the muck to run the job.

"It's muddy, but it'll clear up before my outfit gets here," he panted. "I'll build her high and strong, sir. I'll leave you something worth owning."

"We'll appreciate that," Bonnie said.

Willie touched his hat and smiled a tight smile. "We're like all freight outfits, ma'am—more needed than liked. But somebody has to do the dirty work."

She did not answer. Merrit made small talk for a few minutes and drove on.

"You sure don't like him," he said. "I take it he made his try."

She tossed her head. "It's hard being a widow. You know —nobody notices fresh tracks in an old lot."

He cringed. "I don't like that kind of talk."

"I'm not deaf and dumb!" she blazed. "I know how men talk. I know what'll be said now, too. 'You're too late—Merrit's already got her staked out.' "

It had to be said. He said it carefully, in a slow, measured voice: "Oh, I don't know! I remember five nights in a row when you were so glad to be out of the wagons that you cried yourself to sleep every night. And all I did was hold you and keep you warm."

"Oh, don't. . . !"

"It's the truth. I wasn't going to touch you until we could get married."

"That was only your idea—not mine. I was so grateful to you I'd have been your slave. But never again. No man in the world is worth that. Gratitude—how I hate the word! Grateful's one thing I'll never be."

"Not even to Dick Keller?" Merrit could not help saying.

"Oh, drop that. If you'd been half a man——"

He went crazy. He bunched the lines in one fist and reached for her. He only meant to shake her up—that being as close as he could come to hitting her—but she made a fist and struck at his nose and eyes. He got his arm around her waist and held her elbow.

They fought body to body, while the team ran on. He saw the livid hatred in her face, and he remembered how he had stepped aside so she could be happy with Dick. It was more than human flesh could stand. He felt the lonely years demanding their recompense, an earthquake of savage desire strained beyond all resistance.

He pushed her forehead back with his and reached for her lips. She whimpered when he kissed her—then she bit him. Nothing had ever felt so good as the pain of her bite. Nothing. The buggy creaked rhythmically and the spring-green land flew passed them.

He kissed her again and again. The madness passed, although somehow without depletion. He let go of her and said unsteadily, "Don't ever say anything like that to me again. It's one thing I won't take from anybody."

She straightened her hair unsteadily. "That proves what a hell of a man you are, I guess."

"Go ahead, sound tough."

"How do you expect me to sound? I was born in a mover's wagon. I had my honeymoon in an oat field. My husband was shot in the alley back of a whorehouse."

"Bonnie, if you don't respect yourself——"

"Do you respect me? Does your friend Willie Phelps? Does Aaron Davidson? Oh, what a hypocrite you are, George. You won't marry me . . . you won't live with me . . . you won't leave me alone. Make up your mind what you want!"

"I want what Ma Keller left me. No more, no less."

"Ha! Good old Ma, she paid you off at last—a ranch for your woman, and you take it. Eight years late, but you'll still take it. You fool, don't you know why she left you half of this place?"

"I only know what Newt Price——"

"What does he know about it? The only thing that counted with Ma Keller was holding the PK together. I inherited half of it from Dick and there wasn't anything she could do about that. But there was one man who had a sort of half-interest in me, too. One man she could count on to come back and fight the battle she left behind her. George, she tried to mate us—breed me to you the way she bred her buggy horse to the Irish stallion! She wasn't in her right mind about this land. She and old Pat Keller held this place against Kiowas and Comanches, Mexican rustlers and Union raiders, dry years and low prices and the tax collector. She tried to save it by breeding me to Dick. That didn't take. What was left but you? But I'll tell you this—the PK doesn't mean that much to me. Just let the rails reach Strickland, so I can get my price for my half, and Aaron's welcome to it. But for once, I'll get my price. I'm only a mover's slut, but they'll pay me my price!"

By the time she had finished she was screaming it at him, startling Buck and Mike until they fought wide of the tongue and had to be hauled down by brute strength. Merrit was busy controlling them for a moment, long enough to collect his wits.

When the horses were loping evenly again, he said, "Bonnie, you take money too seriously."

"Ha!"

"I don't underrate it. I just don't underrate you, either. Money can never give you self-respect. And the lack of it can't take yours away from you, either."

"You certainly acted it a minute ago."

"It won't happen again."

"Word of honor?" she said mockingly.

There was that word that Albine Anderson had used in that same tone of mockery. He thought, Damn women! But there is something to it. . . . "Word of honor," he said.

She studied him a moment. "All right. But some cold night, you just remember that I asked you, and you turned me down." She pointed to some wooden wands stuck in the ground. On them were tacked bits of cloth that had faded from a bright red to pink. "What are those?"

"Line stakes and grade stakes. This is where the rails will run, likely. Haven't you ever been out here?"

She shook her head. "George, I was never north of the hayfields before. I don't even know what I own."

He gestured with his hand. "PK range runs far north of this. You own half of all you can see, Bonnie."

"If you can hold it for me," she said. And then she smiled: "I may not know what I own, George, but I know what I owe."

He never knew when she was mocking him and when she was serious. "Forget it," he said uncomfortably. "What I'm fighting for is half mine."

"Meaning you wouldn't lift a hand if it was just mine?"

Now she was teasing him. He could meet her eyes and laugh, too. "Nope! It's purely business with me."

"It wasn't a minute ago."

He wanted to shout, "Will you let me alone!" But he only grinned and said, "I'm right changeable. Like the fellow says, I never know what I'm going to do until I've done done it."

Chapter Seven

THE GRADING camp burst upon them abruptly as they topped a grassy swell, and Merrit hauled in the team and caught his breath loudly.

He had had no idea what it took to make a railroad! Far, far to the north stretched the straight red scar of the new roadbed. On the horizon he could see the smoke of the locomotive of the work train that was laying ties and rails. Much closer, four-horse graders trod a methodical pattern, robbing dirt here and dumping it there. Men swarmed like ants, fine-grading with shovels.

Less than a mile away was a city of shanties, tents, and house-wagons. A puff of black smoke shot out of the hillside, and then another, and another. The ground trembled, and Buck and Mike went up on their hind legs as the roar of the explosions came to them. Merrit fought them down and felt Bonnie's hand on his arm. She pointed.

"I've seen the maps. Yonder is Twenty Plus range, and it's a shortcut to Strickland." She laughed joyously. "Ma would love to see this! Did you hear how she foxed the Twenty Plus?"

"No."

"She stole the railroad from under their noses! The Twenty Plus paid a hundred dollars a mile for right-of-way through state school lands. That was the going price. That was all the Twenty Plus wanted. Ma gave it to them. *Gave* them the right-of-way! For a few hundred dollars, Aaron Davidson lost the chance to fence us off from the rails. Oh, Ma was smart!"

She clutched his arm in a stronger grip. "And what I can't see for the life of me is how Aaron expects to stop them now. Look at that! How do you stop something as big as that, once it's started?"

I don't know, Merrit thought, but there's a way to do everything. . . . "Let's go closer," he said.

Buck and Mike had run it out, but they were still hard to handle as he forced them toward the busy camp. Merrit counted fifteen horses and mules running loose. Several limped, but the loose ones would be the disabled, abandoned ones. The mares could still throw colts.

He had to get down and lead the wild team to the house-wagon that was identified by a sign as the chief engineer's office. He stopped in front of it, put his fingers in his mouth, and whistled.

A man of average height, city-bred but as tough as he had to be, came to the door of the house-wagon. "I'm Merrit. I thought it was time we got acquainted," Merrit called to him. "I've got a wild team to hold, though, if you'll excuse me. And this is Mrs. Keller."

The engineer leaped down. He took off his hat to Bonnie and shook hands with Merrit. "Lloyd Rolf's the name. Heard they'd located you, sir. Glad you're here, glad you're here." He waved both arms proudly at his camp. "What do you think of it?"

"I think it's a railroad, Mr. Rolf."

"I'll be glad when it is. It's a lonely job," Rolf sighed.

"I hope you don't mind our just dropping in like this. It's such a thrill to see," Bonnie said.

Merrit thought, Why you little devil—you're going to show me how to make friends, are you. . . ? Rolf beamed up at her.

"This is the way it's done, ma'am. A shovelful at a time.

Anything we can ever do for you, I just hope you'll let us do it, ma'am."

"There is one thing," Merrit said. "What happens to your used-up horses?"

"We turn them out this time of year, when there's grass. Now and then one comes around sound for work."

"I'll take them off your hands for the brood mares I'll find in them."

"Make me an offer."

"I just did. I said I'll take them off your hands."

Rolf laughed. "They're yours. I don't like to leave old horses out, to be pulled down by wolves. See anything of my wagon train? They should have hit Strickland yesterday or today."

"They won't reach you tonight. They're nighting at the spring where the willows and cottonwoods are, south of you."

Rolf said, "I take that kindly. It was too long a haul. What do we owe you?"

"Your used-up horses, sir. You've got work to do and so have we. I won't keep you, and I'll wait to hear from you if there's anything you need."

They shook hands again. Buck and Mike were eager to be gone from here, and Merrit gave them their heads. Bonnie turned for one last look at the grading camp before it went out of sight beyond the hills.

"Who would have thought of asking him for his used-up horses?" she murmured.

"Grain farmers always follow the rails. We'll have horses to sell them when they get here."

"I never thought of you as a businessman, George. Or as a politician. You were one with Rolf, you know."

"So were you."

She did not answer. Merrit let the horses run. She braced her feet against the endgate and kept her own thoughts. Prairie chickens arose with a thunder of wings around them. Now and then he heard a meadow lark. A strange sense of peace came over him—or something more than mere peace, something sweeter and somehow exalted. He looked at the woman beside him and shaped his mouth to say her name.

And then he thought he heard something else. He leaned back on the lines, hauling Buck and Mike to their haunches.

The horses' ears shot forward. Bonnie heard it, too. She looked at him questioningly.

"Shots? Is somebody shooting?"

"Sounds it. There it goes again!" Merrit cried. "And it's not all six-guns."

"But who—?"

"Davidson has made his move," he gritted. "Bonnie, can you handle this team?"

"Of course, but I—"

He handed her the lines and jumped from the buggy. "It's at Willow Springs. If I remember rightly, there's a coulee yonder, full of brush. You can whip the team through it if you mean business, and with luck, you won't be seen. Get to the house. Find Lawler. Tell him Willow Springs, and to run like hell!"

"George, wait a minute."

"We haven't got a minute! You saw the railroad change its mind once to save a few hundred dollars a mile for right-of-way. Do you think Rolf will risk trouble that could hold him up until snow flies, if he can avoid it by taking the short way through Twenty Plus range?"

He slapped the near horse on the rump with his hat. Bonnie braced herself as the team hit their collars at a dead run. Merrit held his breath lest the buggy overturn as she hauled them sharply to the right, heading for the brushy coulee over under the horizon.

But she lined them out safely and let them run. Merrit swallowed his fear for her. It's a hundred to one in her favor, he told himself. They won't even see her! But Lord, Lord, let her get through. . . !

He heard more gunfire. No use running. He hit a swift walking gait, shuddering every time he heard the boom of the big rifle. Not an old Sharps buffalo gun, he thought now. Sounded more like a big Army Springfield .45-70. Hell of an arm. You could gut a horse from a quarter of a mile away with it.

He heard no more volleys—just scattering shots that made him sick to his stomach, because it meant they were hunting down the scattered horse herd. There was not a tree, not a rock, not a bush to give him cover. He broke into a light sweat and could not help running. How about getting caught out here in the open, with somebody after him with that long-range .45-70?

But he came in sight of Willow Springs without having seen a living thing. He counted eight dead horses and mules before he reached the spring, but the living ones had been stampeded miles away by now.

Here the flat land broke up into myriad shallow ravines. Merrit slipped into one and kept running, and not until this moment did he remember that he had a wounded leg. He burst out at the spring, and what he saw told him that he had been right about the long-haired man. No whole man could have ordered this!

Willie Phelps had finished his dam. He had tried hard to get at his guns and had missed them by a jump. He lay on his back under them, riddled with shots. Two of his men had been shot as they worked in the muck of the pond. Their bodies floated, polluting the water with blood. The others had been gunned down without returning a shot.

It had not been a fight. They had been ambushed, murdered in cold blood, and then the killers had turned to meet the horseherd. The big, clumsy draft brutes probably had been coming hard. They smelled water. They suspected nothing.

And they had died hard. Some had not yet died. Gut-shot, the big, helpless beasts lay or hobbled or sat and looked around blindly, wondering why they hurt so badly. Merrit counted a dozen that had yet to die.

That big rifle boomed out again, and Merrit dived for the cover of the willows. He heard more pistol shots, but they seemd to be moving away from him. And then he heard the heavy beat of horses, and he knew that all he had to do was wait. The poor crazed creatures would head for the nearest water—here.

Five horses and two mules came in sight. They were wet with sweat, they slobbered dry froth, and they ran so unsteadily they were ready to drop. A few hundred yards behind them came two riders. Neither carried a rifle.

The big draft horses and mules plunged into the pond backed up behind Willie Phelps' dam. The two riders came on. Merrit stepped out of the willows. The man in front saw him, screamed, and reached for his gun.

Merrit shot him in the chest. The impact tore the man out

of the saddle and flung him under the feet of the other man's horse. The horse reared. The rider had his gun out, but he had no chance to use it.

Merrit's second shot was low. It struck the other rider in the hip or side. He fell out of the saddle and rolled twice as he hit the ground. Merrit was on top of him in one jump. He smashed his fist into the man's face and felt him go limp. He tore the .45 out of the man's hand, threw it away, and stood up.

In a moment, the man opened his eyes. Merrit said, "Who was shooting the rifle?" The man closed his eyes. Merrit stirred him with the toe of his boot. "God damn you," he said. "I asked you—who owns the rifle?"

"I'll see you in hell," the man said.

Merrit kicked him in the ribs. He raised his foot and drove the heel of his boot into the man's breastbone.

"Who owns the rifle?"

The man passed out. Merrit waited until he became conscious again. Again he stirred him with his boot.

"*Who owns the rifle?*"

"Aaron Davidson," the man said.

"Was it Davidson shooting it today?"

"Nobody tetches that gun but Aaron," the man moaned.

In a few minutes he was dead. Not many more passed before Lawler and five PK men came pounding up. Merrit threw up his hands to signal them—slow down, it's all over. He pointed to the brands on the horses ridden by the two men he had killed.

"Sure, Twenty Plus. That's no surprise," Lawler drawled.

"No, but now we've got proof. Where's Bonnie?"

"To home. Couple of men watching things."

"See anything of the wagon train?"

"They're all right. I told them to push right along. Might as well night here after all."

"Good. Leave a couple of men with me. We'll bury these men and try to police things up. Take the rest of your men, Lawler, and catch those two Twenty Plus horses. Now this is important: I want you to take them on to the grading camp. The boss is called Rolf—Lloyd Rolf. He's going to spook, I know that. You can't prevent it, and don't lie to make things sound better than they are. Show him these two branded

horses. Get it through his head that he can't duck the fight—
it's here. He has to face it! If he has a yellow streak—and I
think he has—let's find it out."

Darkness had fallen before the men were buried. The wagon
train still was not in sight. Merrit sent the two men Lawler
had left to help with the burial detail back to the ranch.
"Check on the wagon train. Make them see they're better off
here than anywhere else," he said. "Then one of you can
bring a horse back for me."

The two men rode off. Merrit spent the dusk hours counting
dead horses and mules, and putting wounded ones out of
their misery. He counted eighteen within a quarter of a mile's
walk from the waterhole. How many more would be found,
he did not like to think.

An hour later, Lawler returned, still leading the two
Twenty Plus horses. He was in a furious mood.

"You can't get nothing through that man's head!" he snorted.
"All he can think about was that it happened on our prop'ty,
at the springs you own. He's weak, Merrit."

"What do you think he'll do?"

"I know what he'll do. He sent a man back to the work
train with a message to take up to the wires, asking New
York what to do."

They heard horsemen coming, riding hard. Lawler and his
men tumbled from the saddle, pulled their horses out of sight,
and waited on foot with Merrit.

In a few minutes, Merrit heard his name being called. The
hoofbeats ceased. He heard it again, with an accent he could
not mistake: "Meestair Merrit . . . Meester Merrit, where
you are?"

Merrit stepped out of hiding. *"Hola! Quien es? Que
quiere?"*

"Soy Emilio. Somos amigos!"

Merrit said to Lawler, "It's Bonnie's maid's gentleman
friend. I told him there was a job for him, but just in case—
cover my back."

There were three Mexicans, badly mounted, and one
carried a man's dead body across his horse behind the
saddle. They rode toward Merrit with their right hands held
high in the air, handling their sorry horses with the left.

"I am Emilio," said the tallest of the three men in Spanish. "These are my cousins, as worthless as I, beyond doubt, but hungry and willing."

"They have a welcome, if they can fight," Merrit said.

"They can fight. Here is a fourth, not a cousin. Pancho, dump your trash on the ground."

The man with the body behind his saddle let it fall.

"Who would this be?" Merrit said.

"Not a cousin, as I say," Emilio said. "I know him well. He has sinned much. His soul is now in hell, if there is a just God."

"Where did you find him?"

"Riding a Twenty Plus horse, Señor Merrit. He came lately from Sonora. We had some talk before he died. It may be that you know his face."

Merrit struck a match and turned the dead man over. He was not surprised to recognize the man who had shot him as he came up from Sonora to claim his inheritance. So I didn't hit him after all, Merrit thought, but I was still right—somebody meant to see that I never claimed my inheritance. . . .

The match went out. He said, in Spanish, "Emilio, who is this man?"

"He works for Davidson," said Emilio.

There was no use asking him anything more. Merrit had always gotten along with Mexicans. You had to go along with them on most things, their way, but they would surprise you with the ferocity of their loyalty once they got over their suspicion of you.

By their dress, these three came from southern Chihuahua —tall peaked hats, sleeveless cotton ponchos, leather pants, and long-sleeved shirts. There was one sure way to the heart of such a man.

"Emilio, we do not ride such miserable horses as those on this ranch. Tomorrow you will be given better horses."

"God will repay you," Emilio said.

"Your job will be to guard Señora Keller, whether she likes it or not. Never let her go from your sight. It may be that you will never sleep, but that is not important. If she ever gets more than ten meters from you, and comes to harm, I will kill you. I will kill your girl, too."

"Maria? She would kill herself, Señor Merrit."

"Let's hope that never becomes necessary."

Lawler understood Spanish too. He said dubiously, "Bonnie will have a fit about this, Merrit."

"Let her," Merrit said.

Chapter Eight

THEY MET the wagon train less than a mile from Willow Springs. It had no second in command. The outfit had been too cheap to pay an assistant trainboss. The men were leaderless, almost demoralized. One burly, red-haired man spoke for them, if anyone did. He got hold of Merrit's stirrup and dared him to dismount.

"You took a whuppin'. We don't aim to," he said. "We ain't stopping at the springs and we ain't going to take this! We's going on to the grading camp and get some boys, and come back and take that town apart."

"That's fine," said Merrit, "only the town had nothing to do with it. You damn fools, it was the Twenty Plus outfit that whipped you and whipped us! You're playing right into their hands, like the dumb farmers you are."

"Call me a farmer!" the redhead said thickly, and tried to drag Merrit from the saddle.

Merrit calmly put the muzzle of his .45 against the top of the man's head. "You want your brains all over your clothes, you're off to a good start," he said. "Now stand back and listen to me. There's a way to handle this, but it takes sense. You think I'm going to take a whipping and do nothing about it?"

"What then?"

"The moon will hold for hours yet. Push on to the grading camp. Your problem is with Rolf, not me. He'll want to do nothing, just sit, wait for New York to find an easy way out for him. You boys keep busy. One thing. You've got horses and mules scattered from hell to breakfast. They've got to be rounded up and delivered to Rolf. He must have no excuse to stop grading."

"Who gives a damn if he grades or not?"

"I do! The Twenty Plus does! How are you called?"

The burly redhead said sullenly, "Duffy, Red Duffy. But to you it's 'Mister.' "

"All right, Mr. Duffy, you're in charge. While you're on my land, I say who runs your outfit—get me? Now get those wagons moving and get to the grading camp. Round up those horses and mules. The next move is Rolf's. He's not going to make it."

"And after that?"

"After that, it's my move. On your way!"

There is, as the Scripture says, a time to sow and a time to reap—a time to be silent, and a time to speak. Red Duffy glowered at Merrit a moment, then turned to the irate teamsters.

"You heard the man. Roll them wagons!" He looked up at Merrit. "But this ain't over. Somebody's going to pay for what they done to them horses."

"That's right, it's not over. Anybody spoiling for a fight will get one. Only use your heads! We pick the time and the place."

"Good enough for me."

The wagons began rolling immediately. Merrit talked briefly to the two men who had been handling the horse herd. Neither had been hurt. They said they had just sighted the cottonwoods and the horses had barely scented the water when the firing began. They heard the big rifle first, then the six-guns. They counted nine men. None got close enough for them to see one with long hair.

"One of 'em kept laughing though. You could hear him nigh a quarter of a mile away. Loud, fool giggle I'd know anywhere," one of the herders said.

That would be Harmon Griffin. Merrit saved that information for himself. He saw the two herders ride out ahead of the train to begin rounding up what horses and mules they could find by moonlight. Suddenly one of the herders galloped back and pulled up beside Merrit.

"We picked these three up. Maybe you can find use for

them. I can, if I ever meet the feller whose gun throwed them," he said.

He dropped three empty .45-70 casings into Merrit's hand and galloped away again.

Merrit had time to think things over by the time he reached the house. He avoided Bonnie. The cook had steak, eggs, and potatoes ready, and Merrit discovered that he was ravenously hungry and that his leg ached. He had overdone it, and now he probably would pay for it.

"Have a fast team harnessed to the buggy," he told Lawler. "I'm going into town and see what kind of sheriff we've got."

"I can tell you what kind," Lawler said. "Nice fellow. Honest as the day is long, but mighty damn legal. What have you got to show him? Couple of cartridges, couple of Twenty Plus horses."

"That's the point. Let's see what he says. Lawler, it's time a few people stood up to be counted."

"I'm going with you."

"You'll stay here," Merrit snarled.

Lawler thought it over. "Then you'll take Whitey with you. He's old, but he's a steady head, and he knows that town and them people."

There was no use arguing. By the time Merrit had eaten, a fresh team was fidgeting on the buggy tongue. As Merrit climbed into the buggy, sparing his bad leg all he could, Bonnie ran out of the house. Behind her, in the shadows, Merrit could see the peaked-hat silhouettes of the Mexicans. It seemed to him that there were now eight or ten of them, but that figured, and it made him feel better.

"Where are you going?" Bonnie demanded.

"Town."

"I'll go with you. You're crazy mad. You haven't got any sense when you're mad! You'll ruin everything. I'm a Keller! I've got friends in Strickland."

"You've got nothing," he said flatly. "Come on, old man."

Whitey, the old rider, got into the buggy, carrying a .30-30 lever-action carbine, which he propped between his knees. Wordlessly he shook the lines. The team bolted, leaving Bonnie standing in the moonlight. Merrit saw the Mexicans come out and surround her before the buggy wheeled out of the yard and out of sight.

"Mind telling me what you aim to do?" Whitey said.

"Put it up to the sheriff."

"Don't allow he'll do much. What then?"

"We'll go from there, Whitey."

·A long silence. Then Whitey said, "I fit with Sherman in the war. Now there was a general! Drove his men hard when the time came, but when he fit, he usually found a way to fight on his own terms. Sometimes it's powerful hard to wait, Mr. Merrit. But it's worse to take a licking."

Merrit said absently, "Yes . . . yes."

Whitey went on ramblingly, "They's two ways to fight a battle—offensively and defensively. Best way is to combine the two. Make the other fella attack you, but be ready to go over to the offensive when he has spent his attack. You win more fights thataway and you live longer."

"What about it?"

"Why—nothing, I guess. On'y I seen too many good men shot to death because some captain or colonel or general got mad."

"You drive the horses. I give the orders."

"Yes, Mr. Merrit."

The team settled down to a rhythmic run that threw the light buggy roughly from side to side. Little by little, Merrit's rage subsided. Funny thing, he thought—I haven't got a lick of sense when I'm mad, but it grated to have Bonnie tell me that. This old Whitey is no fool. I can't let myself be forced into the wrong fight. . . .

They saw first a tall pillar of smoke in the moonlight, then brief flickers of red. Both vanished as they reached the town. "The Speece House, I guess," Whitey murmured. "Somebody got drunk and tipped over a lamp. Was bound to happen."

Merrit shook his head. "The Speece House is adobe. It wouldn't make that much of a blaze. I have a bad feeling I know what it was."

He was right. It was Billy O'Shea's bar, and it had already been destroyed by the time they reached it. There were a few men standing around the smoking shell of the building, but he recognized none of them. He crossed to the Speece House and told Whitey to wait for him and stay out of trouble.

The door of the Speece House was locked for the first time in history. Merrit pounded on it savagely. A strange girl's voice asked him, through the closed door, what he wanted. "I want to talk to Albine," he said, "and I'm coming in if I have to kick the door down."

"You don't have to do that," came Albine's voice, wearily. She opened the door and looked at him coldly. "You finally catched it, didn't you? You wanted trouble and you got it. Now you want to drag me into it."

"You're already in it. You always were." He pushed her aside and stepped into the lobby, closing the door behind him. Three of her "girls" were there. One was Bessie, the woman from room number 3. All looked terrified. Bessie pleaded with him, with her eyes, not to make any more trouble.

He took Albine by her upper arm, like a policeman. "Start talking. Where's Billy? What happened?"

"They took him home. He——"

"Where's home?"

"He boards with that old woman, Mrs. Huey. She——"

"I know where she lives. How is he?" Abline shrugged and looked away. He went on roughly, "What happened? Why did they burn him out?"

"Listen, you son-of-a-bitch, you're not hazing me!"

He took her by both arms and shook her hard, at the same time forcing her backward until her back was against the wall. He kept shaking her, gritting, "Albine, if you talk up like a lady, I can treat you like a lady. If you want it the other way, I can do that, too. Try me!"

Real astonishment and fear came into her eyes. She struggled weakly to get loose, then surrendered. He did not release his deep, biting grip on her arms.

"All I know, Merrit, is what I heard. Bunch of Aaron's boys rode in, whooping and hollering and having the time of their lives. They——"

"Was Aaron with them?"

"He rode on. He didn't get off his horse, Merrit. He left them there and rode on, and they went inside."

Now he knew who it was, if Davidson had been with them. It was the crew that had shot up the horseherd, those left of them. He knew why they wanted to drink, too. A man got a bad taste in his mouth after a job like that, if he really was a man.

"Then what?"

"Nobody knows what started it. Some of the boys got to fighting among themselves. That fellow Griffin—do you know him?—well, him and a big Dutchman by the name of Jake Seeck and another fella, I don't recall his name——"

"Rob McKesson?"

"That's the one, yes. There was a fight. They walked out. I seen them ride away myself, long before the fire started. That's when I locked up. I don't want no bunch of fighting drunks in my place, no time!"

"You're one hell of a friend in need, Albine. Then what happened?"

"I don't know for sure. I heard somebody was talking about shooting up somebody's horses. You know Billy and horses. He ordered them out of his place, is what I hear. He tried to back it up with that chunk of lead-weighted pitchfork handle he keeps as a persuader, and they jumped him and worked him over and set fire to the place."

"And then rode merrily out of town."

"I reckon. What else would you expect?"

"Why," Merrit said, "I would expect the sheriff to put somebody under arrest. I would expect some legal action to redress a breach of the peace."

Albine had her composure back. "Get off your soap box, Merrit. Get yourself a bowl of soup. You're plumb light-headed."

"If it's any comfort to you," Merrit said, as he went out the door, "you told me nothing. You haven't taken sides."

"Thanks for that, anyway!"

He hoisted himself into the buggy. "You know the Widow Huey's place. Let's go there."

He had never been at the tiny, ramshackle place where old Billy had boarded and roomed for nearly thirty years. A lean, hard-faced, gray-haired woman opened the door a crack at his knock. "You don't have to beat the house down," she drawled in a white-trash Southern whine. "They's a sick man in here."

"I'm Merrit. I want to see him."

"I'll see if he's able. He'd prob'ly like to talk to you. Come in."

"Will I be getting you mixed up in my troubles?"

"I make up my own mind. Nobody mixes me into what I don't aim to mix in. Come in, I said."

She picked up a kerosene lamp and led the way through the low-ceilinged house, which was crammed, old-woman style, with the gimcracks and knicknacks accumulated over a lifetime. Merrit saw an ancient .44 in her apron pocket as she opened Billy's room and stood aside.

"G'awn in. Reckon he's conscious."

The woman put the lamp down on the bureau, closed the door, and went outside. Nothing Albine had said had prepared him for the bloody, beaten wreck he saw on the bed. One of Billy's eyes was smashed in, its sight lost forever. His nose was crushed and filled with clotted blood. He breathed noisily and with difficulty through cut and swollen lips. His white hair was matted with blood.

Merrit sat down beside the bed and put his hand on Billy's arm. "How are you, Billy?"

"Hello, Merrit," came Billy's faint voice. "Nice of you to come see me."

"Nobody else did?"

"Only Albine and one of her girls. That Bessie."

I'll be damned, Merrit thought. That took guts. . . ! He said, "Don't try to talk, Billy. I know why this happened. I'll take care of it, don't worry."

"I'd expect that of you, but listen, Merrit——"

"No, save yourself. Your job is to get well."

"Will you listen?" Billy said hoarsely. "I'm not going to make it. I'm all stove up inside. Listen while you've got the chance."

"I'm listening," Merrit said soothingly.

"Merrit, you're up against a crazy man."

"I know that."

"No you don't—not how crazy he is. I always did say that any man who liked to kill was crazy. I been keeping bar for fifty years. Never was anything I couldn't handle, until that bunch of bloodthirsty bastards tonight. Been out shooting down horses—laughing about it, telling about how funny it was, those horses dragging their own guts around and walking on them—" Billy shuddered.

"I saw it," Merrit said. "It was the work of a crazy man, yes. And I'll take care of it."

Billy was silent a moment. Then he said, "I've got to skip a lot. I haven't got forever. Merrit, you think this fight is about the railroad, don't you?"

"Well, isn't it?"

"You damn fool! It's about Mrs. Keller."

"Bonnie?"

"Bonnie. She spit in Aaron's face once. He told it around. What kind of a man would do that? Don't listen to Albine. She can't believe he'd give a damn about another woman. She thinks it's money, money, money. Money's important to Aaron, sure. But it's nothing—nothing!—to making that girl pay for spitting in his face."

"I didn't know about that," Merrit said. "Where did it happen?"

"Outside of church one day is all I know. She never went to church again."

Billy closed his eyes. Merrit watched him a few moments and then, in alarm, threw the door open and called the old woman. She came shuffling rapidly to the room.

"I'm scared it's all over," Merrit said.

Mrs. Huey felt Billy's face. She bent down to listen for his breath, then pulled the blanket up over his head. "He held out longer than I expected," she drawled. "Long enough to get it said."

"You listened?"

"I listened. But I already knowed."

"About Bonnie spitting in Davidson's face?"

"About that, yes. What do you aim to do?"

"Why," Merrit said carefully, "see the sheriff."

"What good will that do? Jack Van Sant, you mean. He'll write out a report and promise to investigate."

"He'll do more than that. By God, he'll stand up and be counted! So will a lot of others."

The old woman picked up the lamp, and he followed her out of the deathroom. He heard her mumble, "Well, the fool killer has got his work cut out for him."

"Talk sense!"

In the tiny front room, she put the lamp down. "Billy tell you Aaron Davidson is crazy?"

"I already knew that."

She muttered a contemptuous vulgarity. "That's too easy.

I's the only person in this town that knowed Aaron years ago, when he come through the first time. He——"

"Davidson was here before?"

"Ain't that what I just told you? Come through with a bunch of movers. Horse-traders, they called themselves. He was maybe twenty-two. He——"

"Davidson came from the movers' wagons?"

"Sho'ly! They was some trouble about some groceries that was stole. The people here burned the wagons for them and run them out of town. Last I seen of Aaron, he had a coat of tar and feathers in his hair. He was runnin' barefoot, but he clipped it off pretty good. I don't know if you got any idea the kind of trash them movers was. . . ."

"I have."

"Then you'll know why he came back, and what kind of crazy man he is. Ambition's a funny thing, even in a normal feller. You take one that come from the wagons——"

"I know, I know."

"Will you want to take care of burying Billy?"

"Yes. I've got lots to do—things Billy would want done. But I'll stand the bills, and I'll be there, if you could kindly make the arrangements."

"How about ten in the morning? Want I should hire a preacher? Billy would take it kindly. I can get that young Pastor Schneider. The fool-killer's going to get him someday, too. He's plumb fond enough to figger he can make a Christian out of anybody, but it'll take a fool to get up there and say the words over Billy."

"Get him. I'll be there."

He went out to the buggy and lifted himself into it with a grimace of pain. "The sheriff's office," he said. "I suppose he's home having fried chicken, biscuits, and gravy, but we'll try the office first."

"You bet, Mr. Merrit," Whitey said.

The buggy rolled. Merrit thought sickly, He came from the movers' wagons. He's got the same shamed poison in him that she has, only a million times worse, and she spit in his face. She spit in his face! That poor, sweet fool of a girl. Couldn't she tell. . . ?

Chapter Nine

THE SHERIFF's office was in the rear of the new courthouse, on the ground floor. As Whitey stopped the team in front of the lighted door, Merrit saw Newton Price reeling down the street. He waved to him, and the lawyer came to the buggy. "My legs are drunk, Mr. Merrit," he said, "but from the neck up, I'm stone sober."

"That is a relief," Merrit said. "This sheriff—Van Sant—what's he like?"

"He's been eating regularly since he was elected. He didn't always."

"The judge—does he amount to a hill of beans?"

"His Honor, David Day Gillespie, late major in the Confederate States' Army? He's foxy. I've known better lawyers."

"Have you ever known a worse one?"

Price thought this over gravely. "A few, yes. Why this juridical survey? Do you contemplate a civil suit, or is your interest criminal?"

"I don't know. I like to know where people stand. So far, the only man I've seen who has the guts to stand anywhere died for it."

"Billy O'Shea."

"Yes. Is he the only one in town?"

"Mr. Merrit," the lawyer said softly, "you're asking that people commit themselves to a dispute that is not yet theirs. Oh, it will be eventually, I grant you that. When it's too late, most of them will take a stand. A few may do so before it's too late—a few never will. It isn't cowardice or dishonesty you're protesting against but inertia. We find our mossy nitch, and we dislike being dislodged from it."

"By God, I'll dislodge a few! I'm going to see a division

69

of the house—the ayes on one side and the nays on the
other. We'll know the sheep from the goats," Merrit said.

"Yes, yes. Admirable, but difficult. You may count on me
for anything a drunk can do."

"Thank you."

"One thing more. I have legal custody of your last will and
testament, even though you put it in the bank for physical
safekeeping. You are a suspicious soul, Mr. Merrit. It occurred
to me that you might not be above suspecting me of taking
liberties with your testamentary directions. To protect myself,
I mailed a fair copy of your will to your brother Clint, your
chief heir. If you're not here to finish this fight, you needn't
worry about being betrayed by a drunk."

"You call me suspicious." Merrit grinned. "By the eternal,
at least I don't suspect myself."

Price closed his eyes and recited sonorously:

"This above all, to thine own self be true,
   And it shall follow, as the night the day,
   Thou canst not then be false to any man!"

"I like that," Merrit said.

"Balderdash! Aaron Davidson is true to himself. And I'm
true to myself." Price waved a hand toward the courthouse.
"The sheriff is in. Pray take a seat, sir. The toga of high
office fires many a faint heart. You may work a miracle."

He stumbled on down the street. Merrit went into the
sheriff's office, into a small reception room with a desk, a
chair, and a bench. A pimpled-face youth, barely old enough
to vote, wearing a deputy's star, sat behind the desk. On a
corner of the desk sat a portly man with prematurely gray
hair and a young, plump but handsome face. He carried a
half-opened umbrella.

"I take it you expect rain," Merrit said.

Sheriff Van Sant blinked. "Not necessarily. But I go prepared. What's on your mind, cowboy."

Merrit said, "You can start out by getting used to calling me
by my name. I'm George Merrit. I've got three empty forty-
five seventy shells in my pocket. I've got a couple of Twenty
Plus horses tied out at my place. There are a couple at the
railroad grading camp. These shells and these horses are

evidence that Aaron Davidson's crew shot up a horseherd that was on its way to the grading contractor. They killed, I figure, up to fifty or sixty expensive horses and mules. What'll mean less to the railroad is that they killed four men, too. We killed three of theirs. I'm reporting the crime, sheriff."

The handsome face sagged. A cloud of dread came into the sheriff's eyes as his whole inner personality collapsed. He fumbled with his umbrella and licked his lips. "Now wait, now wait," he said. "You seen all of this? You witnessed it personally?"

"I didn't see them hit the horseherd—no. I didn't see them kill any men. But I can give you witnesses for everything I told you."

"You're sure they'll testify? It's more than most would do. Can they swear the men that killed them horses and men were the ones on them Twenty Plus horses? S'pose we start at the beginning, Merrit, and tell me just what *you* can testify to."

"You'll have to do better than that," Merrit said. "Those teamsters will be coming back through here in a couple of days. Do you want them to take this town apart?"

The sheriff ignored that. He said stolidly, "Now wait a minute. As I see it, you are accusing the Twenty Plus of trying to wreck the railroad. Be resonable. A big outfit like that, with maybe a million dollars at stake? Is that the way you see it?"

I can't, Merrit thought, take one thing more. . . . He said quiveringly but softly, "No, the way I see it, Van Sant, is that you're just a yellow son-of-a-bitch."

He lunged against the sheriff with his shoulder, knocking him across his own desk. He knocked the gun out of the sheriff's holster and let it fall, ignoring the young deputy's weapon. He got the sheriff by the lapels and banged him up and down on the desk, saying thickly, "They say you're an honest man, but the only thing worse than an honest coward is one who's a fool besides. I came in here to tell you about a damned bloody raid no Comanche would be guilty of. All right, you untie my hands when you weasel out. Just stay to hell out of my way when I handle it myself!"

He threw the sheriff aside as the young deputy reached for his gun. Merrit snaked out his own gun and jammed it in the kid's belly. "Stay out of it!" he said. "Don't make me kill you. And if you mean to stay in this business, take a lesson from this. If you're afraid to stand up and be counted, go back to punching cows."

The kid took his hand away from his gun. Merrit let him keep it. The sheriff had fallen across his umbrella, bending it. He stumbled to his feet, his face pale and his jaw quivering. And yet he had his own kind of guts, Merrit thought.

"You have no call to jump me like that," the sheriff said doggedly. "I've taken an oath. I'll look into this, just like I'm going to scald somebody's ass for beating up on poor old Billy O'Shea, but——"

"You don't know that Billy died?"

The sheriff sagged still more. "No. I'm right sorry to hear that, and it'll go hard with them that done it when I do catch them. I'll arrest somebody and I'll try to see to it that they're hanged for it. And I'll look into this horse-shooting. But you get this, Mr. Merrit: I am not your partisan or anybody else's. If you think because you've fallen heir to half of the PK that you can ride my tail—why, you think again! I only know of one man shoots a forty-five seventy. He's going to tell me where he was when those empty shells was fired—if you really got them."

Merrit tossed him the empty shells. "You do it your way," he said. He looked at the kid deputy. "What's your name, in case we meet again?"

"M—Milt Sedgewick," the deputy stammered.

"This is a good place to get killed, Milt. Some men feel strongly enough about law that it's worth it. If it's just a job to you, better quit it fast, before this fool gets your head shot off."

It was hard not to show a limp as he returned to the buggy. He said, "Home," and old Whitey turned the horses and let them run. More than an hour and a half later, Merrit held the team, to save his bad leg, while Whitey got out and opened the gate across the road that led to the house.

There were several lights in the big house, but when Whitey looked at him questioningly, Merrit shook his head. A small Mexican came out of the shadows under the trees, barring their way with a rifle. Merrit leaned out and said, "I'm Merrit. Who are you?"

"I am called Elodio, Señor Merrit."

"I don't know you, do I?"

"I am a variety of cousin, señor," Elodio said apologetically.

"There are perhaps other cousins here—cousins I have not yet met?"

"Perhaps."

"Then eat well!"

"God will thank you."

Merrit said to Whitey, "Take me to the little barn. Then you go to the bunkhouse, and in my bunk you'll find a brown paper sack. Bring it and a lantern to me, and it's nobody's business but your own."

He waited in the dark barn until Whitey had unharnessed the team, turned them loose in a corral, and gone plodding up toward the bunkhouse. He dropped his pants and drawers, and looked at his wound. There was no pus, but it had broken open again in front and was trickling blood. The exit wound, behind, was fiery sore to touch, but it was dry.

Instead of Whitey, it was Lawler E. Lawler who brought the brown paper bag and the lantern, and caught Merrit examining his wound by moonlight.

"All right, now you know," Merrit said savagely. "But keep your mouth shut. If they know they've got half a man to deal with, we're through."

"You can't ride with that."

"I have to ride with it!"

"Why? You're the boss man now—act it! I'll have Whitey drive you. Why should a man as rich as you straddle a horse like a hired hand?"

Merrit took the bandage lint out of the sack, but Lawler knelt and did the bandaging for him. "Nice clean hole. You got healthy blood. Stay on your butt in the buggy for a few days, and you'll have the prettiest little scar."

"I'll look like a fool."

"You'll look like a man that's rich and ain't ashamed to show it."

Merrit slammed his fist into his palm. "Aaron Davidson doesn't ride in a buggy!"

Lawler finished the bandage and stood up. "Suit yourself, but if that leg plays out on you when you need it, it's Bonnie that'll pay for it."

The fight went out of Merrit. He pulled up his pants and buttoned them, and handed the paper sack back to Lawler. He saw no sign of the Mexicans as he stalked toward the house, but he knew they were watching him. He knew that any stranger who approached this way would have been covered—head, heart, and vulnerable abdomen—by half a dozen guns.

He rapped on the door, and immediately Bonnie flung it open. "George! What's wrong?" she cried.

He pushed into the house and closed the door. She was in a nightgown and apparently had been sitting in one of the big chairs with a blanket around her. Her hair was in curlpapers, and the pallor of her face made her look about thirteen years old.

"Bonnie," he said, "why did you spit in Aaron Davidson's face?"

"He was fresh."

"You said Willie Phelps was fresh. Did you spit in his face too?"

"No."

"But you did in Aaron's. What did he say to you?"

"I'm not going to tell you."

He reached for her shoulders. She pulled the blanket closer to her and stepped back, exclaiming, "Now George, we've had enough of this. I don't have to explain things to you or anybody else."

"Listen to me, Bonnie, listen. I suppose Lawler told you about the horseherd."

"Yes. It's typical of Aaron."

"Tonight that same bunch beat Billy O'Shea to death and burned his place out."

Her hands went to her white cheeks. The blanket slipped. She clutched at it wildly. "Oh God, no!"

Mimicking her, he said, "Oh God, yes. I'm going to the funeral tomorrow."

"I'll go with you."

"No you won't. Bonnie, you haven't been fair with me, and it cost me a good friend. I'd believe Billy O'Shea on anything he said, and his deathbed words were that this fight isn't about money, or the railroad, or anything but you. Do you understand that? You!"

"Aaron's crazy!"

Holding his temper, yet wishing he could backhand slap some sense into her, Merrit said, "That's right, Aaron's crazy. But not the way you think. That long-haired man has got a twist in his mind, and do you know why?" She only stared at him as he repeated harshly, "Do you know why? Did you know that Aaron was a mover's kid? He came out of the wagons, too. And you spit in his face!"

"Aaron, a mover?" she said stupidly. "Oh you're lying!"

"Bonnie, you really didn't know?"

"How could I?" Then she shivered and looked away. "Oh, but I should have, I should have! When you're trash, you know other trash." She looked at him. "So that was it. A mover's kid!"

"What did he say to you that made you spit in his face?"

"That doesn't matter. He——"

"What did he say to you, God damn it?"

He was left standing with only the blanket in his hand. She was across the room from him in her nightgown, screaming, "Oh, you fool! You high-and-mighty fool! George, there was always something missing in you, and now I know what it is. You're a *gentleman!* Oh, go sleep in the bunkhouse. Do you think if Aaron had inherited half of the PK, he wouldn't have taken everything that goes with it? What do you care what he said? You wouldn't understand it anyway. You're a *gentleman!* Or ask Albine Anderson. She knows!"

"Bonnie, when you come to your senses——"

"My senses! Oh, dumb, dumb, dumb—what a fool you are! I should have taken Aaron up on it. We're two of a kind, he and I. Go sleep in the bunkhouse."

He said wearily, "All right, but keep it in mind that I don't mean to lose any more friends like Billy O'Shea because of your trashy tastes."

Another time, the look of pain on her face might have weakened him, but not tonight. As Merrit left the house, Emilio came out of the shadows and saluted him silently. Bonnie was well guarded, he thought. Against everything but her worst enemy—herself.

Chapter Ten

THEY WENT to the funeral in style. He and Whitey both wore white shirts and dark pants. They had bits of black in their hatbands and their boots were polished. Whitey had put up the top of the buggy—even blackened and shined it. He drove Buck and Mike, with the black dress harness and the brass-bound hames wrapped in black.

It might rain, Merrit thought, before the morning was over. They did not reach the cemetery until a few minutes before ten. Merrit knew that O'Shea had been a well-liked man, and he had expected a good crowd. He could have counted them on the fingers of both hands.

What surprised him was the absence of Albine Anderson. Bessie was there, but none of the other girls. A still greater surprise came just as the young preacher began the opening prayer. Harmon Griffin, Rob McKesson, and Jake Seeck rode up, tied their horses to the fence, and came forward, pulling off their hats.

"I am the Resurrection and the life. . . ."

The young preacher, Pastor Schneider, had a deep Dutch accent, but guts, too. He asked the Lord to receive a good man who had come to death in a bad way. Then he took off on a sermon that made Merrit's hair stand on end.

"I am not going to beat around any bushes. We are all witnesses to murder. We are burying more than a man. We are putting our own self-respect in the dirt. We are covering up the pride and honor of a town. I came to this country because they told me it was a free country. It was a nation of law and of people who live by the Golden Rule. Well, I tell you, if this is an example—how Billy O'Shea was murdered—then I say, God's curse on the hypocrites who stand by and let it happen."

"Amen!" came a woman's voice.

Merrit looked around furtively and saw that it was Bessie. Well, Billy, he thought with pride, there are a few who aren't afraid to stand up and be counted—a whore and a preacher. Good for you, young reverend. . . !

Afterward Merrit stayed and helped fill Billy's grave and stamp it down. Harmon, Rob, and Jake did not help, but neither did they leave until the job was done. Merrit watched them go to their horses and swing up into their saddles. "You boys are in mighty big business," he said then. "I wonder you had the guts to show up here."

"Go to hell," said Jake Seeck. They whirled their horses and rode away.

Merrit sensed somebody behind him. He turned and saw Bessie. He smiled at her. "Glad you could make it, Bessie," he said. "Billy would appreciate it."

"I didn't come for that. Albine sent me. She wants to see you."

The woman was so frightened Merrit was afraid she might faint then and there. "I'll be right over," he said.

Bessie shook her head. "She's not there. The place is closed—for good, I guess. The others all left town on the early stage this morning. I—I'd have gone, too. But somebody had to stay with Albine."

"What's the matter with Albine? Where is she?"

"Shh! Not now. She's at the Empire House, room two-twenty. She wants you to take her out to your place."

"To the PK? Why?"

"Aaron had her beat half to death last night. Oh my God, Merrit, she looks horrible, and she's scared—so scared! Can —can you take her?"

"To the PK? Sure. But why?"

"I don't want to talk about it. I don't know anything about it. But can I come too?"

"Sure. Calm down, Bessie. You stick with Whitey and me. Get in the buggy. We'll go get Albine right away."

"Not now. She's in no shape. Can't you make it later today?" Bessie said piteously.

He had things to do, but he was not altogether his own master. "Whenever you say, Bessie. Wait in the buggy."

The woman went to the buggy and stood there with Whitey. The young preacher waited until Merrit was alone.

"You are Mr. Merrit," he said, offering his hand. "I am pleased to know you. I am sorry Mrs. Keller could not come."

"It wasn't the time or the place, but she wanted to," Merrit said. "You have got guts, Pastor Schneider."

The young minister shrugged his beefy shoulders. "Anybody can have guts. But you need sense to go with them. Could I ask what you are going to do now?"

"I don't know."

"Could I give a suggestion? File a lawsuit!"

Merrit smiled. "I'm afraid that wouldn't help."

"Are you sure? There is such a thing as right and wrong, Mr. Merrit. People do respond, one way or another. If the law is no good here, why let's find it out! Somebody has got to stand up for what's right. Maybe this time they will."

Just what I've been saying, Merrit thought. Stand up and be counted. . . ! "You're probably right," he said. "If my lawyer can think of anybody to sue. I thank you, and we'll see what he says."

Pastor Schneider smiled. "Is better than shooting, if it works. I have wanted to meet you a long time. As Mrs. Keller told me, I have been taking good care of your little boy's grave here, every time I have a funeral."

"My little boy? I'm afraid you're mistaken."

"You are Merrit? George Francis Merrit?"

Something cold and frightful went through Merrit. His mind went back eight years, and his cold heart went with it, to a time when Bonnie never could remember his middle name. When they were both kids, fugitives, broke and hopeless tramps, and she was trying to learn all she could about him in the shortest possible time. His name was George Fallon Merrit, and yet she never remembered it. To Bonnie he was always George *Francis* Merrit.

"You have not seen the grave?" Pastor Schneider was saying. "This way."

Merrit knew where the Keller plot was. Ma Keller had had a big obelisk of Vermont marble put up over old Pat. When she died, apparently Bonnie had been unable to duplicate the stone. Ma's stone was the same size and shape, but it was of native sandstone. And next to Ma was the smaller stone that marked Dick Keller's grave.

Beyond the Keller plot was another, with a small cube of granite, polished only on its slanting top. On it were only the words and the dates:

GEORGE FRANCIS MERRIT
April 9, 1881—January 18, 1882

It came to him with a shaming shock that this little fellow could not possibly be Dick Keller's son. He went blind to the world around him and dropped to his knees, clutching at the stone with both hands. Oh, you poor little child, he thought, and I never even knew you were on the earth. They never told me. . . .

He tried to remember, and eventually did. She would have been pregnant, then, when Ma took her up to the house. Bonnie had no sense—she wouldn't know about such things. But Ma Keller did. Ma Keller wanted an heir for the place, any way she could get him.

"Didn't you know about him?" Pastor Schneider said.

Merrit looked up, shaking his head. "Nobody told me, before or after—then or now. That old woman stole him. She stole my son before he was born!"

"It was before my time. All I heard is the gossip."

"Why didn't Bonnie tell me?" Merrit burst out. "When I came back, I mean?"

"I don't know. Neither do I judge."

"How did he die?"

"I would rather you asked Newt Price that."

"I'll ask him, all right! He knew and didn't tell me either."

Merrit did not remember going to the buggy, but when he felt it stop and looked up, he was in front of Newt Price's law office. Bessie was between him and Whitey, and young Pastor Schneider had ridden standing up on the trap behind. The preacher dropped off and took Merrit's arm, and Merrit knew there was no use trying to shake him off.

Newt Price was writing at his desk when Merrit went in, the preacher a step behind him. The lawyer started to smile a greeting, but he saw the look on Merrit's face. Merrit put both hands on the desk and leaned across it.

"You helped steal my son," he said thickly.

Price dropped his pen and narrowed his eyes. "You walked away from him before he was born—before I ever came here. Don't shift your guilt to me."

"You held out on me!"

"I never refused to answer a question of yours, Merrit. If Bonnie did not choose to tell you, I sure as hell wouldn't."

"And I have to find out I had a son from his gravestone!" Merrit hit the desk with his fist.

"You poor devil."

"No, no—I don't want your pity. I want to know about that baby."

"I'll tell you what I can. I knew you the minute you walked in this door, Merrit, because he was the image of you. Black hair, black eyes, your forehead, nose, and mouth—it was a little hard on Dick Keller. No, you wanted to know about it, so listen to me!" Price said.

"Ma wanted the child registered and baptized as a Keller, and she could have handled Dick. Anybody could handle Dick. But she couldn't handle Bonnie. The child bears your name on the records, Merrit—George Francis Merrit. Ma still made the child her heir. I drew the will myself.

"Your baby—not you—would have inherited the PK, had he lived. Ma idolized that child. She knew by then that Bonnie would never have a child by Dick. If I may be a trifle indelicate, it would have been a physical impossibility because they never lived together as man and wife. Even Ma Keller had to accept that."

"The hell with Ma Keller! How did the baby die?"

"I'm coming to that. They were in town here to buy some things, Ma and Bonnie and the baby. Bonnie was patient with the old lady. She let Ma hold the child, baby it, fuss over it. They were in here to let Ma sign a lease on some school land she leased. The baby was all right when they left here.

"From here they went to the hardware store. The old lady had the kid on her hip—sidesaddle, you might say—the way country women tote their kids. She tripped on a damned rotten board and fell, that's all. The child's head struck a pile of bolts, with the old lady on top of him—and Ma was a heavy woman.

"The doctor said the child died instantly, if that's a comfort to you. It wasn't to Ma."

Merrit closed his eyes. "It's not to me either."

The lawyer said compassionately, "You can see the vengeful hand of God in it, if you're of a mind—but if you do, you've got to be consistent. Show me a man who never stumbled, yourself included, and I'll show you the prophet Elias returned to earth."

Merrit had fallen into a chair. He stood up again and leaned across the desk. "Don't make excuses for her. That old woman killed my child!"

Price stood up, too. "That she did."

"And Bonnie let her, and didn't tell me."

"Yes-sirree-Bob, and you're the son-of-a-bitch who got her pregnant in an oat field and then rode off and let a whelp like Dick Keller marry her."

"Now God have mercy on you, Price——"

Merrit jabbed out with both fists, but the lawyer was sober and, today, sure of himself. He hooked a solid right to Merrit's temple. Merrit went down on the desk, but came up swinging again. I'll kill this flabby drunk, he thought. He can sting me, and that's good. It feels good to hurt, but I'll get him. . . .

The lawyer hooked again, then again. When Merrit came to, he was lying on the desk. Pastor Schneider was mopping his face with lukewarm water. The lawyer waited implacably until Merrit struggled to get up.

"Do you want some more, Merrit, or will you listen?"

Merrit said, "I'll listen."

"After that baby was born, Dick Keller came to me for a divorce. I threw him out, told him to get another lawyer. There's another one in town, Alec Whitman. I never knew him to turn down any case, however grubby. He threw Dick out, too. Not because he was afraid of Ma Keller, but because that's the kind of friends Bonnie has in this town. After the baby died, Dick tried to make up with her. She wouldn't have it. She stayed married, for the old lady's sake. But she lived in the big house and Dick slept in the bunkhouse.

"Now I'll tell you something else, Merrit. After Dick was killed, I asked Bonnie to marry me. She turned me down. Not because I was a drunk. Not because I wasn't making any money. And not because she owned half of the PK—Dick's half. Do you want it in her own words?"

Merrit covered his face. "No," he choked.

"You'll get it anyway. She said, 'Someday George Merrit will come back. We'll both be older then. I have to wait and see if he still wants me.' That's what she said."

Even with his eyes closed, Merrit could still see Ma Keller —fat, always beaming and smiling, always talking of love and ambition and fair play and suchlike. He groaned, "That damned old woman."

"All in all," Price said, "I wasn't one of her critics, Merrit. Grace Keller was what she had to be. She survived where a dozen—fifty—a hundred!—cattlemen failed. She would have made your little boy a rich man. She has made you a rich man."

"That's another thing. How do I get rid of that property?"

"You can deed it to Bonnie. If you do, I'll ask her again to marry me, and I won't let her alone until she does. Put that in your pipe and smoke it, you stiff-necked son-of-a-bitch!"

Merrit's whole neck, head, and jaw ached from Price's punches, but he felt scoured clean inside. "No man was ever close enough to talk like that to me before," he said. "I'll think this over—when I can think. Then I'll come back, and we'll shake hands or maybe I'll kill you. I have yet to decide."

"Whatever you like," Price said. "I'm really sorry for you. I saw your son, and you didn't. He would have been a real man. Not so much from you, Merrit, as from Bonnie. She's not a quitter."

Chapter Eleven

MERRIT WAS too badly shaken to give an order when he got to the buggy. The news of his child's birth and death had driven everything else from his mind. It was Bessie who reminded him that he had promised to bring Albine from the Empire. He agreed absently.

They found the woman in her room. Merrit had seen badly beaten people before, but never anything like this. He thought her nose and cheekbones had been broken. Her mouth was a twisted pulp.

She had been drinking steadily. "It's the only thing that helps. I told you, didn't I, Merrit? You're a troublemaker. Oh, you righteous fools. *You* never get hurt, but you sure raise hell with everybody else!"

"Why did he do it, Albine?"

She began crying. "What do you care? Go on, let me alone! I can take care of myself."

"You sure don't look it, Albine."

He tried to persuade her to come out to the ranch, but she refused to go, and Merrit was in no mood to argue with a drunk. When he returned to the street with Bessie, the stage was just loading up. She began crying too. "I want to get out of here, Merrit. Did you see what that long-haired man did to her? She'll never be the same again."

"Your clothes, Bessie. You haven't got time to pack them."

"The hell with clothes!" she screamed. "What good are clothes with a face like Albine's?"

He gave her $50 and flagged the stage for her just as it started past the hotel. He watched it out of sight. Pastor Schneider came up to him. "Don't worry about the woman in the hotel, Mr. Merrit," he said. "I've got a few friends. I'll see she's taken care of."

"You're fixing to get your head shot off, mixing in Davidson's affairs," said Merrit.

"I take my chances. How about that lawsuit?"

"What lawsuit?" Merrit didn't even remember. When the young preacher reminded him, he said, "Some other time. I've got other things on my mind now."

But all the resistance had gone out of him. He could not just walk away from Schneider, although he felt like it. He seemed to be numb, without a will of his own. He let the preacher lead him back to Price's office, Whitey following in the buggy.

Price had started to drink, and he was in a bad mood. "It

seems to me you're going out of your way to make enemies for other people, Merrit," he said.

"What other people?"

"Myself, among others. What do I owe you?"

"It is not what you owe Merrit," Schneider said. "It is what you owe the town, the people, the law—above all, yourself."

"Nonsense. Oh, if we had a suit, I don't mind another enemy or two," Price said. "But this isn't Merrit's idea, Reverend. This is yours. And a cold client makes a weak case."

"Give me time, Price. I'll warm up," Merrit said.

"What do you hope to accomplish?"

"I want to see every mother's son in this town stand up and be counted. That goes for the Judge. That goes for you. Listen, Price—if Rolf panics and stops building the railroad, I'm hurt. Maybe Bonnie and I can last out the summer, but we'll be worth ten thousand dollars apiece less than we are now, if snow flies before the rails get here. Rolf told me——"

"What he told you in private, and what he'll say on the witness stand, are probably two different things. Merrit, the overwhelming fact here is that the railroad is bigger than you, me, Bonnie, Aaron Davidson, and Judge Gillespie put together." He looked at the preacher. "The giant, Goliath, was slain by a smaller man with a slingshot only once. Since then, the giants have won consistently."

Merrit said, "Price, I will give you five hundred dollars to file a lawsuit. Any kind of lawsuit."

"When?"

"Today. Let's go to the bank now."

Price suddenly laughed. Shaking his head, he said, "I have often wondered what Gillespie would do if I came before him with a writ of mandamus. I'm not sure he ever heard of one. If you are fool enough to pay for it, I'm just fool enough to file it!"

"What kind of a proposition is that?"

"It is a form of injunction, but it prays for an affirmative action, rather than the forbidding of one." Price suddenly looked animated, happy, cold sober. "I will ask that the court forbid Aaron Davidson and the Twenty Plus from interfering with the construction of the railroad. That is an ordinary restraining order. I will further ask that the railroad —and its agent, Rolf—be ordered and directed, under pain of contempt of court, to proceed forthwith and as expeditiously as possible with the construction of the railroad upon the right-of-way previously announced."

"Whew!" Merrit said. "What chance has it got?"

"None, I'm quite sure. I will allege a plot to deprive you of your property—namely, the value of your half of the PK— illegally and without due process of law. It is an *ex parte* proceeding, Merrit. By this I mean that all I have to do is make a showing that the plot exists and that it damages you, and I am entitled to the writ.

"Whether I get it or not is another question. The Judge may do one of three things. One, he may issue the writ immediately, on a temporary basis, and set a trial date for a hearing on whether or not it shall be made permanent. Two, he can turn me down. Or three, he can set a date for a peremptory hearing within twenty-four hours after the defending parties have been served."

"What do you think he'll do?"

Price said, "Turn me down. It's your money. I do not solicit litigation."

Merrit stood up. "When can you file it?"

"It will take me the rest of the day to prepare the complaint and petition. It will probably be the best legal effort of my life, and it will be wasted on our learned ignoramus of a Judge. But you are a stubborn man, Merrit. You may want to appeal. If you do, I want to go up on a sound record."

"Then what happens?"

"I'll take it to Gillespie tonight, and ask him to sign it. I think he'll probably throw me out. I *hope* he'll at least give me a temporary order." Price laughed ringingly. "You understand, if he does admit me to court, Jack Van Sant is the man who must serve the defendants. I don't know how energetic he'll be, considering who the plaintiff is."

"Let's make him stand up and be counted, too. Come on, let's go get that money."

"This is the right way!" Pastor Schneider said.

"There will still be a fight," said Merrit.

"But you will have tried."

Merrit rubbed his forehead. "Reverend, I find myself

doing and thinking and saying things that are strange to me. I've heard of people being heartbroken and going mad from it. I never took any stock in it before, but that baby—my child—I feel it in my guts, and it's like a steel band being tightened down around my head."

Price said, "He was Bonnie's baby too. She has had it in her guts all these years."

Merrit almost ran out of the office. He clambered into the buggy and said something, and Whitey took one frowning look at him and let the horses run. They did not speak all the way home.

He slid out of the buggy in front of the house and almost ran to the door. Bonnie heard him coming and flung it open. "It's about time," she said hotly. "I want these damned Mexicans out of here. Who do you think you are, keeping me a prisoner in my own home?"

He pushed her back into the room and kicked the door shut behind him. She began walking backward, staring into his burning eyes, until she stumbled against one of the big chairs in front of the fireplace. She screamed, "Don't you lay a hand on me!"

"Don't you ever worry—I won't," he said softly, almost in a whisper. "If I felt the touch of you now, I'd kill you. I just heard about my baby. I saw his grave. I——"

"*Your* baby?" Her face flushed. She stood her ground. "I like your guts, George. After all these years, you come back here and talk about *your* baby. Where were you when he was born?"

"How did I know he was born!" he shouted at her. "You never told me you were going to have him."

"I didn't know." She confronted him boldly, not giving an inch, but the fury went out of her face. She made a gesture of contempt. "If Newt told you, he told you everything. Ma stole the baby from you before it was born, and I didn't know any better than to let her." Her voice rose. "But you— where were you? You let her run you off the place. You believed everything she told you. Oh, what a hell of a man was George Merrit!"

He covered his face with his hands, not from shame but from hurt. "That damned old woman," he said thickly.

She said wearily, "It's too late to blame her. It's too late to blame anybody, George. I suppose this hurts you, and I'm sorry. But sweet Jesus, I watched him die! I saw his little eyes turn back—I saw him stiffen and then go limp. I knew he was dead, but I still ran all the way to the doctor with him."

"Bonnie, tell me about it."

"There's nothing more to tell," she said in a dull voice. "The doctor said he died instantly. All I could think of was, *Well, that'll be a comfort to George, when I have to tell him.* . . . He didn't suffer, George."

Merrit found he was crying. "I'm sorry, Bonnie. I'll tell you this—no power on earth could have run me out of here if I had known."

"Well, I didn't know either. Movers' women breed like street dogs, but I was that ignorant that I didn't know I was pregnant. Ma didn't tell me what was wrong until after she'd married me to Dick."

She came closer to him. "And I'll tell you something else, George. I never lived with Dick—not an hour! The day we were married he was 'laid up,' something he'd caught at Albine Anderson's place. And you had the nerve to come in here and tell me that's where you were staying when you came back here! That was one thing Ma couldn't do—she couldn't get me to live with Dick. Finally, she quit trying."

She watched in silence as he took out a bandana and wiped his eyes and face. She said compassionately, "I had some pictures taken the week before he died. We were in town, Ma and I, and a photographer's wagon came through. Would you like to see them?"

"I would be very grateful."

She ran and brought the pictures, a whole handful of them, postcard size. He saw his own face staring back at him in them. Some were with Bonnie, some with Ma Keller, but most showed the child in a satin-covered chair from the photographer's wagon. Again the tears choked Merrit, and he handed the pictures back to her quickly.

"Oh Lord, oh Lord—and I didn't know!"

"You can have one if you want it." She put her hand on his arm. "George, I'm not heartless. I know how you feel. But I nursed him. I still wake up in the night, thinking he's in bed with me, and that was almost seven years ago."

He put his arm around her. "Poor Bonnie."

"Oh, don't lose any sleep on my account."

She tried to squirm out of his embrace. He held her and made her face him.

"Bonnie, for everything I've done wrong—and that's plenty—I'm sorry. My only excuse is that I was young and dumb too, and that damned old woman——"

"No, George. We can't blame her for what we did to our own lives. That's too easy. At least I face what's wrong with me. I'm trash, a movers' woman. But you—you never did anything wrong in your life, did you?"

He shouted, "We did *not* do it to our own lives! Ma Keller did it for her damned old land and money."

"Think that if you like. I know better."

"You insist on being trash. You insist on carrying more guilt than Christ took to the cross," he said passionately. "I tell you it's not so! I don't blame you for the baby. I don't blame you for marrying Dick. I did when I came back here, yes. Bonnie, listen to me. You're a good woman—a *good* woman. You——"

"Next you're going to say, why don't we try it again?"

He swallowed. "Well, why don't we?"

She shook her head. "No. Don't you see, George, it's dead. There's nothing left—not in you, not in me. You're all upset now because of the baby, but you'll get over that, and you'll be just like me. And George, I just don't give a damn what happens to you anymore!"

"No, no. When I look at you——"

"Oh sure, you'd like to have me again, just to show me. But when the new wore off, you'd be on your way. And I wouldn't care. I wouldn't care!"

She walked to the window, turned and looked back at him. "I'll tell you something else, George—Ma Keller was right. It's not people that count—it's the land! People are no good without land. Believe me, it takes a mover to know that."

He thought, She really believes that. Old Ma had a true daughter, whether she knew it or not. . . . "I guess that's the difference between us, Bonnie," he said. "The land doesn't mean that much to me. There are three things a man wants— freedom, money, a woman. Sometimes they get in the way of each other. I guess few men get all three."

"And you'll take freedom."

"I'd take you, if you felt the same way."

She shook her head. "I don't. I don't want to hurt you, George. When I heard you were coming back—oh my God, how I hoped! When I saw you, I wanted you back on any terms. But I don't like the man you have become, and I'll never again let myself care for anyone the way I once did for you. It's just not worth it."

He nodded. "I feel the same way about the property. I've had the feeling of being a rich man. It's like getting drunk—everybody ought to try it once. But it's more trouble than it's worth."

"Are you going to sell out?" she cried.

He nodded. "But not till you're ready, Bonnie. There is one long-haired son-of-a-bitch I'm going to get first!"

Chapter Twelve

HE FOUND HE could sleep after all—deeply and restfully. He found that he could get up in the morning and go about his work.

He found that, now and then during the day, he could take the child's picture out of his pocket and look at it without going weak all over.

He left three of the Mexicans to guard the house, and when he told Bonnie that she must put up with it, she nodded seriously. "All right. I won't make any more trouble for you, George," she said.

He took the others and spent the day combing the hills east of the railroad right-of-way stakes for stray horses and mules. They brought back more sound ones than Merrit had dared to hope.

It was late in the afternoon when they got them bunched at Willow Springs. Merrit counted 177 head, most of them fit to work. He sent Whitey back to the house with most of the men. He, Lawler, and two of the Mexicans drove the tired and now gaunt herd to the grading camp.

It had rained a little, but not enough to stop the work. The idle teamsters were playing cards and shooting dice on piles of ties and bridge timbers. They whooped as the big horses came thundering through the camp. Duffy, the redhead, waved to Merrit.

"Don't expect any gratitude for this," he said.

"Gratitude?"

"From Rolf. First he told us there'd be jobs for them as wanted them, soon as he got his teams back. Last night, we heard the whole gang is bein' laid off."

"They're shutting down?"

Duffy nodded. "That was the last gossip. Some feller is in the office with Rolf now. They been arguing for the best part of two hours, and the word is that it's bad news. I don't know what kind." Duffy grinned. "But I wouldn't say it's the best time you could pick to talk to the chief engineer."

"The hell with him," said Merrit. "I brought him back his horses. Let's see what's scratching him."

He spurred forward to the office wagon. Before he could dismount, Rolf flung the door open. "Merrit, what's the meaning of this idiocy?" he sputtered.

"What idiocy?"

"This tomfool lawsuit."

Merrit's heart leaped. "I don't know what to tell you until you tell me what's wrong with you."

Behind Rolf a tall, broad-shouldered, paunchy man with a solemnly handsome face appeared. Sheriff Jack Van Sant said, "I was coming to your place next, Mr. Merrit. Judge Gillespie set the hearing on your case for tomorrow at ten. I'll tell you the same thing I been trying to tell Mr. Rolf—you will be there, or I'll haul you in at the point of a gun."

"I'll be there," Merrit said, trying not to grin.

"Well, I won't!" Rolf snapped. "I'm an employee. I don't make any decisions. I merely follow orders, and——"

"That's what the hearing is about," Van Sant interrupted. "To give you orders, if the Judge feels so inclined. I can't serve the railroad in time to have their responsible executives there. But this is personal, it is directed against you, and you will be there!"

"Merrit," Rolf said quiveringly, "I want this nonsense ended. It will go hard with you if it isn't."

"I take that as a threat," Merrit said, holding his restless horse so that he could cover Rolf with his gun if necessary. He did not look behind him, but he heard movement, and he knew that no man in Rolf's position would be without personal bodyguards.

"Take it any way you like!"

"Then if you are going to threaten me, sir, in the future you'll call me *Mister* Merrit. I am not one of your flunkies, Mr. Rolf."

Behind him, he heard Duffy sing out, "Hold it! Hold it there, feller!" Merrit slapped his hand down and caught his .45. He levelled it at Rolf's belly and said softly, "One move against me is your last one, Mr. Rolf."

"You're all right now, Merrit," Duffy called. "We catched him in time."

Sheriff Van Sant shoved Rolf roughly aside and stood in the door of the office wagon. "Now y'all put them guns away," he said. "If they's any gunplay, I start it, and I finish it. Mr. Merrit, that goes for you too."

Merrit looked behind him. A man with a rifle had come out from behind one of the tool shanties, but Duffy had pulled down on him before he could level it. The rifleman had lifted the weapon high above his head and was shaking his head in surrender.

Merrit holstered his gun. "If you say so, Sheriff."

"I say so," Van Sant glowered at him. "You called me some raw names. That don't go ag'in you in this matter. I served your papers, and I'll bring the people into court, but now I want you to get out of here. Go home."

"Davidson—has he been served?"

"He was the first one."

Merrit said, "Sheriff, I owe you an apology, it appears."

"You owe me to get your boys and get the hell out of here, like I said."

"That I will. Mr. Rolf, I've brought you back your horses. I won't request a receipt," Merrit said turning away. "Come on, Lawler. Pancho—Martin—*vaminos!*"

They were halfway home before slow-thinking Lawler said, "You're suing somebody?"

"Just about everybody."

"Won't do you no good. I come up before Judge Gillespie once. A bill for a suit I bought that shrunk up to half my size when it got wet. He is ag'in the poor man every time."

"But we'll call the roll, anyway. Lawler, I'm in over my head. I never asked for trouble, but my hand was forced. And by God, I'm going to force a few other hands!"

In the morning, he left most of the crew at the house, with Lawler in charge. He went to court in the buggy, in the same clothes he had worn to Billy O'Shea's funeral, with Whitey driving. Behind them rode Emilio and Pancho. "They'll stay out of trouble," he told Lawler. "It's not their country, and they know it. I can handle them."

"But can you handle the Twenty Plus?" Lawler said.

"No, and neither could our whole outfit. We are in the hands of the court. If it can't—or won't—protect us, we're outgunned anyway."

He did not even see Bonnie before he left. The town of Strickland was full of horses wearing the Twenty Plus brand. He kept an eye out for Harmon Griffin, Rob McKesson, and Jake Seeck, but he did not see them. There was no room to tie the team near the courthouse. Even the hitchrail in front of Newton Price's office was filled with Twenty Plus horses.

"He has got an army, that's what," Whitey said. "What do I do with the team?"

"Put them in the town stable, and then I want you to come back here to Newt's office. If we're not here, come to the courthouse. I'll take Pancho and Martin with me. And Whitey—stay out of trouble!"

"If I can."

"You had better."

Price came to the door as Merrit dropped out of the buggy. He was beaming happily, and Merrit thought he was stone sober.

"At least we get a hearing, Merrit," he said. "He didn't throw me out of his office—but he didn't sign the writ either. I'm afraid it's a Roman circus. He'll turn us down today."

"Then he'll have to do it in front of people. Is there anything we have to talk over?"

"No. I'm going to base everything on common public knowledge. If the Judge himself hasn't heard that Davidson is out to get you, he's deaf as well as dumb. There will be no testimony taken unless the Judge himself requests it. Just arguments on law and equity."

They waited at the office until Whitey returned. Then they crossed the street to the courthouse together. Short as the notice had been, the biggest crowd Merrit had ever seen in Strickland had gathered. He might have recalled a few faces from eight years ago, but mostly they were strangers to him. And most of them were poor men, small ranchers who ran a few head of cattle and hoped there would be rain enough to make feed for them.

You poor devils, he thought, I know how you feel. You need the railroad more than anybody. You're more scared of the Twenty Plus than I am, but you're not on my side either. You don't want any trouble at all, because no matter who wins, you always lose. . . .

It was too bad, but he was at the end of his own rope. Let them stand up and be counted, too!

"Here comes opposing counsel, with the only two of his clients who could be subpoenaed," Price murmured. "Counselor Alec Whitman, ornament of the legal profession and a blabbermouth. I will have to introduce you."

The opposing lawyer was a tall man gone to fat. His face was florid, his sharp blue eyes overgrown with sandy eyebrows. He walked with his long black coat open, one hand clutching his checked waistcoat.

"Counselor," he said resonantly, when he saw Price, "how good to see you. I hope you are in good form today—but then you always are."

Price in turn said, "Counselor," and shook hands as though meeting a long-lost brother. "I beg to present my client, Mr. Merrit."

"I am honored." Whitman's handclasp was damp but firm. "Mr. Merrit, I must say you have entered upon a bold course, sir. Poses an intriguing question of law—yes, it does."

Merrit said something. Then he spoke civilly to Rolf, who merely nodded.

It was Aaron Davidson that he watched—not furtively, but not belligerently either. He felt his revulsion rise again at the sight, the nearness of the man, and he wondered what he would do if he had been called upon to shake hands with him.

Davidson's taut-skinned, ruddy face still showed the marks that Merrit had left on him in the bank. His eyes had a hot glitter in them that made this day's proceedings a personal thing. His hair had been brushed until it shone, and his hat—a new one—had been pushed back on his head to show it to best advantage.

But he said nothing. Whitman linked his arm with Davidson's and swept him toward the courthouse steps. Price deliberately slowed down to let them get ahead. Then he took Merrit's arm in the same fashion.

"Try not to look so damned serious," he muttered. "If we lose this, you still have to fight. Don't let anyone think it means so much to you."

"I don't know that it does—or rather, I'd forgotten. You go into something like this, and you find yourself taking it seriously," Merrit replied.

At the top of the steps stood the young Deputy Sheriff, Milt Sedgewick. "No one may enter who is armed—no one may enter who is armed," he was chanting.

Inside the door, shoulder to shoulder, stood Harmon Griffin, Rob McKesson, and Jake Seeck. Merrit said, "Howdy, boys," but only Harmon answered.

"Howdy yourself, Merrit. Since when you taken to the law? 'S 1 remember it, you used to shy away a right smart from courts and judges and the like."

A lonesomeness went through Merrit. He said, "It is a change, Harmon. Be a-seeing you."

The courtroom was crowded, although not yet full. Sheriff Van Sant stood in the center of it, near the railing that separated the audience from the legal arena, with his hands on his hips.

"How many people you got with you, Mr. Merrit?" he called.

"Three, Sheriff. And they don't have to be inside, if you're crowded."

"It ain't a sideshow, but I figure you're entitled to a few seats. He'p yourselves."

"Sit on the aisle, Whitey, and get out quick if you have to," Merrit whispered.

Whitey and the two Mexicans sat down, looking around uneasily. No doubt Whitey knew many of the other spectators—knew them to be Twenty Plus men. To Merrit they were all strangers.

The county had done itself proud in the courtroom of its new courthouse. The Judge's bench was elevated high above the rest of the courtroom, and it was flanked by the flags of the United States and the State of Texas. The jury box was elevated, too, and since this was not a jury case, today it was filled with spectators, mostly women.

There were two tables inside the railing, facing the Judge's bench. Whitman, Rolf, and Aaron Davidson had already sat down at the one on the left. Price took Merrit's elbow and guided him to the other one. They sat down.

"Hear ye, hear ye, hear ye, this honorable court of the State of Texas is now in session, the Honorable David Day Gillespie presidin'," Sheriff Van Sant said loudly. "You will all remain seated."

A door next to the Judge's desk opened, and a small man in a gray suit came out. Merrit's heart fell.

This was not the kind of puny man who gained stature by high office. His mouth was tight, and it turned down at the edges. His eyes were too cold, and too close together. His skin had an unhealthy, papery look, and he had cut himself shaving this morning and had pasted a small triangle of brown paper over the cut.

Oh, but he's narrow, Merrit thought. A bitter man, full of prejudices. There are few things he believes in, and one of them will be money and high mortgage rates. The others will be mostly hatreds. . . .

"The Honorable Judge," Price whispered. "Ain't he a peach?"

"He hasn't had an idea in forty years," Merrit whispered back.

"Longer than that!"

It's funny, Merrit thought, but now that I've seen what I'm up against, I don't mind losing. It was something I had to go through, is all. Now let's see where this little son-of-a-bitch of a Judge stands. . . .

Chapter Thirteen

JUDGE DAVID DAY Gillespie's voice had a whining nasal quality to it. "Are the parties ready?"

"Ready for plaintiff," Price said rising.

Alec Whitman rose and bowed elaborately. "Ready for defense. I hope this tomfool proceeding is not going to get bogged down in a lot of stump speeches, Your Honor. We have all got more important things to do."

"If you have more important things than this, you shouldn't have accepted the brief," Gillespie said. "Go ahead, plaintiff."

Price began, "I have alleged a conspiracy here to defraud plaintiff of his property. I have alleged that the danger of the extinction of his rights is imminent. I have alleged that such conspiracy is common knowledge. If I can make a showing that these three facts exist, plaintiff is entitled to the relief that only a writ of mandamus can provide. Now, I could call the citizens of this town, one at a time, and ask them one question. I don't have to rest on hearsay evidence that I would adduce from them. I need only show this court that there is widespread hearsay."

"Just a minute," the Judge said. "Is there or is there not a conspiracy? You've got to prove that."

Price said ringingly, "If the court will excuse me, I do not! As Abraham Lincoln said about Justice Taney's opinion in the Dred Scott decision, if several persons separately saw pieces of wood, and when they are all brought together, they fit to build a house, it doesn't matter whether they conspired in advance who would saw what boards. The law is skeptical of such miraculous coincidences, Your Honor. All I have to prove is that the boards fit."

Merrit saw the former Confederate officer's face freeze,

but the Judge said nothing. Newt droned on. He admitted cheerfully that he could not *prove* that the Twenty Plus would fence plaintiff off from the railroad, if said railroad changed its course. He could not *prove* that the railroad was a gutless New York corporation interested only in profits. He could not *prove* that the absentee owners of the Twenty Plus, in London, were determined to possess the PK range, overgraze it, and cash in fast.

"If these things are true, however, plaintiff is entitled to the relief prayed for. If they are not true, how would the defendants be hurt? If the railroad means to live up to its franchise and extend the rails here by September, why should it object to doing so under the supervision of this court? If defendant Davidson and the Twenty Plus have no designs on the plaintiff's property, why do they not stipulate to the issuance of this writ?

"Your Honor, I don't need to tell this court that this is a country where we take a man's word until he has proved himself to be a yellow dog. Now we——"

Whitman jumped to his feet. "Now just a minute, here! Who're you calling a yellow dog?"

Newton Price smiled and tossed the graying hair out of his eyes with a mocking nod. "Whoever shot up the railroad's horseherd, that's who," he said. "If defendants wish to disavow that shameful, savage, bloodthirsty act, I invite them to stipulate to this writ right now!"

"Horseherd, horseherd!" Whitman sputtered. "We have nothing before us about any horseherd being shot up."

"Is that a request that I put on witnesses? I can drag this proceeding out until hell freezes over if I start offering testimony to the slaughter of those horses. I can walk horses into this very court bearing the Twenty Plus brand. I can ask the sheriff of this county to turn over to the court the empty cartridges of three forty-five seventy bullets that connect directly with said slaughter.

"However, before I am jackassed into wasting our time with a hundred hearsay witnesses, I am going to try to prove common knowledge by asking just one person one question. The court stands aloof from common gossip. It would be a rash man indeed who would go to Judge David Day Gillespie and ask him if he wanted the latest gossip on a case pending before him. If the court has heard of the savage slaughter of these horses, surely to God *that* proves common knowledge!"

"The court has heard the stories," the Judge put in. "Does defendant wish testimony to prove them? Does defendant wish to take this opportunity to disconnect himself from such rumors, whether true or false? Plaintiff has made what I consider an offer of proof."

Whitman said, slowly and sonorously, "I don't know where counsel learned his law, but I have never heard of any such powerful writ issuing on the basis of village gossip. I'm going to move right now that the writs be denied without further wasting our time."

"I'll hear your argument first, I think," the Judge said. "A ruling is reserved."

Whitman smiled. It seemed to Merrit that this was what he had wanted and expected. Anyway, Merrit thought, slumping lower in his chair, we are going to make a few people take sides. . . .

"We are told," Whitman said, "that 'everybody knows' that the Twenty Plus is gunning for the PK—that 'everybody knows' that it will delay the railroad a year to get possession of what has always been known as the Keller range—that 'everybody knows' that this man Merrit is a lone knight in armor, singlehandedly fighting the battle that all the good citizens of this town are too yellow to fight.

"I say to this court that the opposite is true. I say that it is Merrit who came here to make trouble—Merrit who deliberately and maliciously assaulted one of these defendants and invaded the grading camp of the other with armed men, subverting their own employees, the teamsters who were in charge of the horseherd, to his own——"

"Just a minute," the Judge said. "Let's find out a couple of things. It's common knowledge that plaintiff Merrit beat up on defendant Davidson. I believe that's part of plaintiff's case. Plaintiff himself alleges common knowledge of trouble at the grading camp. What I want to ask your clients, counselor, is very simple. Is that railroad going to reach here by September first? I would like Mr. Rolf to answer that himself."

Rolf stood up. "If it is humanly possible, I will have scheduled trains in Strickland by that date."

"Fine. Now let me ask Mr. Davidson if he intends to impede the construction of the railroad to prevent the consummation so devoutly desired by Rolf."

The long-haired man stood up. "Your Honor, the company I represent is critically interested in finishing this railroad. The sooner the rails reach here, the happier my employers will be. I have orders from them to assist the railroad in every way I can. I have given orders to my own employees to this same effect. I can only——"

"That is a God-damned lie, Your Honor!"

Like everyone else in the courtroom, Merrit turned so quickly that his chair scraped noisily on the floor. It was a loud gust of sound that was beyond the power of the court to forbid.

Just inside the door, Albine Anderson was wrestling with Milt Sedgewick, the young deputy. At first, Merrit thought she was reeling drunk. She slapped Milt with a roundhouse right that had the violence of a blow with the fist. She slammed him backward and came rapidly down the aisle.

She was stone sober, but her face would never be the same again. Her nose had been crushed. The cuts on her lips would never heal cleanly. The livid bruises that had closed her eyes would be weeks healing, and even today she could barely see through them.

Jack Van Sant bustled toward her, saying over his shoulder, "Your Honor, if we could have a short recess——"

"We will not recess!" the Judge snarled. "Madam, this court is in session. You are in contempt."

" 'Madam' is right," Albine said loudly. "Everybody in this court knows me, or knows of me. I want to testify. Not to gossip—to what I know. Aaron Davidson wrote a letter to those stockholders in London, saying he was going to marry Bonnie Keller. He offered them the PK for a hundred thousand dollars. He——"

"You will be silent!" Judge Gillespie shouted.

"I will like hell! Aaron is twenty thousand dollars short in his accounts with the owners of the Twenty Plus. He has got to get hold of the PK, or they'll send him to the pen. He offered me five thousand dollars if I'd stick a knife into Merrit, and he promised me witnesses to testify Merrit was trying to rob me. And look at what he did to me, just for saying . . . just for saying . . ."

She dwindled off into silence. She looked around helplessly, the fury that had driven her here dying suddenly in her. The Judge said, "Just for saying what, madam?"

"If the court will excuse me," Whitman put in quickly, "I don't believe what Aaron Davidson is alleged to have said to this disreputable woman is relevant. If plaintiff wishes to put her on the stand, that's another matter, but——"

"The court can question witnesses," the Judge snapped. "For saying what? Answer the question, madam."

Albine began crying, not prettily. "For saying I'd cut his heart out if he looked at Bonnie Keller!"

Whitman smiled. "We have, it appears, a case of the woman scorned, an infatuated——"

"I don't think we need to go any further into this," Judge Gillespie said, disdainfully. "I am not going to hear any more arguments. I will set August fifteenth as the date for arguments on whether or not the writs will be made permanent. Meanwhile, they will issue."

Merrit did not understand. He felt Newton Price clutch his arm in a grip that hurt clear to the bone. Alec Whitman reeled on his feet.

"What?" he shouted.

"You heard me!" the Judge snapped. "The writs will issue. I further set bond to guarantee compliance in the following amounts: The railroad has pledged to have trains here by September first. For every day after that on which no trains run, the railroad is in contempt of court and will be fined the sum of one thousand dollars. Let me make it clear that this is one thousand dollars *per day*.

"Additionally, the railroad is ordered, in such event, to state under oath the reasons for its failure to comply with these writs. If the Twenty Plus ranch, Aaron Davidson, or any employee of either the ranch or Davidson is responsible for such delay, said employee, said ranch, and said Davidson will be in contempt, and will be fined the sum of one thousand dollars *per day*.

"These fines will accrue until scheduled trains are running. This ruling stands. I will not entertain any motion for rehearing on error or otherwise. These writs will be enforced unless and until a higher court overturns them.

"By that, I don't mean I expect one sheriff and his deputy

to enforce the building of a railroad, but if it is necessary to request the militia to back up this court, I will ask the Governor for ten thousand armed men. Now one word more:

"Plaintiff rested his case on common knowledge. I think both sides missed the main point of this case, which is common knowledge far beyond the borders of Texas. We have to have the railroads, yes. But we don't have to put up with their damned overbearing insolence. A franchise is a contract, and railroads are notorious in their contempt for contracts they have made with the sovereign people. If you want to appeal, Mr. Whitman, appeal and be damned! This is one county in which a multimillion-dollar railroad has no more standing in court than a ten-dollar-a-month hired hand."

He picked up his pen and scratched his signature on something. Merrit caught his breath. He leaned over Price's shoulder to whisper, "I was in error again. Never underestimate any man."

"I told you he was prejudiced," said Price. "But I didn't know his prejudices ran counter to the railroads."

They stood up. Merrit said, "He wasn't afraid to stand up and be counted. But where's Albine? I've got to find her."

He pushed his way roughly and violently through the crowd. Pastor Schneider was leading Albine down the courthouse steps. Merrit caught up with them and said, "Albine, you're coming home with me."

"To Bonnie Keller's place?" she said. "I'll see you in hell first!"

"Where'll you go, Albine? Your girls have all left town. The reverend can't protect you now. You know Davidson better than I do. Do you think you're going to get away with this?"

She swayed as her knees crumpled. Her broken face turned gray. Merrit and the preacher caught her. Merrit said, "Whitey, bring the buggy! We'll wait in front of Newt's place. Bring a horse from the town stable for me, too."

Newt, the preacher, and the Mexicans carried her across the street to the lawyer's office. As Merrit followed them, someone spoke his name. He kept walking and let the man catch up with him.

It was Rolf. He did not offer his hand, but he said, "If you thought this lawsuit was necessary, I suppose that was your right. I want to tell you that I mean to live up to its terms."

"You may have your problems, sir."

"I will not anticipate trouble," the engineer said irritably. "If it comes, I'll try to be ready for it. I'll also live up to our agreement on the used-up horses. There are probably eighteen or twenty ready for you."

The man was a good deal of a man in his own way. Merrit said, "I thank you. If you don't mind advice——"

"I'll listen."

"You have a teamster by the name of Duffy——"

"With red hair. I know the man. A troublemaker."

"You can use one, believe me. He has a grudge against the people that shot up your horseherd. So have the others, but Duffy's a leader. Put him in charge. Tell him to organize you a militia. Your mistake, Mr. Rolf, if you'll pardon me, is in believing that these writs mean the same thing to everybody. The Sheriff himself will tell you that they are no good unless enforced."

"I'll think about it," Rolf said, irresolutely.

"No longer than it takes you to get back to camp," Merrit warned. "That's about how long you have, I figure."

The banker, Champion, came up to Merrit to shake his hand. There were a few others, but most of the crowd, while Merrit thought they were pleased, did not want to be seen in a partisan posture.

Whitey came with the buggy, leading a rented horse. Albine was able to help herself into the seat, but there she collapsed again. Merrit and the preacher shook hands, grinning at each other. Merrit said, "You, too, think the writ ends it, don't you?"

"It's a start," Pastor Schneider said. "It is what your little boy would have wanted you to do, in years to come."

A swift ache streaked through Merrit. His face darkened, and he swung up into the saddle. "Let's go," he said.

He rode behind the buggy. The Mexicans did not have to be told to flank it, one on either side. Merrit was glad when they had left the town behind. What worried him was that Aaron Davidson had simply disappeared, taking most of his men with him.

"Trot 'em, Whitey," Merrit said. He thought, I don't

know what Bonnie's going to say about bringing this woman out there, but I don't much care, either. . . . The buggy team stepped along smartly.

Two miles from town Merrit heard riders coming behind him, pushing hard. He thought he recognized them. He nodded to Whitey to keep trotting, the Mexicans with him, but he slowed his own horse.

He was right. It was Harmon Griffin, Rob McKesson, and Jake Seeck. He twisted his horse around in the road to face them. "Hold it, boys!" he said. "What's this?"

"We're changing sides," Harmon said, gruffly.

"Little sudden, isn't it?"

"Not too." Out came that braying giggle that always meant that Harmon was either in trouble or looking for it. "We talked it over, Merrit. We don't want to work for that long-haired man no more."

"I'd admire you more, boys, if this had happened before those horses got all shot up."

Jake Seeck dug his heels into his horse and pushed it up within arm's reach of Merrit. "We wasn't in on that," he said thickly. "Them renegades knew better. They should ask us."

"You just hired yourselves out," Merrit said. "I probably don't pay as well as Davidson, but there are no bugs in the beds, and the food is plentiful."

He turned to go, but Rob McKesson said, "Wait, before we catch up with Albine. I don't know how much you can believe of what she says, George, but I do know that she kept his books for him. Aaron can figure faster than any man I ever knew, but he is hard put to read and write a simple letter."

"And——?"

"If he told the corporation he was marrying Bonnie and would sell them the PK for a hundred thousand, it's news to me. If he offered Albine five thousand to stick you like a pig, that's news, too. But she's right about one thing—he is twenty thousand short on his books."

"Where would the money come from?" Merrit said. "Where did it go?"

McKesson said, "Year and a half ago, the corporation had your place appraised at forty thousand. They put that much in a New York bank, at Aaron's disposal, but they told him to go as high as fifty-five thousand if he had to. George, there's less than twenty thousand dollars of that money left."

"How do you know this?"

"Never mind, I know it."

"Where'd it go?"

"Your guess is as good as mine."

"Albine? She kept the books."

"Your guess is as good as mine," McKesson said again. "She always did hate a dollar like her right arm. I don't know if she'd double-cross him. On the other hand, I don't know that she wouldn't. But there was a time, after he started galivanting around after Bonnie Keller, that she would have put poison in his cup."

And I'll bet I know how you know, Merrit thought. Albine never was exactly a one-man woman, and she talks too much when she's drinking. Well, well—so she turned that long-haired man's pockets inside out for twenty thousand of the company's money. . . .

"What do you think now, George?" Harmon said, that giggle of his almost breaking through again.

"I think the sooner we get that woman home, the better I'll feel."

"My own idea exactly."

They galloped after the buggy. Albine looked up at Merrit with a crumpled smile. "How are you going to explain this to Mrs. Keller?" she said.

"It's half my place, Albine."

"It ain't going to be any picnic."

You're right about that, Merrit thought. I wonder how much money you've taken out of this town? How much you cleaned Dick Keller for, before Ma cut him off at the pockets. . . ? But one look at her ruined face, and he could not be her judge. "Does it hurt to get shaken up, Albine?" he said. "I won't rest easy until you're home."

"Nothing will ever hurt me again, Merrit. He . . . he gave me the boots. My face is nothing to what's busted up inside me."

"Whitey, run them," Merrit said. "If it hurts her too much, you'll have to slow down again."

Whitey shook the lines. The horses put their bellies down

in the harness, and the buggy spurted ahead. Merrit rode a dozen yards to the left of it, where he could watch in all directions. He saw that while Albine was suffering, she could still stand it. His own nerves were on edge to get her home, and by the way Harmon, Rob, and Jake kept glancing about, he knew their hunch was the same. That long-haired man would never . . .

He saw a glint of movement on the hillside, against the sun. He yelled and pointed.

The whistle of the big slug and the battering thud as it struck Albine seemed to come at the same time. It drove her back against the seat of the buggy, then let her slide down. Then came the billowing boom of the big rifle.

"Don't try to foller him!" Harmon yelled. "He's got the range on you. He'll pick you off like a turkey!"

The rider on the distant hillside had not waited. He went over the hill and out of sight. Merrit rode to the buggy. Whitey fought the team to a standstill. "No use, Merrit," he said. "She never knowed what hit her. God almighty, but that man can shoot."

"Run 'em!" Merrit said. "Let's get home."

He leaned over to slap the buggy team with his hat. Whitey put the two lines in one hand long enough to move Albine's body closer to him, so it would not fall out of the buggy. Poor woman, Merrit thought, what good does her money do her now? But this is just one more thing Davidson owes me. One more. . .

Chapter Fourteen

"I BELIEVE in the Bible," Bonnie said. "I'm going to believe she was forgiven. I'm going to pray that I can forgive her myself."

"Oh, cut that out, Bonnie" Merrit said impatiently. "You're not going to do any such damn thing. You're going to go right on hating her past the grave."

"All right then, I am. She was welcome to Dick. She was welcome to Aaron. As far as that's concerned, she was welcome to you."

He caught her by the arm and shook her. "Listen, Newt and the Sheriff are waiting. We have got to——"

"Let them wait!" she screamed. "You've kept me locked in the house with those damned Mexicans guarding me. You go to court and don't even tell me. You bring that miserable bitch home for burial. This is my place as much as it is yours—more, in fact. If you'd been half a man——"

"Go on, see if you can hurt me," he said wearily. "You're wasting your breath, Bonnie. There is no way you can bother me anymore. Get it said if it makes you feel better. Then I have work to do."

She folded her arms. It was late in the afternoon now, and they were in Bonnie's bedroom. The Sheriff and the lawyer were waiting in the living room—with more patience than he could have shown himself, Merrit thought. How word had gotten back to Strickland that Albine was dead, Merrit did not know. But two hours after he reached the house with her body, Sheriff Jack Van Sant and Newton Price had ridden in, saying that Pastor Schneider was on the way.

Bonnie was still pressing him.

"What kind of work?" she said.

"I am going to see if Rolf is building that railroad."

"I'll go with you."

He smiled coldly. "You can guess again."

"I said, George, I am going with you! I am not some chippy like Albine. I am half owner here."

"All right," he said. "But first I want you to go undress Albine and get her ready to bury. Take a look at what a forty-five seventy slug does to a woman's breast. You fool, all Albine did was steal his money—you spit in his face!"

She did not know how to answer. He seized her by the arm again, saying, "Either go prepare her for burial or shut up. Bonnie, you will stay here if I have to tell Emilio to chain you to the wall."

"You'll pay for this, George," she seethed.

He looked at her a long time and thought, Oh, to hell with it. . . . "I'll pay, all right," he said. "You earned the whole shebang. As soon as I have taken care of a few things, I'm riding on. I'll tell Newt to draw up a deed to it." He pointed a finger at her. "And if that makes you richer than Albine, I hope you enjoy it."

She paled. "You didn't need to say that."

"I don't know what I'm saying, anymore, and that's the truth. You started it, Bonnie. I don't want to fight. I just want to finish my job and get the hell out of here."

"Finish your job," she murmured, half turning her back and folding her arms again. "You mean kill Aaron."

"Among other things."

She closed her eyes. "Oh God, what a fool you are. What if he kills you?"

"He won't."

"He killed that woman." Merrit did not answer. Bonnie rubbed her face with both hands, hard. "How will killing Aaron help?" she whimpered. "Let the Sheriff do it."

"He can't."

"You're always the better man."

"No. He's a good man. Maybe that's the trouble."

"You did love me once. I loved you. In a way, I guess I still do."

"You don't want me to fight Aaron," he said, smiling, "because if I'm killed, you'll still have that long-haired man on your hands. And he is not man enough for you, is he?"

"And you are?"

"I am, Bonnie. I can handle you. Nobody else that you know can, and you're going to take handling all the rest of your life. Five or ten years from now, when you're head of a family, with a husband like Dick Keller, you remember I said this."

"You sure hate yourself."

He put his hand under her chin and tipped her head back. "Ma Keller the Second."

He walked out of the room and closed the door firmly behind him. Newt Price was dozing in one of the big chairs, with his feet on the other. You can't wait until you're installed here, Merrit thought bitterly. . . . Lawler came into the room.

"What's doing?" Merrit said.

Lawler made a helpless gesture. "Whitey has took charge. He says we're gonna be overrun. He sent Griffin and Seeck to the grading camp to find out what they know. The rest of the boys are just setting around."

Merrit smiled. "Whitey's right. Where's the Sheriff?"

"He'll be up in a minute. He's been eatin'. My stars, how that man can stow the grub."

Newton Price awakened and yawned. "Where's Bonnie?"

"Pouting," Merrit said shortly.

"This always was a homely place," Price said. "I mean that in the old-fashioned sense, a real home."

"Glad you like it."

Price grinned. "You're touchy, Mr. Merrit."

"Newt, I don't feel jokey."

"What are you going to do now?"

"Wait. It's Davidson's move."

"I don't see how he can win, however he moves."

Merrit said savagely, "He can't. But what do you expect him to do, become a fugitive? I told you from the first that the man is crazy. I can't tell you how I know, but he couldn't be in worse trouble. Like all maniacs, he thinks he can whip the world—and he'll try. Let him."

" 'Whom the gods would destroy, they first make mad.' Where does this leave Bonnie?"

"She spit in his face."

Price nodded soberly. "Is there nothing I can do?"

Merrit began pacing. "Not now, but you make it easy to bring up a thing I hate to talk about. There's nothing here for me. I'm going to kill Aaron Davidson, and then I want to be rid of this place. You said I could deed my half of it over to Bonnie."

"I can. I said, too, that if you did that and ran for it, I would do my best to marry her."

"You do that."

"*What?*"

"She'll make you miserable," Merrit said, over his shoulder. "I don't think you can handle her, but you'll be kind to her. She's not in a marrying mood now, but she will be one of these days, and when a woman takes the notion, she can make a bad mistake in a man. One more is all Bonnie needs. Keep her out of trouble if you can, Newt."

"I think you really mean that."

"And how I mean it. You draw the deed. Soon as it's ready, I'll sign it." He saw Price studying him and went on haltingly, "I've never felt whipped before. I feel whipped now. I tell you the truth, I'm afraid to go up against Aaron Davidson, feeling this way."

"Then why do it?"

Merrit shook his head. "Oh, I'll kill him. I'll make him come to me, because my nerve is better than his, and then I'll kill him. Face to face, if I can—in the back, if I have to. But I am still a whipped man."

The Sheriff came in without knocking. "You feed well here. I had heard that, and it's the Gospel truth!" he rumbled. "Did you know it's raining a drizzle?"

"No, but I couldn't stop it anyway."

"I hate to take a human body out in this weather. I would like to borrow a tarpaulin from you, to put over Albine in the spring wagon."

The Sheriff had his own integrity, but he got on Merrit's nerves today. "Anything you want. Don't bother me—just take it."

"I wonder if she had any family. Do you know?"

"I know nothing about her."

"I was her attorney," Price said. "It was hardly a gold mine for a lawyer—Albine had four cents of the first nickle she ever made, and she wore the other cent out counting it. She had a couple of grown kids in New York, and there's a blind trust in a New York bank for them. If she has any property, it goes to the trust. But there won't be more than her clothes, a couple of pieces of jewelry, and maybe a few hundred dollars in the bank."

"If my information is correct," Merrit said cautiously, "Albine was worth a lot of money."

"I was her lawyer. I didn't know about it."

"Then let me ask you this. Suppose there had been a lot of money, but it was sent to the trust in New York before you drew the will. Suppose it's stolen money—what could the victims do about it?"

"First they'd have to find it out."

"They'll find it out."

"Well, then they'd have to prove she got it. If they could, and if they could trace it to the trust, they'd have a civil suit, and they would probably win it. The taint of theft does not leave stolen money even when it goes, innocently, into the hands of innocent parties."

Merrit ran his hands through his hair. "That doesn't quite answer my question, but let it go."

"You mean Aaron Davidson," Price said.

"What do you know?" Merrit said quickly.

"Only what you have given away. If it's money belonging to the stockholders of the Twenty Plus, and if it's the twenty thousand dollars she mentioned in court——"

"I didn't say that!"

Price narrowed his eyes. "No, you didn't," he said softly, "but let's assume this is the case. Let's say the money is out of Aaron's reach now, and he knows it—why else would he kill her? Let's say he's got to be able to cover that amount or run—that puts it up to Bonnie, doesn't it?"

The room was silent for a moment. Then Sheriff Van Sant said, "You are just deliberately talking plumb over my head. If there was any money stolen, I want to know about it."

Price smiled. "Sheriff, I give you my word that if I had any such information, I would gladly disclose it to you. We were discussing a hypothetical case."

The Sheriff looked at Merrit. "How about you?"

Merrit did not answer. Price said, "Jack, will you take my word for something?"

"I've always been able to."

"Then listen. I think we know at last what this fight is about. I'm going to tell you something that Mr. Merrit wouldn't say, because he hasn't been able to bring himself to face it. It's not going to be enough for Aaron Davidson to stop the railroad, even if by so doing he could bankrupt the PK.

"Aaron has to get possession of the PK. He *has* to. Only way he can do that is to marry Bonnie Keller, and time has suddenly run out on him. I'll ask Merrit to correct me if I'm wrong, but I think we can forget about Aaron causing trouble at the grading camp. Not because of the writ of mandamus, but because what the railroad does is no longer important to him."

The Sheriff could not wait to speak. "That's ridiculous. Bonnie wouldn't touch the likes of him. Why, she spit in his face!"

"Exactly. But if he can get hold of her, and take her away from here and keep her a week, she won't be the same woman. She'll do anything he says. She'll never hold her head up again anyway."

"Kidnap her?" the Sheriff said. "Force her to marry him?"

"By unspeakable methods. Ask Merrit."

The Sheriff looked at Merrit, who said, "Well, it's out. What makes a man hate to face the truth?"

The Sheriff scowled at him. "You believe this, too?" Merrit only swore at him. The Sheriff said, "How many men have you got? No more than a dozen."

"About that."

"And the Twenty Plus has got forty-some," the Sheriff said, standing up. "I saw a good tarp in the woodshed. I'll just trouble you for it, and a fresher team than mine. Have you got a harness team I can run?"

"Lawler," said Merrit, "give him Buck and Mike."

"I purely hate to run a team with a dead body, but I don't see as I've got the choice. Men, I'm taking your word, and I'm bringing help back here as fast as I can get here."

He went out, moving fast for a man so big and clumsy looking. Lawler followed him, closing the door. Bonnie came out of the bedroom, and Price jumped up and pulled back one of the big chairs for her. She sat down in it with a slight smile, but she did not look at Merrit.

"Why so quiet, Newt?" she said.

"I have my morose moments."

"Then men are as bad as women. So do we."

"Not you, surely."

"Oh yes. I'm one of the worst."

"I have never known you to bottle anything up, Bonnie," Price said. "You out with it. That's better."

"No, I let things fester in me too," she said, in a low voice. "And when they come out, they're worse than they are in other people. Do you know why?"

"I'm afraid I don't, Bonnie."

"Ask George. George knows."

If I just went over and put my arms around her, Merrit

thought, she would cave in. That's what this is all about. But finally I'm thinking clearly, and I can admit that this is what I want to do. Only—someday it would begin again. We'd be right back where we started, and I would rather be dead. . . .

He said nothing. Price started to speak, but someone came running toward the door, and Merrit leaped to open it. It was old Whitey.

He almost saluted. "Quite a bit of fire to the north of us, Mr. Merrit. I reckon it's the haystacks. Boys wanted to saddle up. I had a hell of a time stopping them, but I did."

Bonnie shot to her feet. "The haystacks? My God! And you'll let them burn?"

Whitey said rapidly, "They won't burn. It's been drizzlin' too much. That's what Aaron figgered we'd do—saddle up and ride like hell. I soldiered under Sherman, Bonnie. One of the first rules of war is that you never divide your forces unless terrain, timing, and arms make either of your divisions equal or superior to the massed enemy. We ain't got them advantages."

"But our hay——"

"Be quiet, Bonnie!" Merrit burst out. "Whitey is right. Go in your room and stay there, please."

She knotted her fists rebelliously. "I'm through being ordered around, I told you. Whitey, this is an order—put those fires out."

Buck and Mike came wheeling into view, the Sheriff standing up in the spring wagon and leaning his full weight on the lines until the fine horses ran their edge off. "Hold it, Sheriff!" Merrit called.

He turned to Bonnie. "That's a woman's body in the wagon, under that tarp. You never did see what a forty-five seventy slug can do to a woman's bosom. You go take a look before he hauls her out of here. Then come back and give orders."

She wilted. She turned appealingly to Price, but he avoided her eyes. She sat down in the chair with her back to them. Merrit waved at the Sheriff.

"A mistake, sir. Go ahead. Sorry."

He closed the door. They heard the musical rhythm as Buck and Mike hit their stride. Price went over and put his hand on Bonnie's shoulder.

"What'll I do?" Whitey said, carefully looking between Merrit and Bonnie.

"Whatever Mr. Merrit says," Bonnie said—and put her face against Price's arm to cry.

Chapter Fifteen

THE DRIZZLE DIED, but a sultry spring overcast remained. Merrit discovered that his wounded leg had begun burning like fire, and an examination of it showed a thin trickle of watery blood. He wished briefly and foolishly that he could see a doctor, but he could almost hear the doctor saying, "Stay off your feet for a few days," and he smiled bitterly.

The afternoon dragged on. At about five there was a commotion that sent the Mexicans sprinting out of their hiding places around the house. Merrit was comforted—and amazed —to see how many there were of them. When you hired a Mexican, you hired his whole family, it was said—and here were seven hardbitten, cold-eyed men beside Emilio.

"It's all right. Return to your duty," he told Emilio. "It is more important than ever that the Señora remain in the house. Don't forget that for a second."

"That I am eaten by coyotes first," said Emilio.

The commotion was Harmon Griffin and Jake Seeck, returning from the grading camp and driving nearly fifty horses and mules ahead of them. "Rolf said these was used up, and to give them to you," Harmon said laconically as he swung out of the saddle. "Lots of good work left in them. Reckon he aims to get along with you or bust a gut."

"What's doing there?" Merrit asked.

"They're buildin' railroad. Rolf has issued rifles and shot-guns to some of the rowdies from the wagon train. Fellow by the name of Duffy is in charge."

"Then everything is all right there."

Harmon came over to where Merrit, favoring his bad leg, was leaning against the fence. "I reckon not. Merrit, them teamsters is tough, yes. But you give me just six boys like we had when we was stealin' cows down in Chihuahua, and I could fix it so they wouldn't move a spoonful of dirt for six weeks. And Aaron has got that kind of boys."

"Only that's not where he'll hit. Bonnie Keller is what he's after."

Harmon thought it over. "I can't see that man bein' that crazy about a woman—any woman. But you may be right."

"I'm right."

They stood in silence a moment, watching the big horses and mules wander about, getting acquainted with the big corral. Then Harmon said, "Merrit, me and Jake and Rob have been talking considerable lately. Aaron paid us a hundred a month, and somehow we didn't spend it the way a man usually does. To tell the truth, we never did feel real welcome in Strickland, and the riffraff Aaron has got workin' for him—well, we never cared to be seen with them."

"I can understand that."

"We've got better'n two thousand dollars between us. Did you know Jake's a blacksmith? Well, he is. We reckoned that when this is over, we'd go to California and go in to freightin'. Rob knows of a little town, San Ysidro, down on the border. If we could pick up a few of them used-up mules from you at a fitten price, and a couple of wagons Jake could fix up, we could get there without hurting the teams. I'm of a mind to be my own boss for a change."

"If there is room for a fourth, deal me in."

Harmon raised his eyebrows. "What about the PK?"

"It's not working out, Harmon."

"That's too bad."

"It's too long to explain, but there has to be one boss on a place, and Bonnie is it."

Harmon said slowly, dreamily, "When we was down in Chihuahua together, that was my complaint about you. You always taken charge. It's your nature, and you's generally right, but I was at an age where it smarted like ant bites always to be second-best. You and me came mighty close to having to shoot it out a few times."

"I knew that."

"And you would've killed me."

Merrit smiled. "Well, Harmon, I didn't."

Harmon grinned back, that nervous giggle of his bubbling close to the surface. "I'll tell you something. When Aaron told us to go out there and rough up the stage and scare the hell out of a fellow named Merrit, I asked him, 'Aaron, is this by any chance George F. Merrit?' He said yes, it was. I said, 'Aaron, I'll tell you this, he won't scare for sour apples!' I said, 'Me, I love a little fun, and I'll jostle your stagecoach around for you. But if it's the George F. Merrit I know, there's only one way to scare him, and that's go up behind him with a ten-gauge shotgun and blow his head off'n his neck.' "

After a moment Merrit said, "Harmon, how many men has Aaron got that he can count on?"

"For a hundred a month, he can count on all of them. If Jake and Rob and me wouldn't associate with them, you just know they's pretty miserable people. What have they got to lose? Merrit, what does it matter where you're hanged, here or somplace else?"

"Like Chihuahua."

"Like Chihuahua, only more of them."

"I wish we had Duffy and a few teamsters here."

Harmon shook his head. "They'd only get in your way. I'll tell you about that Duffy. He's the kind of a man who'll bust a whisky bottle over the stove and come at you with the jagged end of the neck, and call it plumb bloodthirsty. There are, I'd say, at least thirty men on Aaron's crew that would only *start* to get bloodthirsty then."

"Thirty."

"At least."

Old Whitey came bustling up, looking thirty years younger. "I told the boys to have ten or a dozen horses saddled up and tied inside somewhere, out of sight. But I told them the first man to mount up, without you or me told him to, I'd shoot him myself."

"Good, but the main thing I'm afraid of is they'll fire the house. Where have you got your men?"

Whitey pointed, "There, and there, and there—and yonder. We're short of rifles, but if they aim to hit us and wipe us out, it won't be until dark. What good is a rifle then?"

"Just keep them away from the house, Whitey. They'll try for Bonnie above all."

"Which is what I aimed to bring up next. Why leave her in the house?"

"Where else?"

"There's an old log smokehouse where Ma Keller used to smoke her bacons and hams. Haven't had a hog on the place for years, but if I was attacking, it's the last place I'd think of. If you are game to let the house burn——"

"Everything on the place can burn, so long as Bonnie is here afterward, Whitey."

"Then you come look at it."

His leg aching painfully, Merrit followed Whitey past the corrals and feedlots to where the hogpens used to be. He remembered those hogpens. No cowboy worth his salt would carry buckets of slop to the hogs, but that was the first job Ma had given him. God, how it had grated! It was bad enough to be broke and afoot, but a stinking hogpen. . . .

There had been no hogs here for years. The smokehouse had been built after Ma ran Merrit off and gave his woman to her worthless son. Like everything else she had built, it was the best. About fifteen by fifteen inside, with wires strung across under the ceiling to hold the hams and bacon sides of a dozen hogs. It was lined with a thick, dry mixture of old soot and the grease that had popped out as the fat pork cured, but there were no windows.

"If you get in here," Merrit fretted, "you stay here. It's a trap, Whitey."

"You want sally ports and sniper's ports. They'd be nice if we had the time. But look, you hide them Mexicans of yours in the brush outside. Tell them to hold their fire until they're attacked. Mr. Merrit, those sons-of-bitches are going to have their backs to this place, waiting for you and Bonnie to be smoked out of the big house!"

"I believe you're right."

"You have to anchor your defense on a strong point. That's where the Rebs fell down at Atlanta. They sent Hood out to fight on a battleground Sherman picked, and he took a whippin'. Lee never made no such mistakes. Like at Fredericksburg, he——"

"Fine, fine. I'll bring Bonnie and the Mexicans. We haven't got forever, Whitey. Let's get it set."

"Now that's sense," Whitey said gratefully.

"What do I do, George?" Harmon said.

"I want you to stick here, too. You speak Spanish. I don't want those fellows to get excited and give themselves away. If when it's all over, you and Bonnie and those Mexican boys are still lying here in hiding without a spent shell in your guns, it will suit me exactly."

He dreaded another showdown with Bonnie, but he saw no way to escape it. He called Emilio to him before he went into the house, and told him the new plan. "You'll take this man's orders," he said in Spanish, pointing to Harmon. "It's as though I commanded you. Whatever he says is my command."

"That is clear," Emilio said.

A nervous sort of dread, heavy and cold, came over Merrit suddenly. He looked around at the darkening landscape, remembering the moon that would not shine tonight, and wondering to whose advantage the poor visibility would be. I just dread taking her out of the house, that's it, he told himself. . . . The old smokehouse suddenly seemed miles away.

"Wait here, Harmon. I'll be out soon—I hope."

Harmon and Emilio began talking softly and easily in Spanish. Harmon lacked a lot of having good sense at times, but he could take orders, and danger only made him giggle. Well, everything in a man's past was part of him. The bleak and hopeless desperation that had driven Merrit himself to Chihuahua and stealing cows had been Ma Keller's work. It came from her taking his woman away from him and giving her to Dick.

But it all worked out in the end. Out of that same past had come Harmon and Rob and Jake. He understood them. They understood him, as Bonnie never could.

Bonnie and Maria, the maid, were in the bedroom that had been Ma Keller's. "Come on in, George," Bonnie called. "I'm giving Maria all of these things. I don't know why I never thought of it before. I guess it's just that Ma never gave anything away, and it seemed sacrilegious to part with anything of hers."

The two women were surrounded by Ma's clothes. "She wore all of them?" Merrit said, in surprise.

Bonnie brushed a loose strand of fair hair out of her eyes. "Half of these things she never had on. I don't know why she bought them. There are even two ballroom gowns. You think of Ma as a fat, homely, tough old slavedriver. But she was still a woman."

Merrit grunted. "I'll have to ask you to put this off a while, Bonnie. We've decided that you'd better go to the old smokehouse for a while."

"We?"

"Whitey and I."

She crinkled her eyes thoughtfully, almost smiling. "You have changed, George. Letting someone else help make a decision. Why the smokehouse?"

No use trying to fool her. He told her, soberly and shortly, what he expected. She kept shaking her head. "Aaron knows better than that," she said, when she could. "I'd die before I'd marry him."

"You would be glad to marry him before he got through with you. He has no choice, Bonnie. He has to do it."

"Why?"

"It's a longer story than I have time for, but he embezzled twenty thousand dollars of the company's money. He can't repay it. He has to have the PK to——"

"Why can't he repay it?"

"Albine Anderson got it."

"Her again! I'm not free from what she can do to me even after she's dead."

"I'm not going to argue. You're going to the smokehouse if I have to carry you."

"No, first I want to know more about——"

"For once you will take orders!"

He picked her up in his arms. She fought him, and to struggle with her slim, wiry body inflamed him almost to madness. He got hold of both her wrists in one hand, saying between his teeth, "Damn it, Bonnie, don't make me hurt you. If I have to tie you and gag you, I will."

She gave up suddenly. "Then Maria goes, too."

"All right, but hurry."

She stiffened her body and slid from his arms. "Tell Maria to bring all these things. We can sort them in the smokehouse as well as here."

Women, he thought. . . . He gave Maria an order, and the woman made a bundle of all of Ma Keller's clothes and swung it over her shoulder. Merrit told her, in Spanish, "The Señora can be stupid. She is not to leave the little house where I am taking you until I return and give permission."

"*Si, Señor.*"

Bonnie escaped him and ran to the kitchen for some sugar sacks. "We can put the clothes in these. It must be filthy there. We——"

"Will you hurry for God's sake!"

He thought she was deliberately goading him. Or was it something deeper than that, some female instinct to go on nesting even while the earth shook? She ran back into the bedroom once more and came out carrying the baby's pictures. Her eyes dared him to say anything.

He pushed the two women outside, shaking his head at one of the Mexicans who would have helped Maria with the huge bundle of clothes. "You need both hands for your gun, boy," he said, in Spanish.

He had forgotten all about Newt Price. The lawyer came slouching around a corner of the house, and one look told Merrit that he had been drinking. Merrit cursed under his breath.

"There's a hen setting on fourteen eggs, in the corner of the fence behind the privy," Price mumbled. "Two of the shells are pipped. One is brown, one white. How will you bet on which hatches first? I'll take either, for any amount up to four bits."

Merrit said, "Newt, what a hell of a time to get drunk."

Price smiled cheerfully. "The one thing you can depend upon about a drunk is that he is incorrigibly undependable. A thirst came on me. Only another drunk could understand the logic of that."

"Go down to the bunkhouse and sleep it off."

"No."

"Newt, you must stay out of our way," Merrit pleaded. "It's Bonnie you're risking."

"It was Bonnie who brought on my thirst. I've been weeping, Mr. Merrit. Oh, I haven't shed a visible tear! But for a few hours, I was up on the mountaintop with Satan, with the world as my purchase price. I did win that case before Judge

Gillespie, Mr. Merrit. On my record, I am a hell of an attorney. And yet, 'The noble Brutus hath said he was ambitious—and Brutus is an honorable man. So are they all, all honorable men!' "

"What the hell are you talking about?" Merrit said, and hit him.

He did not hear the gunfire for a moment because Price took it on the jaw—everything Merrit could swing—and was not staggered. Price smiled and brought up both fists. "I am entitled to something," Merrit thought he heard him say.

Merrit slid under three hard blows, taking them on his shoulders and feeling them rock his whole weight back on his wounded leg. He pumped at Price's belly until the lawyer's guard went down. He measured his man, taking his time, and just as he dropped him he heard the gunshots.

Lawler and Whitey came running into the yard. "Here they come!" Lawler shouted. And Whitey roared, "Get the ladies to the smokehouse before they're seen!"

Emilio crackled some orders. The Mexicans pushed the two women ahead of them at a hard run. Jake Seeck came running back toward the house, from where Whitey had posted him in a weedy gully.

"They are tryin' something slick, Merrit," he said. "Aaron has got more men than this. Better we should expect them to come in behind us likewise."

"Whitey has seen to all that."

Jake grinned. "Hear that big gun? Aaron!"

"Yes," Merrit said. "One thing, Jake—Davidson is my turkey. Pass that word along. Mine!"

Chapter Sixteen

HE HAD NO way of knowing if Bonnie and Maria had been seen, running toward the bunkhouse. At least a dozen Twenty

Plus men had swept in from the road, riding hard. Jake, squatting in a sweet clover clump a quarter of a mile from the house, had waited calmly until they were within range of his .30-30. He loved to shoot, and in his enormous hands, the saddle carbine was like a pistol.

"I fixed two of them so they'll never make another payday," he chortled. "I tell you, it was funny to see them scatter."

Whitey was giving last-minute orders. "Remember, don't fall back until you're ridden down. Let them think we're defending the house to the last man. Delay, delay—that's what we want! Confuse them with delay."

Firing had broken out in the other direction, behind the corrals. The big horses and mules just brought in from the grading camp forgot how tired they were, as they remembered gunfire from another raid. Panicking, they circled the corral in a cloud of dust.

Then it happened, as it had to happen. The fence went down with a splintering crash, and the herd, most of them limping, fanned out toward the prairie. Merrit saw a line of riders break over the top of the hill, and for a moment he felt like laughing.

The crazed draft horses and mules kept running. They did not even see the riders in front of them. The men who had gut-shot the horseherd the other day first tried to stop these maddened survivors by yelling and shooting. Then they only tried to get out of the way.

Merrit saw a long-haired man on a fine bay horse try to twist his mount out of the way. Merrit heard him scream. A running mule that was panting white froth hit the bay horse and kept going. The long-haired man's horse would not weigh a thousand pounds. The mule weighed fourteen hundred.

I've been cheated out of it, Merrit thought. . . . Then he saw the long-haired man get up and pull his long rifle out from under the fallen horse. The runaways were gone now, scattered over the PK range, to keep running as long as there was breath in them.

But four Twenty Plus men were down, and others were fighting to keep their saddles. Merrit heard Whitey yell, "Hit them now! Give them everything you've got! Here come the teamsters!"

There were three wagonloads of them, and their horses were ready to drop in the harnesses. A Twenty Plus man saw the rifles and shotguns that bristled in the wagons. He yelled something, turned his horse, and quit the fight at a dead run. Another followed him—and another.

It will be a slaughter, Merrit thought exultantly. Listen to that Duffy! The teamsters rolled out of the wagons, firing as they ran.

Aaron Davidson dropped to one knee and sighted the .45-70. The impact picked a teamster up and threw him in a backward somersault. The heavy report of the gun threw the teamsters into a panic. Davidson worked the lever and thumbed in another big cartridge.

He fired again. He dropped another teamster. The teamsters' charge broke as they faltered. Duffy was roaring, "Take cover! Take cover! You tarnation fools, make him come to us!"

Merrit ran out of the cover of the trees near the house, carrying his .45 in his hand. He rolled through the nearest corral fence into the still-roiling dust left by the big horse and mule herd. He tried not to limp as he crossed the corral, emerging in the splintered gap where the herd had broken through.

It seemed to him that this was the peak time of his life. He could still see Davidson. He could still yell Davidson's name, and force the long-haired man to turn and face him.

But at the same time it seemed to Merrit that he could see his entire life, in both directions—that which had been and that which was to come. He saw the wasted years, the foolish years of youth, and he saw the long and fruitless waste ahead. If he had been half a man, he would have been raising a son now. But like Harmon and Rob and Jake, like Lawler and Whitey in their time, he had ridden and fought and liquored and womanized, and now the rest would be just waiting for his time to die.

"Davidson!" he yelled. "Davidson!"

There was no place for the long-haired man to run now, except back up the hill. He had come to the final dead end, too. But he still had the big rifle. Merrit saw him run a few yards, turn, and drop to his knee. Davidson put a finger to his mouth, then to the front sight of the big gun. He was sensing the wind, figuring his drift.

You just go right ahead, Merrit thought. You are more than a little bit rattled, old buddy. . . . He knew how it felt to nurse the stock of a big gun against his cheek. It was as though he was the one doing the shooting, bringing that bright, damp front sight to the bead, gently squeezing the trigger. . . .

Merrit threw himself down and heard the big slug shriek over him. He rolled over and came up running, his bad leg raw all over with shock and pain. One thing about those Springfields—they were single-shot guns. Aaron would have to reload, and Aaron was a little bit rattled.

Merrit was close enough now to hear the clack of the action as Aaron jacked the empty out—another clack as a bright new cartridge, as big as a big man's thumb, slid into the massive chamber. The muzzle of the big gun came back on Merrit again.

But you didn't sight in with a .45-70, and snap shoot the way you did with a carbine. Merrit was not yet close enough for his own .45, but he fired once anyway, and saw the long-haired man flinch. He gained a few steps on him that way, before Aaron knelt and put the stock to his cheek again.

Merrit needed his breath for running, but he used some of it to yell. "Wagon trash! Wagon trash! You son-of-a-mover's-bitch. Here's where we settle it!"

He gained a few more steps that way, but he knew now that he was not going to make it. He saw the bore of the big rifle steady down on him. He threw himself down again, on the run, but he knew he was too late.

——And the rifle remained silent. He heard Aaron yell—a scream, rather, high and womanish. He looked up and saw Aaron running. Merrit got to his feet, cursing.

The Mexicans he had left to guard Bonnie, the men he had trusted above everyone else, had left their post at the smokehouse and were running after Davidson. Cursing, Merrit picked himself up and ran too.

Davidson turned and fired once. He knocked one Mexican backward. The man hit hard and did not move. Davidson slipped in another slug and jacked it home.

Then he screamed, and threw the heavy gun away and began running. The Mexicans ran him down on foot and swarmed over him. Davidson did not scream again. There was, in fact, no sound at all.

The Mexicans used their knives. They cut Davidson to ribbons before Merrit could get there. Harmon Griffin and Lawler were not far behind Merrit. Harmon took one look at the bloody mess that had been Davidson. He turned and threw up in the dusty grass.

"I told you he was my turkey!" Merrit shouted.

In his rage he forgot to speak in Spanish. To his surprise, Emilio answered in English too. "He never was, Mr. Merrit. He was always ours."

So, Merrit thought, they'll always surprise you, these people. . . . He said coldly, "A woman, I suppose."

Emilio said softly, "No. Not for some years. She was eleven years old."

"Eleven years old," Lawler said, in a shocked voice.

Emilio winced with pain and shame. Merrit shifted to Spanish. "It isn't something you wish to talk about, is it, my friend?"

"What is there to say?" Emilio answered, with a shrug. "She was my sister's daughter, large for her age, but still only eleven. It would have been kinder had he killed her."

"She still lives, then?"

"If you can call it living, Señor."

And this was a thing Bonnie would never understand, because in her stubbornness she thought that the ultimate shame was to live in a wagon and be a mover's kid. She would never know what she had risked by spitting in Aaron Davidson's face. If she lived to be a hundred, she would never even sense the existence of things that Emilio's niece had learned at the age of eleven.

But Albine had known! There was nothing any man, Aaron Davidson included, could do that would surprise Albine Anderson. And yet, Merrit thought, with reluctant admiration, she still had the nerve to steal his money, then get up there in court and tell on him. And now I know why. I've had a kid of my own. Albine had two. . . .

He put his hand on Emilio's shoulder. "There is one thing

more, my friend. I respect your feelings about your niece, but I told you to guard the Señora."

"Oh, she is well guarded!"

"By whom? Here I see all of you whom I trusted. Here I see those to whom I said I would cut out your hearts, and Maria's too, if harm came to her."

"No harm will come to the Señora," Emilio said gently. "Nor to Maria. I locked both in the smokehouse."

Merrit looked at Lawler. "It's over. You let her out. And tell Newton Price I want to see him in his office the first thing in the morning."

"You going somewhere?"

"Yes," Merrit said shortly.

"I still think you're a damn fool," Rob McKosson said. "I've said myself that there's no woman on earth I'd run after. But Merrit, that's just blab. Some of them are worth it. Bonnie is one."

"And I ran after her," Merrit said.

Jake Seeck said, "One more time won't hurt, Merrit."

Merrit merely shook his head. They were taking it easy, sparing their horses in the dark, heading for town. There had been only twenty-four Twenty Plus men to turn over to Sheriff Jack Van Sant and his deputy, Milt Sedgewick, when they came pounding in at the head of a posse a lot sooner than Merrit had expected them.

It was over. Five of the riffraff Twenty Plus men were dead. At least a dozen had gotten away, riding good Twenty Plus horses which they might or might not be able to explain to some suspicious lawman in Arizona or New Mexico or California. That was how it went. A hundred a month looked good while it lasted—only it never lasted.

"Then you're more than a damn fool, Merrit," Jake said. "You're a no-good bastard."

"Jake, watch how you talk. I'm in no mood for joshing."

Jake kicked his horse ahead in the dark and turned it across the road, forcing Merrit to rein in. Jake said, "Who's joshing? I mean it, Merrit. You've always got to be the one who's right—the big man, him that never makes a mistake. This time I'm telling you though—you're a no-good bastard, and I can whip you!"

"If you want it that way," Merrit gritted, rolling out of the saddle.

Harmon pushed his horse between them as Jake hit the ground too. His high, nervous giggle shrilled out in the night. "That'll be all, you two. I'll bend the barrel of a gun over either one of you with real pleasure."

"Harmon," said Merrit, "I've taken all I mean to take from this marble-headed Dutchman."

"I know what you mean," said Harmon, "only this time Jake is right. You are a no-good bastard."

"Harmon——"

"You can't whup the three of us," Rob McKesson said. "And you're no good to us, when it comes to that. We're going to San Ysidro, California, and be our own bosses. You'd only make trouble. Your heart would never be in it. Here's where you belong. Once a man runs away from what's his, he never can really dig in his toes to scratch a second stake. We aim to work, Merrit. You'd be just a bum we'd have to support."

"Why, you——"

A harness team was coming down the road through the dark at a hard run. Harmon swore and jumped his horse out of the way, and Jake grabbed his horse's bridle just as it bolted. But Rob McKesson stood his ground, shouting, "Hold it up—hold it up, there! This ain't no private road!"

Buck and Mike, Merrit thought, recognized the team. He jumped for their bridles and pulled them down when he saw Bonnie at the lines. Beside her sat Newton Price. Newt would be no help with a horse. Bonnie knew horses, but this pair took muscle.

"You are in a hurry, Bonnie," he said.

"Just so I caught you before it's too late," she said. "Get in."

Harmon Griffin giggled. Merrit said, "It's no use starting anything, Bonnie. We had it all out. You said some mean things I'll never forget, and I guess I did likewise. People can't live, remembering those things."

"You're still unforgiving."

He stood between the two horses' heads, keeping his distance. "No," he said, "but the trouble is, we're two of a kind. What I run, I run. And you're another Ma Keller."

"And love has nothing to do with it?"

"It has plenty to do with it, but how big is the PK? Forty

thousand acres. That's not enough room for the two of us."

"Miss Bonnie, you want us to load him in for you?" said Harmon Griffin.

Bonnie said, "No, let me try once more. George, I don't mind crawling in the dust to you because this is the most important thing either one of us will ever do. I'm sorry, from the bottom of my heart, for the things I said and did. There, now we're even, because you were the first to say 'sorry.' I was too stubborn. I thought it was trashy to apologize.

"Now I know better. George, I can grow up, too! Don't tell me to stop it, because you're going to hear me out. I want another baby. Your baby! That's all that counts with me. George, after you left—after it was all over—Newt took a lantern and took me out to a corner in the fence. There was a hen setting there. She never left the nest, with all the shooting. And . . . and it's like Newt said—is that old hen a better woman than I am?"

"It was the brown egg that hatched first, Mr. Merrit," Price said, "I would have picked the white."

Again that nerve-racking, aggravating giggle of Harmon Griffin, who said, "So long, farmer. If you ever slip your hobbles, come to San Ysidro. We'll set you out a plate of warmed-over beans."

Merrit let go of the horses and jumped around in time to grab the lines while still on the ground. He started to climb into the buggy, but he felt Bonnie's hands on both sides of his face. He was so afraid of shedding tears that he buried his face in her lap, meanwhile leaning back on Buck and Mike's lines and sparing his bad leg all he could.

"I'll make it up to you, George," he heard her whisper. "I'll make you a good wife. I'll never bring you sadness again, nor you me."

THE END

GUN
CODE

by
PHILIP KETCHUM

CHAPTER I

WHAT it was that aroused him, Joe Edison didn't know, but he suddenly was wide awake and after a tense moment he sat up. The night was bright with stars, and a half moon. He could see the homesteader's wagon quite clearly, and near it, the blanket-wrapped figures of the homesteader and his young wife. Not far beyond the wagon, three horses were staked out, his horse and the team that pulled the wagon. Nothing else caught his attention, but in what he had seen, something was wrong. The three horses were pulling back, straining at the stakes that held them.

Joe Edison's holster gun was under the blanket which had served as his pillow. He found it, tucked it in the waistband of his trousers, then pulled on his boots and stood up.

He peered into the darkness to the north. When he had pulled in here at dusk, he had noticed a fair-sized herd of cattle up that way. Now he could hear the faint rumbling sound of their lowing, and could sense the uneasiness which was disturbing them. He took a step toward the horses, then stopped. The homesteader was sitting up, and had reached for his rifle.

"Something gotten into the horses, frightened them," Joe Edison said. "Thought I'd see what it was."

The homesteader whispered something to his wife, then stood up. He was a thin, stooped man, who might have been over fifty. His wife was young and rather pretty. When Joe Edison had pulled in here the evening before, the homesteader had said he was on his way to Unitah where he meant to file a claim on some land open for settlement here in the Unitah basin. His name was Tom Rogers. He called his wife, Kathy.

Up to the north there was a sudden burst of gunfire,

then the distant sound of men shouting. Joe Edison's head came up, his muscles stiffening. His eyes probed the darkness to the north.

"What was that?" Rogers asked sharply.

There was more gunfire up to the north, more yelling, and into the night air came a low, drumming sound. It rolled toward them, growing louder.

"What's going on up there?" Rogers asked.

Joe Edison shook his head from side to side, not wanting to believe the thought that had jumped into his mind.

The homesteader took a quick look at him. "Edison, what's all that noise?"

The drumming sound was louder, now. The gunfire and the shouting sounded nearer. Joe Edison could sense a movement in the darkness to the north, as though the low ridge of a hill was rolling this way. *"Stampede!"* he shouted. *"Get your horses!"*

He started running toward the horses. As he got there, one of the team pulled free and went dashing off madly to the side. He untied the other two and held their halters while he looked back toward the wagon. The homesteader and his wife hadn't followed him. Instead, they were hurrying to the protection afforded by the wagon.

"Here! This way!" Joe shouted.

Neither the homesteader nor his wife paid any attention to him. They stood together near the front of the wagon, Rogers with his arm around Kathy's shoulders.

Joe moved that way, fighting the horses which were trying to pull free. "We can't stay here!" he yelled. "That wagon'll be crushed. Rogers, come get your horse."

But Rogers shook his head. "We'll not be driven off." He stepped away from his wife, levered a shell into his rifle, and fired blindly to the north.

One of the horses Joe Edison was holding pulled free and galloped off, but he held on to the other and took a quick look over his shoulder. He couldn't yet see the onrushing steers but he could sense they weren't far away. The sound they made was like rolling thunder. He glanced at the wagon. It was sturdy and heavily loaded. It might stand up against the stampede if they were

6

on the fringe of it, but he had his doubts even about that.

"Rogers!" he shouted. "We've got to get away from here."

The homesteader paid no attention. He now was kneeling down, aiming his rifle to the north, firing steadily. Joe glanced at Kathy Rogers. She stood near the front of the wagon, her body rigid. She was wearing a long dress, her skirts touching the ground.

A sudden, unreasoning anger swept over him. He stepped toward her and caught her arm. "Get on my horse," he ordered. "Quickly. We haven't much time."

She shook her head, pulled away.

Exactly what happened after that, never was very clear in Joe's mind. He remembered struggling with her, and striking her when she fought back. Then, in some way or other he managed to get her half-limp body over his horse and hold her there until he could climb on behind her. After that, they raced away through the darkness.

Joe looked back. He caught a glimpse of Rogers reloading his rifle and saw the first of the onrushing longhorn steers. He didn't look back again and he didn't hear any more firing.

The thin moon dropped lower in the western sky. The air had cleared of the dust kicked up by the stampede. The night was still again. The only foreign sounds Joe could hear were the sounds of Kathy weeping. She was lying on the ground not far from where he was standing, and she had been crying, now, for a long time. Joe had tried once to talk to her, but she hadn't answered him.

He rolled and lit a cigarette with hands which still weren't too steady. He took a deep drag on it, and stared at Kathy's indistinct figure, wondering if she ever would appreciate the narrow margin by which they had escaped.

He shivered, aware suddenly of the chill of the morning. He took another deep drag on his cigarette. He was a tall, thin young man in the early twenties. He had a shock of rusty-colored hair, and blue eyes which ordinarily looked rather pleasant. But they were troubled,

7

now. He couldn't understand what had happened. There wasn't much question in his mind but that the stampede from which he and Kathy Rogers had escaped had been deliberately managed.

He finished his cigarette, then walked to where Kathy was lying. She still was sobbing, but not so much as before.

"Mrs. Rogers?" he called. "Mrs. Rogers?"

She sat up, and for a moment was silent. She felt her jaw. Joe Edison scowled, remembering how he had struck her. But he had been forced to strike her. Otherwise he wouldn't have been able to get her on his horse.

"Mrs. Rogers?" he said again.

She looked up at him, her face pale and tear streaked in the cold, blue light of the stars. Her eyes seemed enormous. "Why did you make me come with you?" she asked abruptly.

"There ain't no sense in getting killed if you can avoid it," Joe answered.

She bit her lips. A sob caught in her throat. "You mean Tom's dead! Isn't there a chance that—?"

You couldn't soften a thing like this. There were no words he could use to make it easier. There was no point in building up any false hope that Tom Rogers might have survived. He made a blunt, negative motion with his head.

Kathy Rogers stood up, quickly, and before he could reach to help her. She faced him, and he could sense how rigidly her muscles had tightened. Her hands were clenched together at her sides. "I want to go back," she cried. "I want to go back, now. You might be wrong."

He didn't argue with her. It was the thing to do, although what they were going back to might not be a pretty sight. Turning, he led the way to where his horse was tied.

They rode back, the woman straddling the horse in front of him, Joe with his arm lightly around her waist. She had stiffened when he put it there, but he had said, "This is only to steady you. And, anyhow, it's the only way two people can ride the same horse." She didn't like it. He was sure of that. But she offered no further objections.

He had her rein up some distance from the camp. He could identify it quite easily. Several bawling cattle, probably with broken legs, lay on the ground near the crushed wagon. A few others, which Rogers might have shot, were a little distance away.

Joe slid to the ground. "You wait here, Mrs. Rogers. I'll take a look near the wagon. I don't want you on the ground until I'm sure the cattle we see are down for good."

She didn't answer him. She was leaning forward, staring ahead toward the wagon, a drawn, anxious expression on her face.

Joe walked up to the wagon. Near it, lying against it, he found what he had expected to find, the figure of Tom Rogers. The homesteader was lying on his face. His back and his skull were crushed. His legs were twisted into an unnatural angle. His rifle lay half under his body, its stock broken.

Joe straightened, mopped his hand over his face. Kathy had dismounted and was walking toward him, leading the horse. He hurried to meet her, and stood in her way.

She looked up at him and there seemed to be no color at all in her face. She said, "Tom's dead."

He nodded. "Yes, Mrs. Rogers."

"I want to see him."

"I don't think—"

Anger crossed her face. "Get out of my way. I want to see him."

He had no right to prevent her. He stood aside. Then he followed her as she moved up to the wagon. When they got there, however, she didn't throw herself on her husband's body, as he half expected she might. Instead, after a moment she dropped down on her knees beside him, and stretched out her arm to touch him lightly on the shoulder. She whispered, "Good-by, Tom," and stood up, and turned and walked blindly away.

Joe Edison trailed after her. She turned to him and said, quite calmly, "There were some shovels in the wagon. Maybe one isn't broken. Will you dig the grave?"

He nodded. "Where, Mrs. Rogers?"

"Anyplace. It makes little difference where a man is buried. His life goes on in the memory of those who knew him."

Joe had lost his hat. He brushed his fingers through his hair, startled at her words and at the calmness in her voice. He walked back to the wagon, found a shovel, and started digging a grave, noticing the first traces of the morning light creeping into the sky. Now and then he glanced to where Kathy Rogers was standing, and to the injured cattle on the ground nearby. Several had struggled to get up, but hadn't been able to. The sound of their bawling cries was beginning to get on his nerves. He knew he would have to use his gun.

When the grave was deep enough he crossed to where Kathy was standing, troubled in his mind over what kind of service he could hold, over what he could say at the grave of a man he hardly knew.

"I'm ready, Mrs. Rogers."

She sat down suddenly as though her legs would no longer hold her erect. She looked up at him, dry eyed, but with her face still wearing a frozen, tragic mask. "I've already said what has to be said. I said it while you were digging."

He turned back, a hollow, empty feeling inside of him. He lifted the broken body of Tom Rogers and lowered it into the grave, covered his face with a piece of cloth. After this, he filled in the grave.

The sky was much lighter by the time he finished, and now in the east was a yellowish, hazy glow. Sunrise wasn't far off. He set his shovel aside and returned to where Kathy was sitting.

"I'm afraid we'll have to go without breakfast this morning," he said, reaching for something light to talk about.

"That's not important," Kathy said, shrugging.

"We can ride on to Unitah," he continued. "It's the nearest town. From there, you can get in touch with your people."

She shook her head. "I haven't any people."

10

"Then what will you do?"

"Find work someplace. Don't worry about me, Mr. Edison."

She stood up, looked at the mound of the grave he had filled, then looked quickly away.

"Some things from the wagon can be saved," Joe said. "And you've a team of horses to be found. You should be able to realize something from them. When we get to town I'll see if I can find someone to come back here with me and take care of those chores for you."

Whether she heard him or not he didn't know. She was staring off to the north from where the stampeding cattle had come and her body was again growing tense. She wrenched suddenly to face him. "Why did they do it, Mr. Edison? That stampede was no accident. They knew where we were camped."

Joe straightened. "Who knew where you were camped?"

"The men who stopped us late yesterday afternoon, and who told us no more homesteaders were wanted in the Unitah basin."

"What men?"

"There were three. One was big, heavy, wide shouldered and had gray hair. He said the road we were following crossed his range. He said we'd be wise to turn back."

An icy chill raced over Joe's body. He spoke a name. "Henry Tyler?"

"You know him?" Kathy asked quickly.

"I knew him—long ago. I doubt if he remembers me —or if he will be glad when he does."

Kathy, drifting back into her own thoughts, read no significance in his words.

This put a new slant on what had happened. He spoke that name again, under his breath. *Henry Tyler.* Joe Edison had come here to see Henry Tyler. He turned to Kathy. "I'm going to put you on my horse. I want you to ride on down the road a piece, then pull up and wait for me. If you hear shooting, don't get excited about it."

She glanced at the moaning cattle nearby. "You're going to—"

11

"Yes."

A frown wrinkled her forehead. "You've had to do everything. It isn't right you should have had to."

"But that's the way things work out sometimes," Joe said. He managed a weak smile. "Come on. I'll help you on the horse."

"At least I can do that myself." She walked to where his horse was standing, tucked up her skirts, and managed to get astride. Then, without another backward look, started out to the road and turned along it in the direction of Unitah. Some distance away, she pulled up, and sat waiting.

CHAPTER II

KATHY ROGERS was twenty. She didn't know who her parents had been or where she had been born. She had been reared in an orphans' home, and, when she was ten, had been placed with a family who had promised the state officials to give her the love and devotion they would have given a child of their own.

Along with this love and devotion, which never was very evident, they introduced her to a life of drudgery. The mopping, scrubbing, washing, ironing and cooking required of her, never ended, and each day she was expected to work in the fields. As she grew older, the man in the house began to take a personal interest in her. Once, in the barn, she had a terrible struggle with him but managed to escape. After that she refused to go near the barn whenever he was around.

It was Tom Rogers who saved her from what rapidly was becoming an impossible situation. Tom was much older. She didn't love him. But he had been kind, gentle, thoughtful, and she never would regret the year she had spent as his wife.

This morning she was too dazed by what had happened to do any rational thinking. Tom was dead. Beyond that point, she couldn't see. She realized vaguely that she would have to plan a new life for herself. That she would have to get a job somewhere and go to work and look after herself.

She heard the sound of a shot behind her at the camp, then another, and another—and each time she shuddered. She knew what it was like to be hungry, to be muscle sore and weary, but a type of violence such as she had experienced last night was almost new to her. It was like that time in the barn when her foster father had grabbed her in his arms and had started trying to tear off her clothing. It was like that—but worse—for it was Death that had clutched at her last night. But for Joe Edison, she wouldn't be alive this morning. If Joe hadn't carried her away he would have had to dig two graves this morning.

She heard the sound of two more shots but she didn't look back until she heard the scuffle of Joe's footsteps approaching her. She glanced around, then, and took a new look at the young man who had joined them at the campfire the evening before. He was tall, and there was a thin and hungry look about him. His face was bony, sharp featured, but not unpleasant. Freckles showed through the sun and wind tan on his face, and he had clear, blue eyes.

She found herself wondering who he was, where he had come from, where he was going, and what his life really was like. She knew his name, Joe Edison, but that didn't tell her anything. She recalled that he had said he lived here, long ago, but if it had been very long ago it must have been when he was a boy. She didn't think he was much older than she was.

"Ready for the long ride?" Joe asked as he reached her.

She tried to smile. "How far is it to Unitah?"

"We might make it by dusk—or even earlier. This is Wagonwheel land we're on, and will be all the way to town. The Wagonwheel ranchhouse is north of here, so we won't run into anyplace where we can get food. That means we'll be mighty hungry before we hit town."

"I can stand it if you can," Kathy said.

"I think we'll cross several streams on the way. At least we can drink. Move up a little on the horse so I can get on behind you."

Kathy boosted herself forward. Joe climbed on behind her, and they rode on along the twisting road toward Unitah. Behind them, the sun started reaching up into the sky, and grew hot. By mid-morning they came to a tree-shaded stream, where they stopped for a time.

The water was clear and cool. Kathy drank, then bathed her face and hands. After this, she stretched out in the shade. Joe took his turn at the water, then dried

14

his hands. He rolled a cigarette, and sat cross-legged near her.

"What will you do in Unitah?" Kathy asked.

A frown crossed his face. "I've some business to attend to. It's a matter of—an inheritance. One that's been forgotten."

"And then?"

"Then I don't know, Mrs. Rogers. A lot depends on how things work out. Maybe I'll find out that I'm a rancher, or maybe I'll have to look for a job, or maybe—" He shrugged.

"You said you used to live here."

"Long ago."

"It couldn't have been too long ago."

"I'm twenty-three. We left here when I was twelve. I still can remember back to when I was twelve."

He leaned back, closing his eyes. He could recall a good many details of his early life here in the Unitah basin, but three scenes stood out in his memory above all others. The first was of the afternoon when his father's body was found and carried home to the ranchhouse. He never would forget how frightened and bewildered he had been, or the sense of loss he had felt in knowing his father had left him forever.

The second was of the next evening when his mother, in the living room of their home, had hysterically accused Henry Tyler of murder. Tyler had denied it, but his denial had been weak in the face of her anger. And he had beat a hasty retreat.

The third was of their flight, several nights later, and of Tyler's men, pursuing them and firing on them as they raced away. Ben Lindeman had helped them escape. Joe Edison hadn't liked Ben Lindeman until then. Joe's father hadn't liked Lindeman. But then, Joe and his father must have been wrong about Lindeman.

His cigarette had gone out. He lit it again and glanced at Kathy.

"You've been far away," Kathy said.

"No, not far away," he answered. "I've just been remembering some things that happened long ago. When I was a boy, here, the big man in the basin was Henry

Tyler of the Wagonwheel ranch. I reckon he's still the big man in the basin."

"You mentioned that name when I described the man who warned us to turn back."

"Yes. Your description fitted him."

Kathy sat up. "Your business here is with Henry Tyler?"

"Yes."

She shook her head, frowning. "Is it worth it?"

"Yes."

"My husband could have escaped last night. He didn't. He fought to turn the stampede aside. It cost him his life. Is it worth risking your life for land or cattle, or even for a principle you believe in?"

"A man sometimes has to, Kathy."

"Why?"

"That's the way the world is. If some didn't stand for principle, we'd all live as savages and the only law would be the law of the strong."

She still was shaking her head, and still was frowning. Joe got to his feet. "We'd better ride on."

It was fully dark before they reached Unitah. Judging from the lights showing in the cluster of houses and buildings, the town seemed much smaller than Joe remembered. He held to the road which turned into the narrow main street. Joe glanced at the double row of buildings just ahead. Some were dark, some still lighted. By morning, this street and its buildings might look familiar. Tonight, everything seemed strange.

"We'll first go to the sheriff's office and make a report on what happened," Joe said. "Then we'll get something to eat. After that, I'll get you a hotel room."

She looked around at him. "I haven't any money."

"I'll loan you some. You can repay me later, after you've found work."

They were riding down the street. To the right, over a building in which there still were lights, was a sign reading: *Patterson's Store*. Beyond it was the barber shop and bank. On the other side of the street was the stage office and corral, then the B & W saloon; the feed

16

store and the sheriff's office. Joe angled toward the sheriff's office.

He pulled up, slid to the ground, and reached up to help Kathy down.

"Stiff?" he asked her.

"So stiff I don't know if I'll be able to walk."

"It'll be worse later tonight and tomorrow," he said frowning. "But I hope you can sleep." They stepped up on the board walk, crossed to the office door and went inside.

The sheriff was at his desk. He was a thin, under-sized man with a scowling face and sharp dark eyes. Another man was at the desk, talking to the sheriff when they came in. Both looked around. The other man standing at the desk was maybe a few years older than Joe. He was tall and heavy with a puffy face.

"I'm looking for the sheriff," Joe said.

The man back of the desk bobbed his head. "I'm the sheriff. Name's Eli Wallace."

"This is Mrs. Tom Rogers," Joe said, indicating Kathy. "My name is Edison. Joe Edison."

The sheriff's eyes widened. "You're—you're not—"

"Yes, I am," Joe said. "I'm Frank Edison's son, but we'll get to that later. I've something else to report first."

The man with the puffy face turned abruptly toward the door. "Got to go, Eli," he called over his shoulder. "See you some other time."

He gave Joe a hard, searching look as he passed him, then stepped outside.

"Frank Edison's son," the sheriff muttered, wiping a hand over his face. "I just can't believe it. We heard you and your mother were dead."

"We'll get to that later," Joe said. "Before we do, I want to tell you what happened last night. I met the Rogerses a day's ride east of here. They had camped for the night. They invited me to camp with them. I reckon it was a little after midnight that I woke up, and just in time. There was a herd of cattle to the north of where we were camping. Someone stampeded them, straight at us. Tom Rogers was killed, trampled to death."

Sheriff Wallace now was standing. He looked shocked.

17

He glanced at Kathy, then looked back at Joe. "A stampede?" he said vaguely, shaking his head. "You mean someone deliberately started a stampede. It's hard to believe."

"I'll take you to where you can see what happened," Joe answered.

"You're sure someone started it? Maybe some lightning, or thunder—"

"There wasn't any lightning or thunder. Men firing their guns and screaming at the cattle started the stampede. The tracks they left still will be there tomorrow."

"And a man was killed?"

Kathy spoke up. "Yes. My husband."

The sheriff took a deep breath. He shook his head. "I'm terribly sorry, Mrs. Rogers, but accidents will happen. Tomorrow—"

"It was no accident," Kathy said sharply. "I heard the gunfire and the yelling. And it may interest you to know that a few hours before, three men stopped us on the road. One was Henry Tyler. He ordered us to turn back. He said we weren't wanted in the Unitah basin."

Wallace looked directly at her. "Mrs. Rogers, I've known Henry Tyler for many years. He's a hard man, it's true. Maybe he's sometimes a brutal man. But he wouldn't stampede a herd of his cattle across a man's camp. He never would do a thing like that."

"Someone did," Kathy said.

"Not Tyler."

Joe leaned forward. "And I suppose Tyler didn't kill my father."

The sheriff stiffened. "We don't know who killed your father, Joe. I want to talk to you about that, and about why you came back here."

"But not now," Joe said. "What are you going to do about the stampede, and about the death of Tom Rogers?"

Wallace shifted uneasily on his feet. "I'll make an investigation, of course. I'll—"

A voice called in from the doorway, interrupting him. "No, by damn! You'll do more than that, Sheriff. Tyler's gone too far. It's time to call a halt."

Joe swung around. There were several men in the

18

doorway. One, a tall, gaunt, lantern-jawed fellow, Joe recognized instantly as Ben Lindeman. It was Lindeman who had been speaking. The scowl on his face smoothed out and he smiled as he stepped toward Joe, holding out his hand. "Welcome back to Unitah, Joe. Maybe everyone won't be glad to see you, but I am."

They shook hands.

"You're looking well, Joe," Lindeman said. "But we'll have time to catch up on things later on. First, we've got to settle this issue about the stampede. . . . Wallace, what are you afraid of? Henry Tyler?"

A tight, stubborn look had settled on the sheriff's face. "I'm not afraid of Tyler, or anyone else," he threw back. "I'll do what I said I'd do."

Lindeman marched up to his desk. "To hell with your investigations. If there was a stampede that cost a man's life on Wagonwheel land, who but Tyler could be responsible for it. I want him arrested. Now. Tonight."

The sheriff seemed to stiffen even more. "I'll do things my way, Lindeman. Long as I'm sheriff, I'll do things my way."

"You may not be sheriff very long."

"But I am now."

Lindeman wrenched angrily around. "That's what we run up against here," he shouted. "We've got a sheriff who's Tyler's man. He'd arrest me quick enough, if I got out of line, or he'd arrest anyone else. Tyler can get by with murder—and has. It's high time we changed things."

There was a stir in the crowd at the door. Someone else came in. Lindeman's eyes widened. He swept back his coat, dropping his hand to rest on his holstered gun.

Joe glanced quickly at the door, and stood very still. The man who had pushed his way into the room was big, wide shouldered, heavy. He had a tired, deep-lined face, but his eyes were as hard as black agate and his lips made a stern line above the stubborn bulge of his jaw. Joe didn't have to ask who the man was. He recognized him as quickly as he had recognized Lindeman. Joe spoke right up without hesitation.

"Tyler, I want to talk to you. I came here to ask you some questions."

Tyler nodded. "Glad you did, Joe, but we'll have to let them ride for the present. What's this about a stampede, and why should I be arrested?"

Joe looked at Kathy, who was staring wide eyed at Henry Tyler. He could tell from the expression on her face that she recognized him.

"Mrs. Rogers," Joe asked quietly, "did you ever see this man before? Is he one of the three who stopped you yesterday afternoon and warned you to keep out of the Unitah basin?"

Kathy moistened her lips. "Yes. He's the one who did the talking."

Tyler glanced at her, then looked at Joe. "So I warned some homesteaders to keep out of the Unitah. We'vc got more along Lignite creek now than I can put up with."

"That's hardly the point," Joe said. "Here's what I'm driving at. A few miles from where you warned Rogers and his wife to turn back, they made their camp. During the night a herd of cattle was stampeded straight at them. Tom Rogers was trampled to death."

Tyler's head came up. "That's hard to believe, Joe."

"I was there," Joe said bluntly. "I heard and saw what happened."

The boss of the Wagonwheel jerked around. "Lou," he called to one of the men behind him, "take Kim Ellis with you and head down the road to where we saw the homesteaders. If you find any signs of a stampede, stay there and send Kim to the ranchhouse for me."

"On my way," Lou answered.

Tyler then looked back at Kathy. "Mrs. Rogers, I don't know anything about any stampede. That your husband was killed, I'm sorry. If the blame for such a stampede can be pinned down, I'll help pin it down, and see that whoever is guilty is punished. That's a promise I'll keep."

Kathy said nothing, but there was a thoughtful or puzzled look in her eyes.

"It's a promise I'll make, too," Lindeman said harshly.

"You've gone too far this time, Tyler. You're finished in the Unitah."

There was a threat in those words, but Tyler only shrugged. "Time will tell." And then he added, "Joe, I've a room at the hotel. Will you come to see me, tonight, soon as you can?"

"After I've had something to eat, and found a place for Mrs. Rogers to stay," Joe answered.

"Mrs. Holcomb's boarding house would be the best place, Joe. I'll send a man there to tell her to fix up a room."

Joe nodded his thanks.

Tyler turned to the door. He stood there for a moment with his back to those in the room, and in his attitude there seemed to be a definite gesture of defiance.

Joe felt suddenly uneasy. After leaving here when he was a boy, he had been brought up to hate Henry Tyler. Yet he couldn't help but admire the man for the way he had faced the men in this room.

Lindeman was again talking to the sheriff about what ought to be done. There was a blustering, nagging note in his voice. Joe scowled, and turned to where Kathy was standing. He took her arm. "Come on, let's go get something to eat."

CHAPTER III

BEN LINDEMAN found his daughter at Ellen Romney's.
He was a little surprised at this. When Myrt Lindeman
came to town with him and left him in the evening, she
usually said she was going to Ellen's—but often she
didn't. Where she really went on such occasions he didn't
know and this sometimes worried him.

When he was truthful with himself there were a great
many things about Myrt which worried him. She was
tall, slender, beautiful, and twenty-one. At twenty-one, a
girl should have been married, but she showed no interest
in anyone whom he would have considered a good catch.
That didn't mean she avoided men. On the contrary, she
was too much interested in men, and in too many men.
But more fundamentally, she wasn't truthful. She could
lie beautifully, and she was hard. As hard as he was.

He asked her out on the porch when she came to the
door, and as was his custom, he came straight to the
point. "Myrt, I don't often ask you to do anything for me,
but tonight I've got a job for you. One that's important."

"A job, father?" Myrt said curiously. "What would
you call a job?"

He squinted at her in the darkness. She was wearing a
divided riding skirt and a sweater that was so tight it
showed the outlines of her breasts quite clearly. He told
himself that, damn it, a girl ought to cover her breasts.
But he knew if he said anything about it, Myrt would
only laugh at him.

"Do you remember Joe Edison?" he asked.

"Faintly," Myrt said. "Wasn't he the son of the man
who was Henry Tyler's partner, and whom Mr. Tyler
shot, years ago?"

"That's right," Lindeman said. "He's back in town,
rode in tonight."

"Then maybe he'll shoot Mr. Tyler, and your troubles
will be over."

22

"Or maybe he won't. And there's where you come in. I want you to interest him in coming out to the ranch to visit us—right away—before he does anything else."

"You want me to what! You, my father, are asking me to pick up a man!"

"You've done it before," Lindeman growled. "Don't be so damned innocent about it."

Myrt laughed. She lifted her hand to brush back her hair. It was coal black and went well with her dark eyes and tanned skin.

"He's in the hotel restaurant, right now, with another woman. Some homesteader's widow. He'll take her to Mrs. Holcomb's, then come back to the hotel to see Henry Tyler. You might be on the hotel porch—and stop him."

"Just like that?"

"Myrt, this is important, damned important. Joe Edison is our key to the Wagonwheel. With him on our side we can take the place over—just like that." He snapped his fingers.

Myrt's eyes narrowed. "You mean—"

"Don't ask me what I mean," Lindeman snapped. "For once, just trust me."

Myrt was silent for a time, busy with her own thoughts. Finally she nodded. "All right, Father. I'll gather him in. But on one condition. I want to know what's going on. I want to know what you're planning."

"Soon as I can tell you."

"Then soon, you'd better. If I can lead him in, I can lead him away. Don't forget that."

He shrugged, feigning an indifference he didn't feel. He wasn't sure how far Myrt could be trusted. "Get your jacket," he said. "I'll walk you back to town."

Joe Edison finished his meal, pushed away his empty plate, leaned back, and looked over at Kathy and grinned. "I really was hungry," he apologized. "I usually don't eat so much."

"I don't either," Kathy said. She shifted her position, carefully, and slowly, biting at her lower lip as she moved.

"Sore?" Joe grinned.

23

"I don't know whether I can stand up or not. I'm not sure I can walk."

"Wait until tomorrow," Joe said. "You'll really feel it then."

He got up, walked around the table, helped her to her feet and crossed with her to the door. They went outside and started down the street in the direction of Mrs. Holcomb's, Joe holding her arm.

The boarding house fronted on the main street beyond the vacant lot next to the saddlers. When they got there, Kathy turned to face him. "Joe, I didn't like Mr. Lindeman. You almost could taste the bitterness in him."

"What about Tyler?"

She shook her head. "Him either. I'm afraid of him. He'd smash anything that got in his way."

"My father and Henry Tyler came to the Unitah basin together when both were quite young," Joe said. "They established the Wagonwheel ranch, and ran it as a joint venture. When they got married they split it in half, but without putting anything down on paper. They still operated it as the Wagonwheel. Tyler kept the books, and twice each year they divided the profits. When they disagreed over something they tossed a coin to decide what course to follow. Their relationship was one of those things you often hear about, but seldom run into. They were close as brothers, closer, maybe.

"Then one day they had a real quarrel. They had quarreled before but always patched it up. This quarrel they didn't patch up. About a month later and while they still were fighting, they left town together. Two men saw them at a place called Rocky Gorge, where their trails divided to head toward their separate homes. A few minutes later they heard a rifle shot, and rode that way to investigate. They found my father lying on the trail, dead, a bullet through his back."

"Mr. Tyler had killed him?"

"No question of it. But Tyler denied it. Then a few nights later his men raided our ranch. Except for the warning brought us by Ben Lindeman, mother and I might not have escaped."

"He meant to kill you, too?"

24

"Yes. Then the Wagonwheel would have been his. All of it."

"You've come back to claim your share?"

"Why not, Kathy?"

"What proof do you have that you own a share?"

"None in writing. None that would stand up in court. But every old-timer in the valley knows of the unwritten agreement between my father and Henry Tyler. It's going to be hard for Tyler to deny it."

Kathy was frowning. "The Wagonwheel must now be quite valuable."

"It is."

"Then do you think Mr. Tyler has changed? Do you think he will hand over half of what he owns on the basis of an old, unwritten agreement?"

"What else can he do?"

"Kill you, or see that someone else does."

"That's a chance I have to take, Kathy."

"It doesn't look like a chance to me," Kathy said bluntly. "It looks like something which surely will happen. I think you're a fool, Joe."

"Why?"

"Half the Wagonwheel isn't worth it."

"But I think it is. And I think something else is important. Bringing to justice the man who killed my father. Tyler has dominated this basin long enough."

"Maybe so, Joe. I just don't know. Tom used to say that the brew of revenge was a bitter tea. Tom was a wise man."

Joe said, "You'd better get some sleep, Kathy. We'll think about a job for you in a day or two, after you get over the stiffness from our ride."

"No—I'll think about the job," Kathy corrected. "Thanks, Joe, for everything." She reached out, dropped her hand on his arm and squeezed it. Then she turned toward the door.

Joe Edison started back up the street which was now nearly deserted. Most stores had closed. Lights still showed from the saloon windows and the hotel, but the street was darker than when he had walked this way with Kathy.

25

He stared ahead toward the hotel, and suddenly came to an abrupt stop. A shadowy figure had stepped out of the narrow passageway between two buildings, just ahead. He caught a glimpse of the man, and of the glistening reflection of starlight on the barrel of the gun he was lifting. There was no time for thought, no time to puzzle about who the man was or what he meant to do. Joe's dive at the ground was an instinctive measure of protection.

He heard the roar of a shot and sensed the scream of the bullet tearing through the air above him. He saw the man ducking back into the passageway again, and he snaked out his own gun and threw a quick shot at him.

The man disappeared from sight. Joe rose to his feet and raced across the street. There, in the deep shadows of the building, he crouched and stood waiting, his eyes raking up and down the buildings on the opposite side. Nowhere could he see any sign of movement. A full minute passed, then part of another. From back of the building across the street, a horse raced suddenly away, the sound of its hoofbeats fading into the stillness of the night.

Joe relaxed, then, holstered his gun, and mopped his hand across his face. Up the street, now, he could hear the sounds of men's voices, and of footsteps heading his way. The sheriff, and probably a few others, were on their way to investigate the shooting. Joe Edison backed away, rounded a building corner, and cut behind it, circling toward the hotel. He didn't want to face the sheriff and say someone had taken a shot at him. He had no way of pinning the blame anywhere.

He came out on the street again in front of the hotel, and, after a brief hesitation, headed that way. There were three people on the hotel porch, one a woman. She turned toward the steps, suddenly smiling as she looked down at him. She was young, and more than ordinarily attractive. She had dark eyes, dark hair and even under her jacket he could see the thrust of her breasts.

She laughed in a low, throaty way, and said, "Hello, Joe."

He stopped, and stood staring up at her, searching his mind frantically.

"You've a poor memory, haven't you," she said easily. "Think back, Joe. Way back to your school days here in Unitah. You could lick every kid in the school. I could lick every girl, and half the boys. Remember?"

A name came to him. "Myrt! Myrt Lindeman!"

"That's right," she said laughing, and putting out her hand.

Joe took it, joining in her laughter, and climbing the porch steps to stand beside her. It flashed through his mind that in her school days, Myrtle Lindeman had been a half-wild creature, a tomboy and always in trouble. There still was a reckless look about her. An exciting look.

"And are you still Myrt Lindeman?" he asked.

"Yes, still Myrt Lindeman. The right man hasn't come along. I've almost given up hope, Joe."

He shook his head. "As I recall it, you never were one to give up anything."

This seemed to please her. "Not if I wanted it badly."

"Same old Myrt, huh?"

"Same old Myrt."

They both laughed. Then Joe, recalling why he had come here, grew serious. "I've someone to see in the hotel, Myrt. But afterwards—"

"You're too late," Myrt said. "The man you came here to see is gone."

"Henry Tyler?"

She nodded. "He went tearing out of here about ten minutes ago, climbed his horse and tore off to the east. Maybe he wants to erase all traces of the stampede before the sheriff gets there."

"It's not that easy to erase the trace of a stampede."

"A man can try, can't he?"

Joe shrugged. He was sorry he had missed Henry Tyler. He wished, now, he hadn't taken so much time eating.

"Where will you stay, tonight?" Myrt asked.

"Here in the hotel, I suppose."

"But why, Joe? You're a marked man, so far as Tyler

is concerned. You'd be better off among your friends. Father's somewhere around town, looking for you. He wants you to come out to our place. It's only an hour's ride from here. You'll get a better bed, and better food than here in town."

It was an appealing suggestion, but not only from the standpoint of food and safety. Joe had a notion that it might be interesting to get to know Myrt better.

"Well?" she asked smiling.

"I don't have a saddle for my horse," Joe said.

"We can borrow one at the livery stable. Come on."

She took his arm and they started up the street together. Joe took a sideward look at her, and instinctively straightened. Myrt Lindeman had turned out to be a damned attractive woman. He wondered again why she never had married.

In front of the sheriff's office they picked up his horse, then walked on up the middle of the street, walking close together. Joe took another look at her. It was too dark to see her face clearly but he was almost sure she was smiling. It occurred to him abruptly that things might work out so that he would be very well pleased that he had returned to the Unitah. He spoke part of that thought aloud, saying, "You know, Myrt, maybe I'm glad I came back."

"Maybe I am, too," Myrt said.

He felt the brush of her body against his side and he laughed softly and stopped, and turned her to face him. "A man should be welcomed back like this."

He pulled her forward, and kissed her, meaning it to be just an experimental kiss. It was more. Her arms went suddenly around him and her lips clung to his and he felt the full length of her pressing against him. He was a little shaky when she stepped away. He reached for her again.

She backed off, laughing. "Don't rush things, Joe. We've all the time in the world."

CHAPTER IV

THEY LINGERED the next morning over breakfast. Ben Lindeman had sent his two hired men to town, getting them started before dawn. They would join the sheriff's posse and ride out to the scene of the stampede. Lindeman had decided against going himself, saying he was so angry over what had happened he didn't dare risk it. And he had insisted that Joe stay here at the ranch.

"It's one of the few places you're safe," he declared bluntly. "Tyler will have all his crowd out at the scene of the stampede. Maybe he can't hide what happened, but he can hide traces of the men responsible. The sheriff will play along with him, too. If you and I were there, Joe, we might speak out of turn and it could easy enough end up in a shooting."

"But I'll not get anyplace staying here," Joe insisted.

"We got to figure out something," Lindeman said.

"What kind of plan do I need?"

Myrt said, "First, let's decide what you want."

She was wearing a dress this morning, a flowing dress which fit tightly at the waist and bust and flared out over her hips.

"What do I want?" Joe repeated. "That's simple enough. I want my father's share of the Wagonwheel. I want an accounting for the past years. And I want Tyler brought to trial for my father's death."

"Simple?" Lindeman said. "You call that simple?"

A wry smile crossed Joe's face. "Maybe not. But it's what I want. Do you think Tyler will deny his unwritten partnership with my father?"

Lindeman shook his head. "Not at all. He never has denied it. You probably can demand and get an accounting for the past years, but a thing like that takes time and Tyler has several gunmen on his payroll, any one

29

of whom could polish you off before another day rolls by."

"Maybe not."

"Do you want to risk it?"

"I have to, don't I?"

"Not if we can figure something else. Not if we can hit Tyler where he isn't expecting it."

"And where would that be?"

"I don't know," Lindeman said scowling. "Give me time to think." He sat at the table, drumming on it with his fingers, still scowling.

Joe glanced at Myrt and surprised her smiling at him. "I think I'll stretch my legs," he said abruptly.

He got up, waved at Myrt and her father, and went outside. The sun was almost two hours high and was growing warm. He stood in the yard and stared off to the east. The Wagonwheel lay in that direction, and north and east of here had been the location of his father's ranchhouse. He could picture it in his mind, quite clearly. He wondered if anyone lived there now, or if it was deserted. It struck him suddenly that there was no reason he shouldn't visit it. He could get there and back easily in four hours, which would leave him plenty of time to get to town before the posse could return this evening.

Myrt came out as he was saddling up. She looked surprised. "Joe, where are you going?"

"Just for a short ride."

She shook her head. "Father won't like it." This annoyed him. He climbed into the saddle. "I'll not be gone long, Myrt. See you this afternoon."

Touching his borrowed hat, he wheeled away, angling to north and east. This was a rolling, hilly country, and in five minutes he was out of sight of the ranchhouse. Five minutes more and he reined up. Ahead of him, through the fold in the hills, two riders came suddenly into sight. Their rifles covered him. He took a quick look over his shoulder. A third rider had crested the hill to the south and was dropping down toward him. A fourth rode into view from the north.

A clammy perspiration broke out on his skin. He was

as completely surrounded as though he had stepped into a box.

The four men drew closer. They pulled up; two behind him, two in front. Their horses wore the Wagonwheel brand, but this didn't surprise him in the least. A moment after he had seen them he had guessed who they were, and that they had been watching Lindeman's in the hope he might ride out alone.

"We'll take your gun, Edison," one of them said. "Toss it to me." He was bearded, middle aged, and had hard, black eyes.

Joe tossed him his gun, then asked in a dry voice, "What's next?"

"The boss wants to see you, pronto. Any objections?"

"Would it do me any good to object?"

One laughed at this, shaking his head. "We'd just have to get rough. The boss wouldn't like that any more than you would."

"Then we're going to the Wagonwheel?"

"Yep."

Joe took a deep breath. He felt better. He knew he had no real grounds for it, but the feeling was there. He nodded and said, "Let's ride."

They headed in an easterly direction to the river, crossed it and rode on over the low, rolling Wagonwheel hills. Another hour brought them to the ranchhouse. It was a low, sprawling structure around which were clustered a barn, a bunkhouse, several cabins and a few sheds. Joe hadn't remembered, very well, what Tyler's place looked like, but he recalled it now from the days of his boyhood in the basin. He had had many a Sunday dinner here and had watched horse breaking and racing in the afternoons.

Two men came out of the bunkhouse when they rode into the yard, one calling, "I see you got him."

"Sure," the bearded man answered. "Don't I always get what I go after?"

"Not always, Jake."

"Most of the time, anyhow. Where's the boss?"

"Not back yet. He said if you got here with Edison to hold him until he showed up."

31

"Hold him where?"

"What's the matter with the barn? We can tie him, can't we?"

That was what happened. They took Joe Edison to the barn, tied his hands and feet securely and left him there.

The hours of the day rolled on. They fed him toward dusk, standing guard over him while he ate. Then they tied him up again, left a lantern burning so he was in its light, and posted a guard at the barn door.

It was nine o'clock before Tyler reached the ranchhouse. Several men came with him. Joe heard them ride into the yard and heard the sounds of their voices outside. A few minutes later Tyler came to the barn, accompanied by several others. He looked tired. The lines in his face seemed deeper than the evening before.

"Sorry about this, Joe," he said gruffly. "But I felt it necessary to talk to you as soon as possible." He turned, then, to one of the men near him, and added, "Cut him loose. Bring him into the house. Did you take his gun?"

The man nodded.

"Give it back to him," Tyler ordered. He turned and hurried away.

One of the men left in the barn, freed Joe's hands and legs, and after he stood up, another gave him his gun. Joe made a brief examination of it, then tucked it in the waistband of his trousers. He still didn't have a holster.

"Ready to go to the house?" the bearded man asked.

He and the others were watching him closely. Joe shrugged. "Why not?"

They went outside and crossed to the ranchhouse. Lamp light showed through its curtained windows. Someone knocked on the door, and, at Tyler's invitation to enter, opened it. They walked in. Tyler had taken off his coat. He was wearing his gun. Red suspenders held up his trousers. His shirt was sweat stained at the arm pits.

"That'll be all, Charlie," he said to the bearded man. "You fellows can go. If I want you, I'll yell."

"This guy's armed," Charlie said uneasily.

"What of it?" Tyler asked.

32

The others left the room. Joe stood where he was, just inside the door.

"Have a chair," Tyler said. "Or walk around, if you want to. Hungry?"

"No. They fed me."

"I've been south and east of here," Tyler said. "Along the Waterhouse road. There was a stampede, all right. We found Rogers' grave. And we found the tracks of the men who could have started it, if that's what happened."

Joe moved forward. "That's what happened."

"You heard the men shouting?"

"And firing their guns."

"Did you hear any names? See anyone closely."

"No."

The older man shrugged. "Maybe you won't believe me, but my men didn't start that stampede."

"Then who did?"

"I don't know. Or at least, I can't prove anything. A real tracker might be able to make something of the trail the men left, but I don't know anyone in the basin who's up to it. We used to have some men who were good at reading trails, but they're not around any longer. Your father was good at trail reading."

"Too bad you killed him," Joe said dryly.

Tyler's head came up sharply. "I didn't."

"Two men saw you with him at Rocky Gorge. A moment later they heard the sound of a shot and rode to investigate. They found my father's body. Where were you?"

"It was more than a moment later when they heard the shot. Your father and I separated at the Gorge. He rode toward his house and I rode toward mine. I heard no shot. Your father was killed some time after he left me. He rode on, then turned back."

"Your story."

"Yes, my story, Joe. And the way it happened. The two men who said they saw us together and who tried to pin the killing on me were two men I had fired from the Wagonwheel and who hated me and hated your father."

"Where are they now?"

"One is dead. One works for Ben Lindeman. His name

33

is Ed Wylie. Roy Maxwell, who was sheriff in those days, tried to pin the killing on those two men. He couldn't, and probably they weren't guilty. Maxwell said a third man was near the Gorge that afternoon, and that this third man was the murderer. He found the man's trail and tried to follow it, but lost it. I don't know who killed your father. I've my suspicions, but suspicions aren't enough. I once beat Ed Wylie half to death to try and get the truth out of him, but he stuck to his story. That was a long time ago. Since then, I've let things slide. Maybe I've been waiting for your return. I was sure you'd come back some day. How's your mother?"

"Dead."

"I'm sorry to hear that. She never liked me but she hid it fairly well. She never could understand the relationship between your father and me."

"I don't understand it either," Joe said.

Tyler sat down in a chair near the table. "It was a very simple and close relationship. We made a team."

"With you running it?"

"No, I handled the business end of the operation. Maybe that made it seem as though I was boss. But your father gave the orders to the men, and directed the work on the ranch. When we disagreed on something, we tossed a coin."

"You had a fight just before father's death."

"Not a fight. A disagreement."

"Why didn't you toss a coin?"

"It was a personal matter. It didn't involve the ranch."

"What was it?"

"I can't tell you, Joe. It's all over now, anyhow, and has been for years. It's best not to rake up the ashes."

Joe shook his head angrily. "I don't believe you."

"Then you don't believe me, and I'm sorry. Let me tell you this, Joe. If I explained matters to you, it wouldn't change the present or the past even a little bit. It wouldn't make you like me better or hate me more. Forget it. Just let it stand that your father and I disagreed over something that couldn't be settled by flipping a coin. Now, let's get down to the present."

Joe moved on forward to the table. He sat down

across from Tyler. What he just had heard didn't satisfy him.

"You didn't come to see me last night at the hotel," Tyler said.

"I came," Joe said. "You had gone."

"No, I was there when you walked off with Myrt Lindeman."

"Then she misunderstood. She thought you were gone."

"Myrt is like her mother was," Tyler said. "The truth isn't in her."

Joe came half to his feet. "And what do you mean by that?"

"She lied to you, Joe. Lindeman didn't want you and I to have a chance to talk things over."

"I don't believe you."

"Then let's get to something you can believe. Do you know of the old agreement between your father and me?"

"Yes."

"How do you understand it?"

"My father and you were joint owners of the Wagonwheel. Twice each year, you divided the profits of the ranch."

"Or the losses. We didn't often go in the red, but there were years when we did. Then there was another phase to the agreement. Each of us agreed not to sell out unless he sold out to the other."

Joe nodded.

"It was a good agreement," Tyler continued. "We never committed it to paper because we didn't feel it necessary. When you were born your father suggested that you be included as his heir. I agreed. If I had had an heir, he would have been included. Anyhow, by the terms of the agreement, half the Wagonwheel is yours."

"Right now?"

"Yes, right now."

"What about the profits and losses since my father's death?"

"I will draw up a statement and make an accounting, year by year, and if you want to, we can commit the agreement to writing."

"Only to me. Do you want to sell?"

35

"I don't know."

"If you do, it'll take me quite a while to get the financing necessary to swing the deal. During that time, you will have to remain as half owner."

"What does that mean?"

"It may mean that you're buying your way into a fight, Joe."

"What kind of fight?"

"A dirty fight. An ugly fight. The last few years times haven't been so good here in the basin. When your father and I moved here, long ago, we took up all the land east of the river. It's a range that's comparatively flat, and where we haven't water, we have wells. Others settled west of the river. It's more rugged country over there. The grass isn't so good. There aren't many wells. For years, the ranchers west of the river have eyed the Wagonwheel. They'd like to move in on us, smash us, and cut up the range to fit their needs. They are about ready to make such a move."

"How can they?"

"I don't know, but Lindeman's got a plan. I see traces of it now and then, but can't yet make out the pattern. In the last year, five families have homesteaded on Lignite creek, bordering the Wagonwheel. Three of the five families, at least, aren't legitimate homesteaders. They're making no pretense of working the land they filed on. They're here for some other reason. Then there was that stampede the other night. I might have been arrested for that. I still may be. With me in jail the Wagonwheel would be without a boss—unless you were here."

"And if I come here?"

"You can stay with me, or at your old home. If you stay at your old home you can take part of the crew with you, or most of them, and work the Wagonwheel from there. We'd have to keep in close touch with each other."

"And settle our disagreements by the flip of a coin?"

"Your father and I worked that way—and got along. We didn't often have to flip a coin. We saw eye to eye on most things. Anyhow, there you are, Joe. Half the Wagonwheel is yours. I'd like you to keep it and move out here and help me run it. How about it?"

Joe stood up. He felt both confused and excited.

"Well, Joe?" Tyler was asking.

"I don't know," Joe muttered.

"Maybe you'd like to sleep on it. We can have another talk in the morning."

Joe hesitated, then nodded. "Yes. Let's talk again in the morning."

CHAPTER V

JOE EDISON had breakfast with Tyler and most of his crew. Two women prepared and served the meal and the coffee was the best he had had in a long time. Afterwards, Tyler introduced him, without saying anything about what his future status would be.

Dan Gomez, a grizzled, middle-aged man, and tophand on the Wagonwheel, spent the next few minutes with Tyler, and afterwards called the men together and laid out the day's work.

"What would you like to do, Joe?" Tyler asked. "You could spend the day with Dan. He could give you a good line on the routine problems we're facing. Or you can strike off on your own if you wish."

"I haven't told you my decision, yet," Joe said.

"Have you reached it?"

"No."

"Then don't hurry it. Take a day or two. Ride the range. Talk to the men who work here. Of course, in a way, you're tied down by the old agreement."

"How's that?"

Tyler laughed. "Half the Wagonwheel's yours, whether you like it or not. Of course I can't make you accept any responsibility, but, as I said, there's no rush. I'm going to Unitah. I want to get Richter, at the bank, to draw up a statement covering what I owe you. Want to ride in wih me?"

Joe shook his head. "What I'd really like to do is ride up to the old house where I was born."

"Fine. Pick a fresh horse from those in the corral. I have a rifle in the house, if you want to carry one, and an extra gun belt and holster too."

Joe walked to the house, scowling. No one, he decided, could seem more friendly than Tyler was acting this morning. No one could seem more honest than he had last night. A doubt was growing in Joe's mind. A doubt that Tyler was the man who had killed his father.

Tyler came in a few minutes later, accompanied by Dan Gomez.

"You want I should saddle a horse for you, Edison?" the foreman asked.

"You can, or I can do it myself," Joe said.

"It's no trouble," Gomez answered. "I reckon you can find your way to your father's house."

"You knew him?"

"Yep."

"Dan's been here close to twenty years," Tyler said. "We have several others who have been here almost that long. Of course some of the men are new. It's always that way on a spread big as the Wagonwheel."

They talked a few minutes longer, then Gomez went outside and Tyler offered Joe the choice of three rifles, and a box of shells. After this he dug up an extra gun belt and holster.

Joe fitted it around his waist, settled his sixgun into the holster, and turned to the door.

"Keep your eyes open," Tyler warned.

"Looking for what?"

"Just keep your eyes open. I still haven't figured what Lindeman's up to. Some of the men are riding into town, this evening. Maybe you'd like to come in with them."

"Probably," Joe said.

He went out into the yard. Gomez had put his saddle on a claybank stallion that had good lines, and looked as though it could run. Most of Tyler's crew had left on various assigned jobs but two still were here, talking to Gomez at the corral. Each carried a rifle. They drifted away as Joe came up, one heading for the barn, one walking toward the house.

"Guards," Gomez said briefly, a scowl showing on his face.

"Are things that bad?"

"Who knows how bad they are? If you got a valuable property and smell danger, you guard it."

Joe nodded thoughtfully, then switched the subject. "You knew my father. Who killed him?"

"Can't tell you for sure, Edison. Want me to make a guess?"

"Make it."

"Ben Lindeman."

"Why?"

Gomez looked down at the ground, scowling. He stirred his toe in the dust. "Can't figure why. Just a hunch I have. I suppose there ain't no way to prove it right or wrong."

"It was Lindeman who helped mother and I escape," Joe said.

"Escape from what?"

"Escape from men who raided our house several nights after father's death."

A narrow look came into the older man's eyes. "Never heard of that before. As I got the story, you an' your mother just picked up and left. If there was a raid on your house, no one knew it."

"I remember the shooting," Joe said. "I remember the chase."

"And you got away? What kind of riders were following you?"

Joe shifted uneasily. He remembered his mother never had liked horseback riding and wasn't a good horsewoman. Yet they had managed to get away. Joe said, "Thanks, Dan," then mounted the claybank and rode away, slanting to the north.

It wasn't a long trip from Tyler's to the house where he had been born and spent the early years of his life. Joe reined up when he came in sight of it, a sudden rush of memory coming back to him, bringing a strange moisture to his eyes and lifting a lump in his throat.

It was a low, square house with a wide, front porch, its windows boarded up. The corral and a shed he remembered were gone. The bunkhouse still was standing, and the walls of the old barn. He rode slowly forward, recalling a dozen childhood incidents involving his early life. It was here he had had his first real lessons in riding, roping, and handling a gun, his mother's face pressed at the window, looking out at him worried and disapproving.

He was frowning when he rode into the front yard and

dismounted, and tied the claybank's reins to the front porch. It just had occurred to him that his mother hadn't liked ranch life. After they left here they had gone to El Paso where she had worked in a hotel and after he finished school she had done everything she could to persuade him to take a town job. He had come close to yielding to her wishes.

He climbed the steps, tried the front door. It was unlocked. He pushed it open and stepped inside, squinting his eyes to adjust them to the darkness of the room. What warned him, he never knew. It might have been some faint, scraping sound, or some sense of motion, but he had the sudden feeling that he wasn't alone in the room, that someone else was here. He threw himself at the floor, snaking out his gun as he fell.

An orange flame spit at him from the side. The roar of a gun deafened his ears and he felt the jerk of a bullet at his coat shoulder. He fired at that exploding flame, then fired again, aiming just below it. He heard a hoarse cry of pain and could see the blurred outline of a figure, staggering toward him. He fired once more and saw the man jerk erect, turn half around, and plunge to the floor.

Joe rolled sideways, then lay motionless for a full minute. His eyes now were adjusted to the darkness in the room and he could easily make out the lump of a man's figure. The man had fallen near the table, and hadn't moved since. Joe came to his knees, his gun still ready for another shot. But another shot wasn't needed.

He stood up, stepped forward, then knelt at the man's side and rolled him over on his back. His eyes had a glassy look and the front of his shirt was blood soaked. He wasn't breathing.

Joe put his gun away. He took another look at the man, and began to feel sick. He recognized the face. He had had breakfast with this man only a little over an hour ago, at Tyler's, and after breakfast had been introduced to him, although he couldn't now recall his name. Joe walked out to the barn. The horse the man had ridden here was tied in the roofless barn, out of sight. He untied the reins, and returned to where he had left the claybank. He climbed to the saddle and headed south toward town.

CHAPTER VI

TYLER, after he got to Unitah, went directly to the bank where he had a talk with Edward Richter. He told him just what he wanted him to do.

This brought a frown to the banker's face. "You mean to turn the money over to Edison, all at once."

"Why not?" Tyler asked.

"It may take almost every cent you have."

"What of it, Ed? I'm buying a partner, and if he's anything like his father, he'll be worth it."

From the bank, Tyler walked to the sheriff's office. He had seen Eli Wallace out at the scene of the stampede, but hadn't talked to him since. He was anxious to get the sheriff's slant on what had happened.

"The stampede was no accident," Wallace declared. "There's no question of that. Someone stirred up the cattle, got 'em started running. I'd say, maybe four or five men had a hand in it."

"And it looks bad for me, huh?"

"It happened on Wagonwheel land. That same afternoon you warned Rogers and his wife to turn back."

"What are you going to do, Eli?"

The sheriff looked troubled. "I don't know. I can't overlook what happened. A man was trampled to death."

"Are you going to arrest me?"

"Damn it, Henry, I don't know."

"I'm not responsible for the stampede. I didn't start it, nor did any of my men."

"Then who did?"

"I could make a guess, but I've no way to prove it."

"If there's any guessin' to be done, let me do it," Wallace growled.

Tyler shrugged. "If you want me, I'll be in town for

an hour or so. But if worst comes to worst, give me a day or two, at least."

He left the sheriff's office and walked to Mrs. Holcomb's, where he asked to see Kathy Rogers. She came out on the porch to talk to him. A day of rest had smoothed some of the lines out of her face and she had washed and ironed her dress. She looked more attractive than he remembered, and was much younger than she had seemed two nights before in the sheriff's office.

"You may not understand this," Tyler said gruffly. "I wasn't responsible for the stampede in which your husband was killed. I don't owe you anything, but if I can help you in some way or other, I'll be glad to. Have you money enough to get home?"

"I haven't a home," Kathy said.

"Then what will you do?"

"Go to work somewhere."

Tyler nodded. "I have two women cooks at the ranch. One is leaving at the end of the month. Would you like her place, starting today? It's hard work."

Kathy hesitated for only the fraction of a moment, then said, "Yes, I'd like it."

"Good," Tyler said. "I'll have a wagon stop by for you in about two hours. If you need any clothing, buy what you need at Harper's store. I'll speak to Harper and tell him to let you charge it."

"Thank you, Mr. Tyler," Kathy said gravely.

Tyler scowled. He was wondering suddenly if this girl wasn't too attractive to last long as a cook. Someone would snatch her up and marry her, and he would have to find another woman to take her place. If he had thought faster, if he had realized this sooner, he wouldn't have offered her the job. But it was too late now to change his mind. The offer had been made and accepted. He said, "See you at the Wagonwheel," and left her and started up the street.

When he was halfway to the hotel he saw Joe Edison pulling in at the tie rail in front of it. He went to meet him.

Joe looped the reins of his horse over the tie-rail,

stepped to the walk, and glanced up and down the street. He saw Tyler coming toward him, and he waited, watching the man closely, but if Tyler was at all surprised to see him, he didn't show it.

"Howdy, Joe," he called as he drew near. "You didn't stay at your father's place very long."

"No, I didn't," Joe said.

"The house is in fair shape," Tyler continued. "Of course a lot needs to be done to it."

"One thing in particular," Joe said.

"What?"

"There's a body in the front room that'll have to be carried out and buried."

Tyler stiffened. "A body? Whose?"

"Where can we go to talk?"

Tyler's eyes narrowed thoughtfully. He hesitated a moment, then said, "My room, here in the hotel. Come on."

Joe followed him inside and to his room. The air was stuffy. Tyler crossed to the window and opened it, then looked around and said, "Make yourself comfortable, Joe. Take that chair by the desk."

"This isn't going to be a comfortable talk," Joe said, shaking his head.

Tyler straightened a little, throwing back his shoulders. "Then plow into it any way you want to."

Joe looked directly at him. "When I got to the old house, a man was waiting for me just inside the door, his gun already drawn. He was one of the men I had had breakfast with, but I don't remember his name. He was forty, or older. Bald. Heavy. He wore a mustache."

The stiffness went out of Tyler's body. He moved to the bed and sat down. He spoke a name under his breath. "Andy Snyder."

"A very dead Andy Snyder," Joe said bluntly.

It was silent in the room. Tyler stared soberly at the carpet, shaking his head from side to side. After a time he looked up. "You think I sent him?"

"Didn't you?"

"No. Of course not."

"Then what was Snyder doing there? I never saw him

44

before this morning. What did he have against me? What had I ever done to harm him?"

Tyler moistened his lips. "I can make a guess, Joe."

"It had better be good."

"I don't know how good it is. I don't want to believe it, yet it's all I can think of."

"Make it."

The older man stood up. He crossed to the window, looked down into the street, then turned to face Joe and he seemed somehow to have aged.

"My wife's dead," he said slowly. "She died two years ago. We didn't have any children, and she didn't have any people, nor do I. Last year I was sick, and got to worrying about the Wagonwheel and what would happen to it if I died. When I got well I had Lloyd King, the attorney here in town write out a will. The will says that if I die, my share of the Wagonwheel goes to the five men on my crew who have been with me longest. One of the five men named in the will was Andy Snyder."

Joe shook his head. "I don't get what you're driving at."

"It's simple enough. Since you're back, the old agreement with your father is in force. If anything happens to me, the Wagonwheel is yours; or if you die, the Wagonwheel is mine. The five men are left out in the cold. All I can see is this. Andy Snyder didn't like it that you were back. He decided to get rid of you."

Joe pulled off his hat. He brushed his hand through his hair, staring hard at Henry Tyler. He told himself angrily that he should have expected something like this—so clever it sounded reasonable, and could be the truth.

"You don't believe me, do you?" Tyler asked bleakly.

"I don't know what to believe," Joe growled.

"Talk to Lloyd King. Ask him the names of the five men listed in my will. Talk to Edward Richter at the bank and ask him about the statement he's drawing up and what I said he was to do about it."

"If you named five men to inherit your ranch, why didn't one of them get you before this?"

"It's one thing to wait for an old man to die. It's quite different when a young man upsets the applecart."

45

Joe didn't know whether to believe Tyler's story or not. He took a restless turn around the room and when Tyler left the window and walked back to the bed, he stepped to the window. From it, he had a good view of the street, and standing there, looking out, he saw Ben Lindeman in the shade in front of the barber shop, talking to two men he didn't recognize. They were tall, gaunt men in old shapeless clothing. After a moment, Lindeman left them and went into the barber shop. The two men drifted down the street to the sheriff's office, and went inside. A woman passed the sheriff's office. Kathy Rogers. She continued up the street to Harper's.

"Don't decide things in a hurry, Joe," Tyler was saying. "Talk to Lloyd King, and to Richter at the bank. Have a talk with Dan Gomez, when he gets to town. Dan knew Snyder pretty well. See what Dan says."

Kathy had entered Harper's store. Joe turned from the window, crossed to the door. He opened it, then looked at Tyler. "I'm going to see the sheriff," he announced. "I'll find out what the sheriff thinks about it."

He left the hotel and walked to the sheriff's office. There, he saw the two fellows Lindeman had been talking to. At close range they didn't look any better than from the hotel window. Each had a seedy, shiftless appearance. Neither had shaved in several days.

"I tell you we know what we're talkin' about," one was insisting when Joe came in. "We saw what we saw, an' we'll stand up in court an' say so. Jist 'cause a man's got the biggest cattle ranch in the country, it don't give him no right to run over a little guy."

Wallace seemed uncomfortable. He looked up and saw Joe. "What is it, Edison?"

"I can come back later," Joe said.

"No. Let's have it now?"

Joe nodded. "I stayed at Tyler's last night. This morning, early, I rode to my father's old ranchhouse. You probably know of it."

"Been there," Wallace said.

"I rode there alone," Joe continued. "And I thought I was alone when I got there, but when I pushed open the door and started inside, some man waiting in the darkness cut loose on me with a gun. I fired back. I was lucky. He wasn't."

Wallace came to his feet. "Who was it?"

"I described him to Tyler, who says it was Andy Snyder."

"Had you had trouble with Snyder?"

"No."

"When why—?"

"I don't know why, sheriff. What do you think?"

Wallace scraped his hand across his forehead, pushing back his hat. "I don't know what to think, either," he said slowly. "Too much is happening, an' I've got a feeling this is only the start of it. What's between you and Tyler?"

"He says he's going to live up to the old agreement he had with my father."

"Then he will. Henry Tyler's a man of his word. Of course I'll have to ride out there to the old ranch. Can you go with me?"

"When?"

"In about an hour."

Joe nodded. "I'll be around when you're ready."

He glanced at the other two men who were eyeing him narrowly, then stepped out on the street. Kathy was just leaving Harper's, a bundle under her arm. She saw him almost immediately, and he was pleased at the smile that came to her lips and at the way her face brightened.

"Feeling better, are you?" he asked when he met her.

"Better?" Kathy said.

"At least you're not limping."

She smiled, remembering how sore her legs had been the day before. They still were sore but she didn't think she showed it when she walked.

"I'm going to work," she told him.

"Where?"

"At the Wagonwheel. Cooking. Mr. Tyler offered me the job this morning. I've just bought two dresses for which I will pay later on. Mr. Tyler said he would arrange credit for me. He hasn't yet spoken to Mr. Harper but Mr. Harper seemed ready to trust me when I told him where I would be working."

47

Joe was more startled than he wanted to admit. A scowl gathered on his face. "Have you forgotten who warned you to keep out of the Unitah basin."

"No, I've not forgotten," Kathy said soberly.

"Then why would you go to work for Tyler?"

"I talked to Mrs. Holcomb, where I'm staying. She's been here for years. She had no idea where I could get a job. When you need a job—really need it—you take whatever's offered."

"Even from the man responsible for killing your husband?"

"Yes—for perhaps at the Wagonwheel I can get at the truth."

"So that's the reason."

"No, that's only part of the reason. I would have taken the job anyhow—because I need it."

"Hey, Joe," Lindeman called from across the street. "Can I see you a minute?"

Joe glanced that way, nodded, then looked back at Kathy. He didn't like it that Kathy was going to the Wagonwheel, but he didn't know what he could do about it.

"I'd feel a lot better if you were working somewhere else," he grumbled.

"Why?"

"Because Tyler's mixed up in trouble he may not be able to handle."

"I'm to be one of the cooks, Joe. I don't carry a gun. I'm not taking sides. Your friend is waiting impatiently across the street."

"Let him wait," Joe said. "When are you going out there?"

"In another hour, more or less."

He shook his head, still uneasy over her decision. But Kathy didn't seem at all bothered. She said, "Come by and see me, if you are worried. Or do you dare come by? What have you learned since I saw you?"

"Tyler says half the Wagonwheel is mine."

Joe wondered what Kathy would say if she knew all that had happened to him since he last saw her. He decided not to tell her. Perhaps, as cook at the Wagonwheel, she wouldn't be involved in whatever trouble might develop.

"I'll drop by and see you one of these days," he said vaguely.

"Please do," Kathy said.

She walked on, holding her body very erect. Joe watched her for a moment, then turned and crossed the street to where Ben Lindeman was waiting.

Lindeman greeted him cordially. "Knew you weren't in any serious trouble at the Wagonwheel," he said. "Did Tyler sell you a bill of goods?"

"I don't know yet," Joe said honestly.

"Tyler talks well, and he can run a good bluff," Lindeman said. "I suppose he offered to pick up the old agreement he had with your father."

"Yep."

"And make a financial accounting for the past years?"

"That, too."

"Seen any of the money yet?"

"Not yet."

"And you won't," Lindeman said wryly. "Would you like to get a line on Tyler? Really get a line on what kind of man he is?"

Joe shrugged. "Why not?"

"Then come out to my place tonight. A few of the smaller ranchers here in the basin will be dropping in. Some of the homesteaders from Lignite creek, too. You'll hear an earful. What are you doing this afternoon?"

"I have to ride out to my father's old ranchhouse with the sheriff."

"Why?"

Joe told him. He was fairly sure what Lindeman's reaction would be, and he was right. The rancher slammed his fist into the palm of his hand. "By damn! What more proof do you need of what you're up against. It's lucky you're still alive."

"Tyler says that he named five men to inherit the Wagonwheel if he died, and that Snyder was one. He figures Snyder didn't like it when I showed up."

"So he's trying to lie out of it that way."

"I can ask Lloyd King if there is such a will."

49

"And King will say what he's been told to say. He gets a lot of business from Tyler."

They went over the situation once more, but Lindeman's attitude didn't change. . . .

After he had had dinner, Joe walked to the sheriff's office. The sheriff was ready to leave. "Dan Gomez is going with us," he said.

It was almost a two-hour ride to the old ranchhouse. By mid-afternoon they pulled up in the yard, dismounted, and went inside, but there a surprise awaited them. There were blood stains on the floor where Snyder had fallen, but his body had disappeared.

The sheriff looked bleakly at Joe Edison. "What do you make of it?"

"Someone's been here and carried him away," Joe said.

"You're sure he was dead?"

"Yes."

They both looked at Gomez.

"I think I know who it was," Gomez said. "Don't ask me to name him, but I'll find out if I'm right, and let you know."

Joe walked out into the yard. He turned to Gomez. "Who were the other men named in Tyler's will?"

"Charlie Ford, Kim Ellis and Lou Murdock," Gomez said.

"And you and Snyder?"

"Yes."

"Then it must have been Ford, Ellis, or Murdock who knew why Snyder came here."

Gomez nodded, then said half angrily, "They're good men, steady men. So was Andy Snyder."

"He didn't mean to give me a chance, Dan. He took a shot at me the minute I came through the door."

Gomez wrenched to face him. "Let me tell you about Andy Snyder, and, in a way, his story fits the others. Snyder was close to fifty. He's been a cowhand all his life, but at thirty a month it's pretty hard for a man to get ahead, particularly if he runs into trouble that keeps him from working or that uses up his savings. In Snyder's case, he had a sister whose husband died and who was left with three kids. A good part of what Snyder could save, went to her.

"Then suddenly he gets a break. Henry tells him that he's one of the five men who will inherit the Wagonwheel. That means that maybe in a few years he'll have a place of his own, something he's always dreamed of. We were going to do just that—cut the Wagonwheel up into five ranches. But what happened. You come along and the whole scheme goes out the window. Now, if anything happens to Henry Tyler, you get all the Wagonwheel, and Snyder remains a ranch-hand at thirty a month. It's quite a blow to a man."

"And to you, Dan?"

"Yes, even to me. Maybe I wouldn't use my gun to change things, but I've got to admit I don't like it. In my place, would you like it?"

"Maybe not. But in my place, what would you do?"

"What you're doing, I suppose," Gomez said flatly. "There's damned little justice in the world."

Sheriff Wallace scrubbed his jaw. "Dan, will you run this down for me? I've got other things to worry about."

"I'll be in to see you in a day or so," Dan Gomez said. And then he glanced at Joe. "Riding my way?"

Joe shook his head. "I may be by later."

"What'll I tell Henry?"

"Tell him I haven't yet reached any decision."

Gomez grunted, and walked toward his horse. He struck off toward the Wagonwheel. Sheriff Wallace started back toward town. Joe mounted and rode west, in the direction of Ben Lindeman's. There was to be a meeting there tonight which should be interesting.

CHAPTER VII

Late that afternoon, at Lindeman's, Joe met the two men who worked there, Ed Wylie and Stu Cardwell. He was particularly interested in Wylie. From what he had heard, Wylie was one of the two men who had seen his father and Henry Tyler at Rocky Gorge, who had heard the shot which had taken his father's life, and who a few minutes later had found his body.

Encouraged by Lindeman, Wylie told the story of what had happened that afternoon. He was a tall, gaunt, sour-faced man who spoke in a dry, rasping voice. His dark, deepset eyes had a hard cast.

"In those days," he said, "Mike Brandon and I worked for the man who used to own the Vardon ranch, north of here. We were on our way home that afternoon, following the road from town. It forks three ways at Rocky Gorge, one branch climbing a ridge then dropping down to the river at a place we call High Bridge. One of the other two forks goes to Tyler's place, one went to your father's.

"We were riding maybe a mile ahead of your father and Henry Tyler and we climbed the ridge from Rocky Gorge, taking our time. From the top, we looked back, and could see two men on the road below us, right at the Gorge. It was easy to recognize them. Your father and Tyler. We had a cigarette. Then we rode on, an' I guess that in less than a minute we heard the shot. We pulled up and listened for more. But there was only that one shot, and it seemed to come from the direction of the Gorge. It was Mike who suggested we ought to take a look-see, and find out what had happened. I wasn't much in favor of it, but we rode back to the crest of the ridge. From there we could see a body, with a horse standing near it. By the time we got there, your father was dead—a rifle slug through his back."

52

Joe took a deep breath. "You heard the rifle shot within a minute of the time you saw my father and Henry Tyler having a smoke together?"

"Maybe less than a minute," Wylie said. "It couldn't have been more."

"You were sure it was my father and Tyler?"

"Each was wearing a new black hat. They bought 'em in town that day, exactly alike. But I'd have known 'em without the hats by the horses they were riding, your father on a paint horse, Tyler on his black stallion."

"What about the tracks of a third man?"

It was Lindeman who answered. "Those tracks were made earlier, or later. The sheriff at that time used 'em as an excuse not to arrest Tyler. And as I figure it, Tyler paid him plenty to smother the case—enough so that he retired and moved to El Paso within a year."

"Is he still living?"

"No."

Joe looked directly at Lindeman. "How did you get wind of the raid on our ranch a few nights later?"

"I figured it out from something one of Tyler's men said in town one night. He'd had too much to drink. He said that Edison's wife and his brat, meaning you, wouldn't be around much longer. Tyler didn't think much of your mother, but maybe you know that."

Joe rolled and lit a cigarette. He took a deep drag and wondered, angrily, why he was still asking questions and looking critically at all that was said.

Myrt Lindeman rode in from town just before supper. She was dressed as she had been the day before, in boots, a divided riding skirt, tight sweater and jacket, and her face had a nice color glowing through its layer of tan. She seemed quite glad to see him. They had no chance to be alone; for right after supper Lindeman's guests started arriving.

Joe was introduced to them as they rode in. Russ Vardon, whose ranch was north of here. Carl Ordway and Sam Russell, whose land was to the south, and Matt Brophy and Ted Oberfelder who had places up on the bench toward the mountains. Three more men arrived from town, and it didn't surprise Joe much to learn that they were homesteaders from along Lignite Creek, the southern border of the Wagonwheel, or that two of them were the men he had seen talking to Lindeman outside the barber shop and later had seen in the sheriff's office.

These ten men, with Lindeman and Joe, crowded the parlor to its capacity. There was no order or form to the meeting. Nearly everyone present had something to say about the Wagonwheel, or Tyler, or the men who rode for him, and none of it was complimentary. And all had been threatened with what had happened to Tom and Kathy Rogers. A stampede.

"Tyler's men started that stampede," Bill Hunnicutt said. He was one of the homesteaders, one of the two Joe had seen in the sheriff's office. "They started it, but who cares?"

"How do you know they started it?" Lindeman asked sharply.

" 'Cause we saw 'em. We was there."

A tense silence gripped the room.

"What was that again?" Lindeman asked, coming to his feet.

"We saw what happened, didn't we, Marsh?" Hunnicutt said.

Arthur Marsh, the other homesteader who had been in the sheriff's office, nodded. "That's right. We was there. Not too close, of course, but close enough to hear the shootin' an' yellin', and to know what was goin' on."

Lindeman took a glance around the room, then stared at the two homesteaders. "How come you were there? The stampede was half a dozen miles from your places on Lignite Creek."

"We been keepin' a night guard posted," Hunnicutt said. "The night of the stampede we heard some men ride past our place. Since we couldn't figure what they were doin' down by Lignite Creek, we followed 'em. We was just about to give up an' turn back, when they camped. I crept up close to their camp an' heard 'em talking. Kim Ellis was there, Charlie Ford, Gomez—an' Tyler, an' two more I don't know by name. They didn't camp long enough for me to do anything about what I heard. They put out their fires an' rode on an' we followed. I wanted to get to the Rogers an' warn 'em, but I didn't have a chance. Soon as the men we was followin' reached the herd of cattle, they started stirrin' 'em up. It didn't take long."

Lindeman cleared his throat. "By damn, the sheriff ought to know about this."

"He does," Hunnicutt said. "We told him, but he ain't gonna do nothin'. He told us to keep it to ourselves until he had time to investigate."

"He what!" Lindeman shouted.

"He said we wasn't to repeat it to anyone. He said his investigation wasn't complete."

"Investigation hell," someone muttered.

"What he means is this," Lindeman said bitterly, "he wants time to discredit what Hunnicutt and Marsh witnessed. He doesn't intend to do a damned thing about that stampede or the death of Tom Rogers."

All around the room men were nodding in agreement.

"Why do we put up with it?" Lindeman demanded. "Here's a perfect case. Here's something Tyler can't dodge. We've got witnesses to what happened. Why wait until the sheriff can find some way to wreck their story?"

The room fell silent, every man there staring at Lindeman.

"Here's what we should do," Lindeman cried. "Go get the sheriff, bring him out here, throw the story we have heard right in his face, and then demand action. Now! Tonight!"

Russ Vardon stood up. "What kind of action?"

"There are enough of us here to form a posse. We'll ride on the Wagonwheel. We'll put Tyler under arrest, and maybe a few of his men as well. We'll make the sheriff go with us, back us up. We'll make him swear us in as deputies. What's wrong with that?"

The excitement in Lindeman's voice was contagious. It hit Russ Vardon, bringing a quick flush of color to his face. Here was a chance to strike back at Henry Tyler. Vardon clenched both fists, lifting them into the air. "Nothing's wrong with it!" he shouted. "I'm with you!"

"Here, too!" Ordway roared.

Russell joined them, then Oberfelder, Brophy, and the three homesteaders.

Lindeman looked triumphantly at Joe. "How about you? Where do you stand?"

What his answer was going to be, Joe didn't know. But a voice in his mind was asking: Why all the hurry?

"Well, Joe?" Lindeman shouted. And then he laughed and said quickly, "Hell, we don't have to ask Joe Edison where he stands. It was Henry Tyler who murdered his father—and got out of it, just as he nearly got out of the charge that he was responsible for the death of Tom Rogers."

Someone—it was Vardon—stepped up and slapped Joe on the back. Others crowded around him to pump his hand. Everyone seemed to accept Lindeman's assurance that he was one of them. And everyone now was talking. The room was in an uproar. Joe shouted for their attention, knowing that what he was going to say wouldn't be understood. But he had to say it. He shouted again, and those nearest him turned to face him and fell silent. Gradually that silence extended to the others in the room.

"What is it, Joe?" Lindeman asked uneasily.

Joe Edison glanced from face to face, then started speaking. "I don't like it. I don't like this idea of a crowd of men, taking the law in its own hands—and riding on another crowd. I don't care if the sheriff's with you and if you're all deputies, I still don't like it. Why the hurry? Why does it have to be done tonight? Why can't we go in to see the sheriff tomorrow, and make him act on his own?"

"He'll never act on his own," Lindeman shouted.

"He will if you put enough pressure on him. Have Bill Hunnicutt tell his story up and down the main street. Spread it around. He'll be forced to act."

Lindeman shook his head angrily. "You don't know Eli Wallace. He's in Tyler's pocket."

"Then how will you get him to ride with you tonight."

"At the point of a gun," Russ Vardon said. "That's how we'll handle him."

"And you think that because Wallace is along, you'll

56

be a posse. You won't and you know it. If Tyler was responsible for the stampede I want to see him pay for it. Legally! Not at the hands of a crowd of night riders, and that's what we'd be."

An uneasy silence fell over the room. Joe had the feeling he was getting someplace. He could see looks of indecision on the faces of several of those in the room. He said, "Listen, I want—"

"No, wait a minute," Lindeman roared. "I want to ask you just one thing, Edison. What kind of proposition did Tyler make to you? Why are you trying to save him?"

"I'm not trying to save him," Joe growled.

"What else do you call it? He's guilty as hell. He belongs in jail."

"Then let the sheriff put him there. Don't take the law into your own hands."

"In our hands? Where has it been? In Tyler's hands, and if it stays there he'll never be arrested. I'm asking you again—why are you trying to save him? What kind of offer did he make to you?"

Russ Vardon took up the cry. "That's what I want to know. What did Tyler offer you?"

Oberfelder stepped toward him. "Sure. What did Tyler offer? Tell us, Edison."

The attitude of everyone in the room was suddenly antagonistic. Borphy moved forward. And Russell.

Lindeman laughed. The sound was ugly. "I know the answer. He bought you off with half the Wagonwheel—and you thought he meant it. That's why you're trying to save him. You want him to last long enough to put it in writing. What do you care about justice—if you can get a fine ranch for yourself."

"I care about justice, but I care about law and order too," Joe said.

"Did Tyler offer you half the Wagonwheel?"

"That's not the point. I—"

Lindeman thrust forward. "Damn it, answer my question. Did he offer you half the Wagonwheel?"

"His agreement with my father—"

"To hell with that. How did he buy you?"

Joe glanced from Lindeman to the others in the room.

He knew there was no answer he could give, and make it seem right. In the eyes of those here, he had sold out. But he still had to try to stop them from what they were planning to do.

"Tyler and I have reached no agreement," he said slowly. "I'm still not sure—"

"Take his gun, Russ," Lindeman broke in. "We don't need him. We want no one with us tonight who's not on our side."

Russ Vardon moved another step forward. He reached out and snatched Joe's sixgun from its holster, then stepped back, covering him with it. He was breathing heavily. His flushed face was perspiring.

"I reckon we'd better tie him up," Lindeman said. "We don't want anyone riding to Tyler with a warning. He'll be safe here in one of the bedrooms. I'll take his gun, Russ."

Russ Vardon handed the gun to Lindeman, and seemed glad to be rid of it. The others in the room stood in a half circle, fencing Joe against the wall.

Lindeman said, "I'll get a rope," and started for the kitchen or the back porch.

"Wait a minute, Ben," Joe called. He stepped forward, and those immediately in front of him let him go. Lindeman had stopped and was waiting. Joe reached him. He knew that if he was going to get away from here, he had to do it now, and before anyone here suspected what he had in mind. He reached Lindeman and lunged suddenly past him, driving the man off balance with his shoulder. He dived for the kitchen door. His escape suddenly was blocked by a man standing in the way, a man who had been there, listening. Ed Wylie.

The gun in Wylie's hand whipped up and down, crashing against the side of Joe's head. He staggered sideways, striking futilely at the man in his way. Pain blinded him and the blow on the head made him groggy. The floor came up and hit him in the face. He tried to get to his knees but couldn't. Another blow crashed against his head, and with it came a smothering darkness.

CHAPTER VIII

B EN LINDEMAN supervised tieing Joe up in one of the
back bedrooms, made sure the window was locked.
He posted Ed Wylie at the door. "If Myrt wants to go
in and see him, let her," he said gruffly. "And don't ask
me why."

Ed Wylie, who knew more about Myrt than her father, and more than her father suspected, showed no
surprise at the order. He could figure a few things out
for himself. Edison might some day own the Wagonwheel.
It would be a good match for Myrt, and it wouldn't tie
her down. Nothing ever would tie her down.

Lindeman walked back to the parlor with Russ Vardon
who had handled the job of tieing Joe's arms and legs.
"I want you to go to town with me to get the sheriff,"
Lindeman said. "But before we leave I want to talk to
Myrt for a minute."

She was on the porch. She had heard what had happened in the parlor, knew that Joe had been tied up, and
was furious about it.

"A rotten way to treat a guest," she said angrily.
"And it wasn't necessary. Why do you have to push
things so fast. Joe would have come around to our way
of thinking in another day or so."

"We can't wait another day or so," Lindeman said.
"Tonight's the night I've been waiting for. We've got a
case against Tyler that will stand up in any court in the
land. As a posse, we can go after him."

"And kill him, I suppose, for resisting arrest."

"That might happen," Lindeman said. And in the darkness, he smiled, fairly sure that it would happen.

"Then what comes next?" Myrt flared. "Joe will inherit the Wagonwheel, and he'll hate you for what you've
done."

"Maybe he'll inherit it," Lindeman said. "He has no claim on paper. But why should he hate us? Or let me put it this way: Why should he hate you?"

"He doesn't," Myrt said.

"Are you sure of that?"

She smiled archly. "He's a man. I'm a woman."

"You haven't had much time to work on him."

"I'm not the kind who needs much time."

"Wouldn't a little more help? I told Ed Wylie to let you in to see him. If Joe thought you were trying to help him—"

Myrt gave her soft, throaty laugh. "Father, you're a devious man. We should have discovered each other sooner."

"Just be sure he doesn't make a fool out of you."

"It usually works out the other way around," Myrt said.

Joe Edison stirred. A low, moaning sound rumbled in his throat. He tried to move his arms, but couldn't. There was a painful, throbbing ache in his head. Then suddenly it wasn't so bad for a cool cloth had been pressed against his forehead and he heard a voice whispering, "Does it hurt terribly, Joe? Tell me, darling—what can I do?"

Someone leaned over him, kissed him lightly on the cheek, and then drew back. He caught the familiar scent of her perfume and his lips formed her name. "Myrt."

She put her lips close to his ear and whispered, "Shh-hhh. I'm not supposed to be here."

At first he couldn't bring his eyes into focus, but after a time he managed it. A lamp, turned low, was on the dresser. He was lying on the bed, Myrt sitting beside him.

She put her hands on his shoulders, whispering, "Joe, don't move. Don't make a sound."

"At least you could untie my hands," he whispered.

She nodded, and started working on the rope knotted around his wrists and arms.

"Where is everyone?" Joe asked.

"Father and Mr. Vardon have gone to town to get the sheriff. The others have started a poker game. Now and then one comes back here to check up on you. I—I can't get these knots untied."

"I've a knife in my pocket," Joe said. "The side pocket near you."

She found the knife, opened it, and started sawing on the rope. Once she stopped, moved swiftly to the door and stood there, listening, then after a minute hurried back to the bed. "My room's down the hall," she said under her breath. "If we can get there—they never would look for you in my room."

When his hands finally were free she started working on the ropes around his legs. Joe sat up. At first he was dizzy, but by the time his feet were free he felt better, able to stand. He tried it, one arm around Myrt's shoulders, her arm around his waist. She had a sturdy, strong young body.

"Ready?" she whispered.

"Ready for almost anything," Joe said grinning.

They walked to the door. She took a quick look into the hall, then glanced back at him, nodding. She led the way to her room. No one challenged them.

Joe stared at her thoughtfully after they got there. It was too dark to see the expression on her face but it was his impression she was smiling, and he thought, *This has been too easy. Why was the hall door left open? Why was no one watching me?* His arm still was around Myrt's shoulders. He pulled her closer. She came to him willingly, and there was a touch of fire in her kiss. Then she pulled away from him, laughing softly and asking, "What am I going to do with you Joe?"

He could see the gray outline of the window, and could make out the dark shape of the bed at the side of the room. He felt shaky. There was a driving urge in his body to reach out and pull Myrt back into his arms again, but a warning voice in his mind was telling him, *That's what you're supposed to do*. He crossed abruptly to the window, stared into the shadowy yard.

Myrt followed him, caught his arm. "Someone out there may see you."

"I don't think there's anyone out there," Joe said. "But if there is—"

61

He turned to face her. "Myrt, do you have any influence with your father?"

"Some."

"Can you stop him from this crazy scheme he has for raiding the Wagonwheel?"

"But if the sheriff goes with them——"

"It still will be a raid. There will be useless fighting. Men will be killed. Can you stop him, Myrt?"

"I can try."

"Myrt, don't just try. Stop him. Do anything you have to to stop him. When I get back——"

She caught her breath, grabbed him by the arm as he pulled the window all the way up. "Joe," she cried. "Joe, don't go out there."

He swept her aside. "I've got to, Myrt."

"No!"

He had one leg through the window and was swinging through it when someone, who must have been just outside in the hall, kicked the bedroom door open. He caught a glimpse of the man coming in. He heard the roar of the man's gun, and heard Myrt screaming, "No, Eddie. No! Don't shoot him." But by that time Joe was through the window, had dropped to the ground, and was streaking toward the horses tied at the corral fence.

Another shot laced at him from the house as he pulled a horse free and swung into the saddle. And as he raced away there was more shooting from the men who had come tearing out onto the porch. But those shots, fired too hurriedly, were wide.

He angled north, then straightened out to ride almost due east, toward the Wagonwheel.

A guard was kept posted at the Wagonwheel throughout the night. Joe remembered that as he rode into the ranch-house yard. He peered into the deep shadows of the buildings, wondering where the man might be.

There was a movement at the front corner of the house. A man covering him with a rifle stepped into sight.

"Edison?" the man called.

"That's right."

"Wasn't sure," the guard said. "Tyler said if you

showed up I was to tell you the house was open and you could have the same room as you had last night."

"Wake him," Joe said.

"Huh?"

"Wake him up. And get the men up in the bunkhouse. Maybe we're about to have visitors."

The man asked no more questions. He hurried into the house and as Joe rode on to the corral and dismounted, he heard him shouting for Tyler. Lamplight came on in the house, and, a moment later, showed at the bunkhouse windows. By the time Joe dismounted and tied his horse, Dan Gomez was marching toward him.

"What is it, Edison?" Gomez asked. "What's wrong?"

"Come to the house with me," Joe said. He walked that way, Dan trailing him.

Henry Tyler, wearing only a pair of pants, met them on the porch. They went inside.

"What's this about visitors?" Tyler asked.

Joe shook his head. "They may not come, now. But there's a chance they will."

"Who?"

"Lindeman and some of his friends."

Tyler seemed to stiffen. "Why?"

"They were going to pick up the sheriff, then ride this way as a posse. The excuse was to make an arrest."

"Of me?"

"Yes. Two men named Marsh and Hunnicutt claim to have seen you with the stampede the other night."

Others were crowding into the room, most carrying rifles. They stood silent as Joe gave a brief description of the meeting at Lindeman's, then repeated what the decision of the meeting had been.

"Wallace won't fall in with their plan," Tyler said when he finished. "He's too smart. He would know he wouldn't be leading a posse."

"They didn't plan to give him much choice in the matter," Joe said.

Tyler's eyes narrowed. He seemed to consider this for a moment, then said, "Joe, those two men, Marsh and Hunnicutt, were lying. I had nothing to do with the stampede, nor did any man working for me."

"They claim they were there," Joe said. "They claim they recognized you, and they named Kim Ellis, Charlie Ford, and Dan Gomez. They said there were two more in your crowd whose names they didn't know."

"A lie," Gomez said sharply. Then he glanced at the man standing next to him, a tall, gaunt, tired looking man. "Where were you that night, Charlie?"

"Right here, sitting in a poker game in the bunkhouse," Charlie Ford said. "Kim was in it, too."

"I was here myself but I turned in early that night," Gomez said.

Tyler stirred. "Joe those two men, Marsh and Hunnicutt, are no more homesteaders than you are. Maybe they've filed on land on Lignite Creek but they're not working it. I wouldn't put it past them to be the ones themselves who started the stampede, but a guess like that isn't getting us anywhere. I'm going to ride into town, and surrender to the sheriff. If he isn't there, I'll wait until he shows up."

"You're going to what!" Gomez cried.

"I'm going to call Lindeman's bluff. I don't think Lindeman wants me arrested. I think he wants what he's got right now—a chance to raid the Wagonwheel and do it legally. If I'm in jail he doesn't have that excuse. Joe, the Wagonwheel responsibility is now yours. What are you going to do when the so called posse gets here?"

"What am I going to do?" Joe was surprised at the sudden turn of events.

"That's right. What are you going to do? You're half the Wagonwheel. If I'm in jail, the full responsibility is yours. Did everyone hear that?"

"We heard it," Gomez said.

He was looking at Joe, scowling. And it seemed to Joe that everyone in the room was looking at him, and waiting to hear what he would say. He took a deep breath, unconsciously straightening. He said slowly, "Reckon we'll form a reception committee."

Tyler grinned. "I'm going out and saddle up. I'll cut across country to town, so I won't run into anyone." He crossed to the door and from it, looked back. "Good luck, Joe."

64

CHAPTER IX

SILENCE fell over the room. It was a tense and uneasy silence. Joe glanced from face to face. Most men were scowling, and watching him uncertainly.

Dan Gomez pushed back his hat. "What do you want us to do, Joe?"

"How many men are on guard outside?" Joe asked.

"One. Sole Cushing."

"Find him and take him with you to the barn," Joe said. "I want you to take half the men to the barn. Half will remain here with me. If the posse shows up, we'll let them ride into the yard and hear what they have to say. Maybe, when they learn Tyler's gone, they'll turn back without starting anything. If they start anything, we'll have them caught in a cross-fire. Pick out the men to go with you to the barn."

Gomez nodded, and made his selections.

"One thing more," Joe said. "There's a chance Lindeman's crowd won't show. They know I got away and must have warned you, so they may call the whole deal off. Don't get too excited. It could be that all we face is a lonesome night."

Several laughed at that. Gomez and those he had picked to go with him started for the barn.

Joe posted a man at each of the parlor windows and at the front bedroom window, told the others to take it easy, extinguished the parlor light, and went out to the kitchen. A lamp was burning there. Kathy stood at the stove, adding wood to the fire. Another woman was at the table, making sandwiches. She had stringy, gray hair and didn't look up when he entered.

"What are you women doing up?" Joe asked.

The woman at the table didn't speak.

Kathy glanced at her, then at Joe. "We're fixing coffee

and sandwiches. If the men are going to be up all night, we thought—"

"Can you work in the dark?" Joe asked.

Kathy promptly walked to where the lamp was standing. She blew it out.

"Good," Joe said. "Call in when the coffee's ready. And if there's any trouble, if any shooting develops, lie down on the floor and stay there."

"Don't worry about us, Joe," Kathy said.

He went back to the parlor, relieved one of the men at the window, and crouched down near it. He listened to the silence of the night.

The first hour passed slowly, and with no sign of the raiders. Meat sandwiches were brought in from the kitchen, and a supply was carried to the barn. More coffee was put on.

"They won't show up, now that they know we're expecting them," Kim Ellis growled. He was a stooped, aging man, and tomorrow would miss the sleep he was being robbed of tonight.

"You knew my father, didn't you?" Joe said.

"Yes, I knew him."

"Who do you think killed him."

"Thinking is one thing," Ellis answered. "Having proof of what you think is another. It always stuck in my mind that Ed Wylie and Mike Brandon knew more than they ever admitted."

"You figure one of them might have done it?"

"Why not?"

"What would it have gained them?"

Ellis shrugged. "It happened long ago. That's a question I can't answer. I'm sure only of one thing. Henry Tyler wasn't guilty. Word of your father's death hit him too hard. They made quite a pair, your father and Henry Tyler."

Another hour slipped by, and then part of another. Joe was beginning to feel that they had nothing to worry about, that the raiders had changed their plans, but until they were sure of it they would have to maintain their guard. Toward morning, and after conferring with Gomez in the barn, three riders were sent out on a scouting trip into the low hills to the east. They returned at sun-up, having found no traces of the raiders.

Joe held a council of war after breakfast.

"If all went well last night," Joe said, "Henry Tyler made it to town and surrendered to the sheriff. What will the next step be?"

"A trial, probably, in the next day or so," Gomez said. "Judge Harlow doesn't waste much time over such things."

"And there are two men ready to swear that Tyler is responsible for the stampede. The same two men are ready to name Gomez, Kim Ellis and Charlie Ford. That means three more of us may be arrested."

"No one's arresting me," Charlie Ford growled.

"Then you'll have to keep out of town," Joe said. "And the same order goes for Dan Gomez and Kim Ellis. But we need a report from town. Who can get it safely? Who can ride in there, talk to the sheriff, Tyler, and his attorney?"

Half a dozen volunteered. Joe picked Solo Cushing, then named two more to ride in with him.

"Next, what about Hunnicutt and Marsh?" Joe asked. "I'd like to talk to them before they say their piece in court."

"I'd like to talk to them, too," Gomez said. "With a gun in each hand."

"Remember how you picked me up the other day, near Lindeman's?" Joe asked.

"You mean we should pick them up like that?"

"Why not?"

"From now until the trial, they'll stick close to Lindeman's, or where they're safe in town."

"They won't be so safe if some of us go in after them," Joe said.

Here and there around the table, men grinned and nodded. Everyone was ready to offer to go after the two homesteaders, and they talked about it for a time.

Kathy came in with fresh coffee. She moved around the table pouring it, then returned to the kitchen. Kathy didn't look at all tired although she had been up all night. She gave Joe an encouraging smile as she passed him.

As a result of their discussion, two men were to be sent

scouting toward Lindeman's, and two others were to ride toward the homesteaders' claims on Lignite Creek, in an effort to locate them. The men who went to town also would keep their eyes open for Hunnicutt and Marsh.

Joe shaved, then went out and saddled up.

Dan Gomez joined him at the corral. "Where do you think you're going?"

"Town," Joe said briefly.

"Think it's safe?"

"What's safe for any of us? What did you find out about Andy Snyder trying to kill me?"

"Yesterday, after breakfast, Snyder had a talk with Kim Ellis. Snyder didn't say much. He didn't like it that you were here. He had been counting on someday having a piece of the Wagonwheel as his own. He heard that you were going to your father's old ranchhouse, and told Ellis he was going to ride up there and talk to you. He didn't say he meant to kill you, but Ellis got to worrying about what might happen and after about an hour, headed that way himself. He found Snyder's body, figured things out, and decided to bury him and say nothing about it. He knew Tyler wouldn't like it if he knew what Snyder had tried, and he was afraid Tyler would change his will if the story came out."

"How could it help but come out?" Joe asked.

"Maybe you didn't know who Snyder was. If his body disappeared, what could you prove. At least, that's the way Ellis lined things up."

"Can I trust him, Dan?"

The foreman shrugged. "Who knows? I believe you can. I'm not worried about him."

"Or the others?"

"No."

Joe mounted his horse, waved to Gomez, and set off down the road toward Unitah.

Ben Lindeman awoke early that morning, after a restless and almost sleepless night. He felt moody over the collapse of the plan he had made the night before. He and Russ Vardon had missed the sheriff in town. They had returned here determined to go ahead without him, only to learn that Joe Edison had escaped. Lindeman still had been ready to go ahead with the raid, but the others had argued him out of it. Joe would have warned the Wagonwheel to expect them. To ride there under such circumstances, would be riding into a massacre.

A good breakfast didn't make Lindeman feel any better. Ordinarily, Myrt had breakfast with him, but this morning she wasn't up. Last night, when he had turned on her angrily for having helped Joe escape, she had asked him how she could pretend to be Joe's friend and at the same time refuse to cut the bonds at his wrists and legs. "Blame yourself that he got away," she had snapped. "You sent me to him."

He went out in the yard, saddled up, and headed toward town, taking Ed Wylie with him.

"I could have dropped him last night as he went out the window," Wylie mentioned.

"Why didn't you?" Lindeman growled.

"Didn't figger it was wise. He stands to get the Wagonwheel if anything happens to Tyler. And if Myrt—" He shrugged expressively.

Lindeman scowled.

"You gonna push the sheriff to arrest Tyler?" Wylie asked.

"Why not?" Lindeman asked.

"Hunnicutt and Marsh won't make good witnesses against him. Both look like liars. A good attorney could make monkeys of them."

"Want to bet on it?"

"So you've bought off Lloyd King."

"I didn't say that."

Wylie shrugged. "But it figgers, doesn't it?"

"There's such a thing as a man being too smart for his own good," Lindeman said bluntly. "You talk too much, Wylie."

"I didn't talk too much a few years back," Wylie answered. "Matter of fact, I ain't never tried to collect for it. I figgered that maybe someday things would work out so I got a good break."

Lindeman said, "You'll get your break."

"Thanks, Ben," Wylie said. And immediately he seemed

more cheerful. He wouldn't have felt quite so good if he had looked into Lindeman's eyes, or had noticed Lindeman half draw his sixgun then let it slide back into its holster. . . .

One of the first things Lindeman heard when he got to Unitah was that Henry Tyler had ridden in during the night, and surrendered to the sheriff. This startled him. It was a move he hadn't expected.

"You mean he's in jail, right now?" Lindeman asked.

Harry Zellerback, who owned and ran the Rimrock saloon, nodded. "Yep. So they tell me."

"He admitted he was responsible for the stampede?"

"Nope. He denied it, but said he wanted to get the whole matter cleared up quickly as possible."

Lindeman hurried to see Lloyd King.

"What's this about Tyler being in jail?" he demanded of King.

"You know as much as I do," King replied. "Just heard about it. I'm going over there and see him."

"And get him out?"

"Is that what you want?"

"No."

"You're going ahead with what we talked about?"

"Damned right I am. And I can produce two witnesses to the stampede who saw Henry Tyler helping to start it."

"Then he'll not find it so easy to get out—but don't lose your witnesses. Without them, we'd be sunk."

"Don't worry. I won't lose them." Lindeman twisted around to the door, and looked back. Lloyd King was a young man in the early thirties. He drank too much, and in his eyes was the haunted look of a man who was running away from something. He had buried himself here in Unitah half a dozen years before, and had managed to find enough work to keep going. He had been easy to buy.

"Don't make any mistakes, King," Lindeman said bluntly. "Don't get too damned smart when you examine my witnesses."

"You handle your end of the deal, I'll handle mine," King said.

Lindeman shrugged, and stepped outside. He hadn't

seen either Bill Hunnicutt or Arthur Marsh since his arrival in town. He started up the street looking for them. As he neared the bank he came to a sudden stop.

Joe Edison was just leaving the bank and had turned to face him.

Lindeman glanced quickly from side to side, searching for Ed Wylie. An icy shiver ran over his body as he saw Joe Edison. He would have liked to turn quickly away, but all he could do was wait.

CHAPTER X

JOE walked toward him, nodded and said, "Morning, Ben."

"Morning, Joe," Lindeman replied. "I guess we got a little excited last night."

"Is that what you call it?" Joe asked.

Lindeman seemed to relax. "You haven't had to put up with what we've had to from the Wagonwheel."

Joe asked, "Any complaints as of this morning? Tyler's in jail—where you wanted him."

"And where you ought to want him. . . . Joe, where did you go when you rode off last night?"

"To the Wagonwheel," Joe answered. "Where else would I have gone? It's half mine."

"You're running it now, for Tyler?"

"For Tyler—and for myself."

"You've been checking things at the bank, and you're satisfied?"

"Yep."

Lindeman shrugged, "Time will tell," he said bleakly. "Maybe Tyler feels guilty enough about the past to want to square things. I wouldn't trust him, myself. You can, if you want to. No hard feelings about last night?"

"None I can't get over."

"Then I'll be seeing you around, Joe. Drop by sometime for supper. Myrt's a good cook."

Joe said, "Thanks, I will."

He walked to King's office, stepped inside, nodded to the attorney and mentioned his name.

"Glad you came in," King said. "Saw you in town the other day, but didn't get a chance to meet you. What can I do for you, Edison?"

"You can tell me what Tyler's chances are," Joe said.

King smiled. "I'll get him off. Don't worry for a minute.

I know both Marsh and Hunnicutt. It'll be an easy thing to poke their story full of holes."

He seemed confident, almost too confident.

"When will the trial be?" Joe asked.

"Within a day or two. No sense delaying it. I'll tell you soon as I've talked to the judge."

"Marsh and Hunnicutt will name Dan Gomez, Charlie Ford, and Kim Ellis as other men who had a part in stirring up the stampede. We have men at the Wagonwheel who can prove they were at the ranch the night of the stampede."

The attorney shook his head. "That won't be necessary. I intend to concentrate on Marsh and Hunnicutt, and tear their story to pieces."

Joe was frowning. He couldn't get over the feeling that King was taking this too lightly.

"Tyler came to see me yesterday," King said. "He instructed me to tell you about his will. He did make one, last year, leaving the Wagonwheel to five of his men, providing you couldn't be found. Would you like to read a copy of the will?"

"No, that won't be necessary," Joe said.

He left the attorney's and went to the sheriff's office, but the door was locked. Eli Wallace wasn't in.

Solo Cushing joined him. "The sheriff must have been called away early," Cushing said. "I been waiting for him myself."

"What are folks saying about Tyler's arrest?" Joe asked.

"Not much. They seem to be waiting to see what happens."

"Are Marsh or Hunnicutt in town?"

"Nope. Or if they are, they're in hiding."

"Do you know them?"

"I've seen 'em around town."

"Are they homesteaders?"

"Homesteaders work the land they file on. Marsh and Hunnicutt spent most of their time hanging around town."

"That takes money."

"They seemed to have it."

"Then tell me this. If they spent most of their time hanging around town, how did they happen to be home the night of the stampede and standing guard over their fields?"

"I'd say they weren't home that night. I'd swear they never stood guard over any fields. Hunnicutt plowed up and sowed a few acres, and so did Marsh, but it was just for show."

Joe nodded, and walked to where his horse was tied. He climbed to the saddle and left town, following the road to the east, the road over which he and Kathy had ridden to Unitah and which would take him to the scene of the stampede. Or there was a branch to the south a few miles out. If he followed the branch road he would reach the homesteaders' settlement on Lignite Creek.

Just as he was reaching this decision, two men appeared on the road ahead, riding toward him. He didn't immediately recognize them, but the possibility that they might be Marsh and Hunnicutt flashed across his mind, and he reached down to loosen his holster gun, and took a quick look over his shoulder. There was no one behind him and he was out of sight of town. He stared ahead once more. The two were Arthur Marsh and Bill Hunnicutt.

Joe continued riding toward them, aware of a tightening excitement. He forced himself to relax, twisting sideways in the saddle. He also managed to get a smile on his lips as he reined up to face them. But the smile was wasted. Neither Marsh nor Hunnicut looked glad to see him. Their eyes met his, then shifted away. It was his instant impression that they were as nervous about this meeting as he was.

"Howdy," he said. "I was headed out your way."

The two exchanged quick, uneasy glances. Hunnicutt, who had done the talking the night before, answered him. "Ain't much to see along Lignite Creek, Edison. We're just gettin' started."

"Tyler's in jail," Joe mentioned.

" 'Bout time," Hunnicutt said.

"He surrendered voluntarily. He still claims he had nothing to do with the stampede."

Hunnicutt glanced at Marsh. "That's a lie. We saw what we saw, didn't we, Art?"

74

"We sure did," Marsh answered.

Neither man wore a gun belt, but Marsh had a sixgun tucked in the waistband of his trousers and Hunnicutt probably had a gun in his sagging coat pocket.

"I think we ought to get this straight," Hunnicutt said. "We ain't got nothin' against you, Edison. Maybe you was right last night 'bout not ridin' on the Wagonwheel, but you're sure on the wrong side if you're backin' Henry Tyler."

"How do the others feel out on Lignite Creek?" Joe asked.

"Same as we do," Hunnicutt said promptly. "How would you feel if you couldn't farm on account of cattle tramplin' down your crops?"

"That happened to you?"

"Sure it did. It's happened to all of us on Lignite Creek."

"Did you complain to the sheriff?"

"What good would that do? Wallace used to work on the Wagonwheel. He's Tyler's man."

"Either of you ever work on a cattle ranch?" Joe asked.

"Nope," Hunnicutt said promptly. "We're farmers. Dirt farmers."

They didn't look it. They sat their horses like men familiar with the saddle and they wore boots with stirrup heels. But this was another line of inquiry Joe wasn't ready to press. He shrugged and said, "Well, I gotta be ridin' on."

"You said you was goin' to Lignite Creek?" Hunnicutt asked.

"Could be I'll go that way."

"Waste of time," Hunnicutt said. "But suit yourself, Edison. Let's be ridin', Art."

They started on up the road and just as they passed him, Hunnicutt dug into his coat pocket and jerked out his gun. Hunnicutt screamed, "Now, Art. Let him have it!"

Joe had no more warning than that. He saw the lifting gun in Hunnicutt's hand as he grabbed at his own. He heard the blast of the man's gun shot as he fired. A bullet

75

jerked at his coat. Joe fired again, then switched his aim to Marsh who was bringing his gun into line while fighting his plunging horse. He took a quick shot at the man, and then another. He lowered his gun. Hunnicutt had pitched to the ground, his horse had danced away. The horse Marsh was on had started running with Marsh swaying from side to side in the saddle. Joe looked down at Hunnicutt. When he looked up again he could see that Marsh's saddle was empty and he saw that the man had fallen about a quarter of a mile away.

He took a deep, shaky breath. Then he dismounted and knelt briefly at Hunnicutt's side. The man was dead. Joe climbed back to the saddle and rode to where Marsh had fallen. So far as he could tell, the unconscious Marsh had only a scalp wound.

He glanced up and down the road, then took a look at the circling hills. No one was in sight. It occurred to him that all he had to do was ride away from here and no one would know exactly what had happened. But if he did that, and if no one came along in the next hour or so, Marsh might bleed to death. This left only one course he could follow. He ripped his shirt to make a bandage for the wounded man's head, fixed it in place, then mounted and started back to town.

At a curve in the road he reined up, and looked back at the two motionless figures. He still felt dazed at what had happened, at the suddenness of it. He shook his head, then rode on.

Sheriff Eli Wallace paced the floor of his office. He seemed worried. When he stopped and turned to stare at Joe Edison his eyes held a flinty look. "I'll have to hold you," he said gruffly. "Ain't nothin' else I can do. I'll have to hold you until I can get the straight of it from Art Marsh."

"You've had the straight of it from me," Joe said. "I tell you, I had no other choice but to fire back. If I hadn't I'd be dead."

"It ain't gonna look right," Wallace said. "Hunnicutt an' Marsh are the two men who say they saw the start of the stampede. It's gonna look like you tried to keep them from giving their evidence in court."

"Would one man jump two?" Joe demanded.

"Not in most cases," Wallace admitted. "But if the one man was wearin' a gun an' the two seemed unarmed—"

"But they weren't unarmed. Hunnicutt had a gun in his coat pocket. Marsh had one tucked into the waistband of his trousers."

"That's what you say."

"It's true."

"I'm thinkin' of what other people will say."

Joe took a step forward. "All right, then. If I'd wanted to silence both of them, why would I have rushed to town to send a doctor out to look after Marsh? I could have finished him, or let him bleed to death."

"We don't know yet that he will live, do we?" Wallace asked. "The doctor isn't back yet."

Joe swung abruptly to the door.

"Where are you going?" Wallace asked.

"Outside to watch for the doctor," Joe snapped. "Damn it, I can't afford to be arrested. What's going to happen to the Wagonwheel if I'm thrown in jail."

"It won't run away," Wallace said dryly.

"You don't know how anxious some people are to smash it."

"Don't leave town, Joe. Don't make me ride after you."

"Don't try it," Joe growled. "If I've got to stand trial for this, I'll stand trial—but not from any damned jail."

He expected Wallace to stop him, but the sheriff didn't. Joe opened the door and stepped outside. The sun was directly overhead, and was hot. He got his horse and struck out through town, and from its outskirts, angled to the east road. About three miles from town he sighted the doctor's wagon, making its return trip. He pulled up when he met it.

"How's Marsh?" he demanded.

"Scalp wound," the doctor answered. "Some concussion. Not serious."

"Is he still unconscious?"

"Came to for a minute, but didn't say anything I could understand."

Joe nodded. "When you see the sheriff, tell him I'll be

77

around. And when Marsh can understand you, tell him if he doesn't tell the truth about what happened, he'll have to answer to me."

The doctor stared at him bleakly. "I'm not good at passing on threats."

"If you were in my fix, you'd say what I said, Doc."

"Maybe—or maybe I'd run."

"I'm not running," Joe said. He stared at the two blanket-covered figures in the wagon, then rode on, scowling.

The first homesteader's cabin Joe came to on Lignite Creek was a log structure and had a substantial look about it. In the fields near it, a man and his wife and two children were working. They broke off when they saw him rein up near the cabin, and came walking toward him. The man was middle aged, stooped, and his shirt was plastered to his body by perspiration. His wife looked tired. She had gray hair, but clear blue eyes and a young body. The boy might have been ten. The girl looked younger. Both were too thin.

"My name's Edison," Joe said. "Looks like a nice stand of wheat you're growing here."

"I'll have a good crop if the cattle don't ruin it," the homesteader answered. "Name's Houston."

"Any trouble about cattle running over your fields?"

"Some. This is a second plantin'. The first was ruined by cattle. I complained to the sheriff but don't know if he ever did anything."

"How about your neighbors."

"Same trouble as me. Schmidt and Henderson both lost their first plantin's."

"And Marsh and Hunnicutt?"

"Don't know much about Marsh or Hunnicutt. They filed on land east of here. Don't know why. They don't seem to be workin' it. Spend all their time in town."

"Do you keep a guard posted at night, just in case cattle might drift this way?"

"Nope. There's just the four of us here. I reckon if Henry Tyler wants to drive cattle over our land, he will. I had a talk with him an' he said he wouldn't. Said he didn't the first time. Don't know why he lied. The cattle that ruined my first plantin' sure didn't get here by accident."

"So you're taking a chance he'll keep his word this time."

"What else can a man do, Edison? Ain't no time this year to move anywhere else."

"Where do Schmidt and Henderson do their farming?"

"East of here. You can see Schmidt's land off that way. Henderson's place is over the hill."

"How far east is it to Marsh's or Hunnicutt's?"

"You're lookin' at Marsh's land now, just beyond mine. He put in a few days plowin', but that's all. Next is Newbold's, then Hunnicutt's. Newbold ain't much more of a farmer than Marsh or Hunnicutt. Why are you askin' me all these questions, Edison?"

"Curious, that's all," Joe said. "Can't understand why a farmer doesn't farm."

"If you ask me," Houston answered, "Marsh ain't a farmer an' never was. Neither is Hunnicutt or Newbold."

"You're talkin' too much, Sid," the woman whispered.

"Can't help it," Houston answered. "Never make any secret of what I think. You know that, Mary."

Joe glanced at the boy and girl, and smiled. "You're raising two good-looking children, anyhow."

"Yep, they're good kids. Good workers. They do their school work nights, too, with Mary. She used to teach school."

"You showed good judgment when you got married." Joe grinned. "Think I'll find anyone home, east of here?"

"Not Marsh or Hunnicutt. They rode off toward town, hours ago. Newbold might be home. He's got a shack under the trees along the creek. Haven't seen him for several days, but he might be around."

Joe nodded. "Thanks, Houston. And don't worry about cattle ruining your new stand of wheat. Tyler meant what he told you."

He touched his hat to the woman, waved to the two children, and rode on. East, beyond the land filed on by Marsh, he saw a shack under the trees along the creek. He turned his horse that way, pulled up near it and dismounted, noticing another saddled horse tied not far away. He glanced at the other horse, his eyes suddenly narrowing. It was branded Circle L. That was Lindeman's brand. A quick apprehension shot through him. He twisted around toward the shack. A man stood in its open doorway. Ed Wylie. And the gun he was holding was pointed straight at Joe.

CHAPTER XI

JOE EDISON stood motionless, still clinging to the reins of his horse. He knew he should raise his arms, but he didn't.

"Let your horse go, Edison," Wylie ordered. "Get your hands up."

Joe dropped the reins of his horse. He raised his hands shoulder high. "What are you doing here, Wylie?"

"Newbold's a friend of mine."

"Then why the gun?"

"I'm not sure just where you stand. The homesteaders along Lignite Creek have been bothered enough by the Wagonwheel."

"And you think I came here to cause trouble?"

"Could be."

"Or it could be you're wrong. I want to talk to Newbold. That's all."

"He's not here."

"Then I'll come back some other time," Joe said.

He lowered his hands a little and turned toward his horse but Wylie's gun followed his movement and the man's voice rapped out sharply. "Not so fast, Edison."

Joe turned back to face him. "Why not?"

"Now that you're here, maybe we ought to do a little talkin'."

"About what?"

"About why you really came here?"

"I said I wanted to see Newbold."

"Why?"

"Could be I wanted to offer him a job."

Wylie shook his head. "No, it wasn't that. I can't make you out, Edison. It was Tyler who killed your old man. Why are you breaking your back to help him? Is it for half of the Wagonwheel? Do you think you'll ever get paid off?"

Joe shrugged. "Why do you care?"

"I don't. I'm just curious."

"And I'm curious," Joe said. "I'm curious as to why Tyler would stampede his own cattle across a homesteader's camp. I'm curious about why you're here and what happened to Newbold."

"Nothing's happened to Newbold," Wylie snapped. "He's gone someplace—maybe to town."

"But you're expecting him back. Is that it?"

"No, I'm just—" Wylie didn't finish the sentence. He broke off, stiffening at a sound from the interior of the shack, behind him—the weak sound of a man's voice calling:

"Bill—Bill, I can't stand it. Where are you, Bill?"

Joe said nothing. He stood staring at Wylie.

A scowl had tightened on Wylie's face. His tongue licked out to moisten his lips.

"So Newbold isn't here?" Joe said dryly.

Wylie had been leaning in the doorway, but now he straightened. "No, he's not. To hell with you, Edison. You're messin' into something that's none of your business. I reckon you're in too deep to get out. I reckon—"

It flashed through Joe's mind that Wylie meant to kill him—that he was building himself up to the point of using the gun he was holding. He could sense it in his voice, in the hard, narrow look that had come into his eyes. Joe leaned a little forward, watching him closely. He had lowered his hands when he turned toward his horse. They still were lowered and his right hand wasn't too far away from his holster gun but he doubted that he could reach it before a slug would knock him down.

The sun sifting down through the leaves of the trees made a pattern of light and shadow on the shack, and on the figure in the doorway. The air wasn't stirring at all, and it was hot. Joe's face was moist with perspiration and he could feel the clammy stuff all over his body. His breath was coming fast. He heard more sounds from within the shack—a whimpering cry—the noise of something falling. And then, suddenly, a louder crash.

Wylie took a quick look over his shoulder. For just an instant his eyes left Joe's. He jerked his head back again as Joe reached for his gun. Wylie's arm steadied, and he fired.

Their shots came almost together. A bullet whipped Joe's hat from his head. Joe fired again, then a third time at the sagging Wylie in the doorway. And then he lowered his gun and stood looking down at Ed Wylie.

"Bill—Bill—are you all right, Bill?" asked that quavering voice from within the shack.

Joe Edison sucked in a haggard breath. He moved forward, knelt for a moment at Wylie's side then stood up and stepped over him, entering the shack. At first it was too dark to see anything inside, but as his eyes grew accustomed to the darkness he saw the man's figure lying half off a straw mattress to one side. A table which had been near his bed was pulled over and the water jar which had been on it now lay broken on the dirt floor.

Joe stepped nearer the man. He stared down into his face. It was a pale, haggard face, darkened by half a week's growth of whiskers. A bloody froth showed on the almost colorless lips. Fever bright eyes looked up at him. "Bill?" the man asked in a husky whisper. "Is that you, Bill?"

"Sorry," Joe answered. "Bill isn't here right now. He couldn't make it. You're Newbold, aren't you?"

The man spoke again. "Did you get the doctor?"

"I'll get you one soon as I can," Joe said. He got down on the dirt floor and lifted the man back onto the straw mattress. Then he opened his shirt, expecting to find a wound. There was no indication of one, but the entire right side of the man's chest was a dark-blue color and was swollen.

"It hurts terribly inside," the man whispered. "Did you bring more whiskey?"

"I'll get that, too," Joe said.

An idea was forming in his mind. No ordinary blow would darken a man's chest like this. But a kick from a horse could do it. *Or the trampling hoof of a steer could have been responsible.* He stared thoughtfully at the figure on the mattress. Newbold hadn't recognized him as a stranger, probably because his mind was wandering. He had called him Bill, which was Hunnicutt's front name. Joe said, "Newbold, remember the stampede?"

The man's lips moved. "What about it?"

"We really stirred up those cattle, didn't we."

"If I hadn't got throwed—"

"But you're going to be all right."

"I don't know, Bill. I don't feel right inside. All my ribs—" His voice trailed off. His eyes closed.

Joe stood up. He was beginning to feel excited.

The man stirred, then opened his eyes and looked at him, then closed them again.

"Feel better," Joe asked.

"No," Newbold said weakly. "Who are you?"

"Joe Edison. Do you want me to get you a doctor?"

"Too late for a doctor."

Newbold seemed perfectly rational now.

"I'm going to see what I can do to get you a doctor," Joe said.

Newbold shook his head. "There was a man here—"

"Ed Wylie."

"I think he was going to kill me."

"So you couldn't talk about the stampede?"

Newbold's eyes opened in surprise. "You know about the stampede?"

"Several people do," Joe said. "How come you got tied up with Ben Lindeman?"

"Did you ever need money?"

"Sure. Who hasn't?"

"That was it," Newbold said. "All we had to do was watch the road for a new family of homesteaders, then stampede some cattle at them when they camped. The road to Unitah runs up a meadow. There were several herds we could have stampeded, depending on where we wanted to drive them. An' homesteaders—hell, I've always hated homesteaders. Been a cowhand all my life."

Here was the story he needed. "Look here, Newbold, I'm going to see that you have a doctor and whatever medical attention you need. But you've got to repeat to others what you just told me."

"Why not?" Newbold asked. "I got hurt an' they were ready to dump me. When a doctor could have helped they wouldn't get one. What do I owe people like that?"

"Just hang on," Joe said. "I'll not be gone long."

He went outside, mounted his horse, and rode back to Houston's farm. "Newbold's been hurt," he told the homesteader. "He's in pretty bad shape. I'm going to try to get help for him, but I don't like leaving him alone. Can you go over and stay with him for a few hours?"

Houston didn't hesitate for even a moment. He spoke briefly to his wife, then climbed up behind Joe and they started back to the shack under the trees.

"Newbold was mixed up in a stampede the other night," Joe explained on the way. "He was thrown from his horse and trampled by a steer. His chest is crushed. If he talks any, I want you to listen and remember what he says. There's another man at the shack, but he's dead."

"Dead?" Houston said.

"I shot him," Joe said flatly. "He tried to keep me from talking to Newbold. He worked for the man who hired Newbold, Marsh and Hunnicutt to start the stampede—a stampede that would be blamed on the Wagonwheel. I think he would have killed Newbold if I hadn't shown up about when I did. It was like this—"

He went on talking, and by the time they reached the shack had given Houston a fairly complete picture of the situation. He didn't know whether the homesteader believed him or not, but it was only fair to take him into his confidence.

Newbold was sleeping, or unconscious when they got back. He didn't wake up when Joe called his name, but his pulse still was steady.

Houston looked at his swollen and discolored chest, then stared bleakly at the body of Ed Wylie. "I'm not taking sides in this," he declared. "But a man's been hurt. I'll look after him until you can get help. That's all."

"It's all I'm asking," Joe said.

"You're going to town for the doctor?"

"Or send someone," Joe said. "I don't know how safe it would be for me to go to town."

He was thinking that by this time Marsh would have recovered consciousness and given *his* version of the fight.

Joe went outside, climbed his horse and wheeled away, angling toward the Wagonwheel ranchhouse.

CHAPTER XII

THOSE at the Wagonwheel listened soberly, but with an increasing excitement to what Joe Edison had to say. They had heard of his fight east of town with Hunnicutt and Marsh, but they had heard what Marsh reported after he recovered consciousness. According to Marsh, Joe Edison had cut loose on them with no warning at all.

"The sheriff was out here with what he called a posse," Dan Gomez said. "He told us he'd give you until midnight to ride in and surrender."

"He's going to have to wait a little longer than that," Joe said. "Think he'll be back here before morning?"

"He might be. Wallace is a stubborn man when he gets his dander up."

"Then I'll camp out tonight," Joe said. "We can't move in on Unitah until we bring Newbold's story out into the open."

"And maybe until we get Marsh, and pry the truth out of him."

"What happened to the men who rode out to Lignite Creek this morning?" Joe asked.

"They inquired around and found Marsh and Hunnicutt had started to town, so they went that way. They didn't stop at Newbold's. They're here at the ranch, now."

"Then I must have passed them as I rode to Lignite Creek."

"It's hilly country. You could have missed them easily."

Joe nodded. "Dan, what about Newbold? I want enough men to head that way to protect him, and I want a doctor to see him as soon as possible. I want some witnesses besides Wagonwheel men to hear his story, too."

"Do you think he could be taken to town?" Dan Gomez asked.

"Reckon so."

"If he's strong enough to make the trip, that's the thing to do."

"Where could you take him in Unitah?" asked Joe.

"To Doc Slater's. Doc Slater's an honest man, and not an easy one to run over. Or there are one or two other places in town where we have friends."

"Then if Doc Slater thinks you can move him safely, take him to town. But go along with him. Is Cushing still in town?"

"And two other men."

"All right," said Joe. "Send someone to town to get Slater out to Newbold's. You and the others from here ride there, now. If the doctor thinks Newbold can be moved to town, borrow a wagon from Houston and take him in, but ride guard on the wagon, and post a guard around the doctor's house when you get there."

"And what will you do?"

"Meet you in Unitah, if that's where you end up."

Gomez turned toward the door, then looked back. "Why don't you go with us, Joe?"

Joe smiled. "I've something else on my mind. Who are you leaving here?"

"Fred Ulrich and Tex Bell. They're both good men."

"I'll have a talk with them later on," Joe said.

"How will you know what we've done?"

"Check on you," Joe said. "Or you might send someone here with a message."

He followed Gomez outside. While they had been having this final talk, the Wagonwheel riders who were to accompany Gomez to Lignite Creek had been saddling up. Joe watched them mount and ride off, then went back into the house and walked out to the kitchen.

Kathy was standing at the stove. She had warmed up something for his supper and as he entered the room she started taking it up.

"Smells good," Joe said. "Have they made you head cook?"

Kathy laughed, her eyes twinkling. "No, and they probably never will. I'm the new woman and the new woman always gets the extra jobs."

He sat down at the table and started eating, wolfing

88

down the food. It was his first meal since morning. Kathy kept his coffee cup full, and when he finished his meat and potatoes, set a slab of pie in front of him.

"Did you hear what I said when I rode in?" he asked her.

"Enough to gather what happened," she answered. "You found someone who admitted he had a part in starting the stampede. That means that Mr. Tyler and the men here had nothing to do with it."

Joe nodded. He sampled the pie and found it good.

"What kind of men could do a thing like that?" Kathy asked. "What kind of men could start a stampede over someone's camp?"

She was frowning, a puzzled look on her face, her lips pressed tightly together. She was wearing one of the new gingham dresses she had bought. It had a blue-and-white pattern and fitted her snugly at the waist. Joe realized abruptly that she looked quite nice this evening, and the same thought occurred to him as had occurred to Henry Tyler after he had hired her—that Kathy wouldn't be left to grieve very long for her husband. Some man would snatch her up.

He leaned back, crossing one long leg over the other. He felt tired, more tired than he wanted to admit. He closed his eyes for a moment.

"You ought to get some sleep," Kathy said.

She had started straightening up the kitchen. Joe finished his pie and coffee, then leaned back again. He heard the sudden sound of horsemen pulling up in the yard outside, then the murmur of voices. He came quickly to his feet.

Kathy looked around at him. "Stay where you are." She hurried to the parlor. She was back almost immediately, a worried look showing on her face. She said, "Sheriff Wallace. And those who were with him when he stopped here several hours ago. They're talking to our men in the yard."

Joe turned to the back door. "Kathy, you haven't seen me."

"Of course not."

89

"When they leave, when the coast is clear, take a walk. Circle out past the corral." Joe stepped outside.

Fred Ulrich and Tex Bell faced the posse in the ranch-house yard. Ulrich, who was the older of the two, assumed the burden of doing the talking. He lied in a manner almost convincing. "Nope, Joe Edison ain't been back."

"Where are the others?" Wallace asked.

"Can't tell you that, either. They didn't say where they were goin' when they left here. I reckon maybe they took off for town."

"We didn't pass them on the way here," Wallace said.

Ulrich shrugged. "Could be, they didn't hold to the road."

"Why the hell don't you know where they went?" Wallace stared at the house, scowling. For some reason or other he was uneasy over the absence of the men he had expected to find here. After a moment he decided that as long as they were here they ought to take a look inside before they left. He glanced around at those who had come with him, detailed three of the men to cover the back of the house and three more to accompany him inside. After this, he dismounted and walked toward the porch. Ulrich and Tex Bell were there ahead of him and stood blocking the door.

"Don't know as I ought to let you go inside," Ulrich said stubbornly. "You ain't got no call to search the house, so far as I can see."

Wallace was instantly convinced someone was inside. He whipped up his gun, covering the two men at the door. "Stand aside," he ordered crisply. "We're going in."

After a momentary hesitation, Ulrich and Bell got out of the way.

Wallace, and those accompanying him, searched the house, and were disappointed. They found only one person there. Kathy Rogers was working in the kitchen, scouring the stove.

"You always scour the stove this late at night?" the sheriff asked angrily.

"When a job's got to be done, it's got to be done," Kathy said, and continued working.

Wallace stared at her thoughtfully. He had been surprised to find her here, working for the man who almost certainly was responsible for the death of her husband. He couldn't help asking her about it. "How come you're working for Tyler?" he demanded.

"A job's a job," Kathy said. "When you need one, you take what's offered."

"I suppose you know Tyler was one of the men who stampeded the cattle across your camp."

"No, I don't know any such thing," Kathy said. She straightened and turned to face him, a stormy look in her usually clear blue eyes.

Wallace sighed wearily. At times, he got no pleasure from his job. At times, he had to do things he didn't want to do. This was one of those times. He glanced at his deputy, and the other three men who had followed him inside to search the house. "Suppose you fellows stay here," he suggested. "When Joe Edison shows up, bring him in."

"What if he gives us trouble?" his deputy asked.

"Bring him in anyhow," Wallace snapped.

He left the kitchen, went outside. A moment later, with the other members of the posse, he was on his way back to Unitah.

Kathy finished polishing the stove, then tested the coffee. It still was hot. She served a cup to each of the men who had been left here. After this, she crossed to the back door.

"Where are you going, Mrs. Rogers?" asked the deputy.

"To my cabin," Kathy answered. "If you want more coffee, one of you men will have to make it."

"I'll walk there with you," the deputy said.

"Thank you, but I can find my way alone," Kathy said, and there was ice on every word.

She stepped outside and walked to the cabin she shared with the other two cooks. And because the deputy was watching from the back door of the house, she entered the cabin.

A woman in one of the beds, stirred, and asked drowsily, "That you, Kathy?"

"Yes, it's me," Kathy replied.

"You'd better get to bed." Her voice trailed off in a sleepy whisper.

Kathy stood in the darkness near the window, watching the house. The deputy went back into the house and closed the door. Kathy went out again. She half circled the corral, and in the darkness beyond it, stopped, and stood waiting. She heard a sound off to her left and looked that way, and an instant later saw Joe's figure moving toward her.

"Four men still are there waiting in the house for you," she said swiftly.

Joe nodded gravely. "I figured some had been left behind. Thanks for letting me know, Kathy."

"What will you do?"

"Slip around to the yard, after a time, take one of the horses tied to the corral fence, and ride off."

"They'll hear you."

"Maybe not."

"Where will you go, Joe?"

"I want to go to Lindeman's."

"Why?"

"I want to frighten him. I want to frighten him so much that he'll run. It's Ben Lindeman who's stirring up all the opposition to the Wagonwheel. I want to scare him off so there'll be no fight when we bring Newbold into town and clear this matter up. If there's a fight in town, a good many people may get hurt."

Kathy smiled. "Joe I'm glad you said that. Some men would have wanted to punish Mr. Lindeman for what he's done, would have wanted to see him suffer."

"He'd suffer all right," Joe said. "He wants to smash the Wagonwheel and he thought he had a sure-fire way of doing it. It'll hurt him to see it fail. It'll hurt him to have to run. I'm not being easy on him, Kathy. It's sometimes harder to have to go on living than it is to die."

"Then the trouble we ran into here in the basin is all over?"

"Nearly all over," Joe corrected.

"Mr. Tyler will be set free. He will give you half the Wagonwheel, which belonged to your father. Will you move back to the ranchhouse where you grew up?"

"I may. I'd need a cook."

Kathy's heart started beating faster. She knew from the tone of Joe's voice that he really meant something else, but it was something she didn't want to think about yet. She tried to answer him in a very matter of fact way. "You'll probably be needing many things to make the house livable. Maybe you should stay here with Mr. Tyler for a while."

"Yes, maybe so," Joe agreed. "We'll talk about it again, someday."

He stood looking down at her, frowning and wondering if she realized what he really had in mind. He was a little surprised at himself. It had just come to him suddenly that Kathy was the woman he would want out there at his father's old ranchhouse. She would fit in perfectly. But he couldn't rush a thing like that. He would have to give her time to get used to the idea.

He touched her arm. "You ought to get some sleep, Kathy. And if I'm going to Lindeman's, I should get started."

"Going to Lindeman's will be dangerous, won't it?"

"Not very dangerous, if I'm careful. Good night, Kathy."

She bit her lips. "Good night, Joe."

He squeezed her arm, then turned away and started circling the corral toward the yard where the saddled horses were tied. He took the first one he came to, untied the reins, and led it away from the ranchhouse. When he was a good distance off, he adjusted the stirrups, mounted it, and set off through the hills to the west.

CHAPTER XIII

It was well after midnight by the time he came within sight of the Lindeman ranchhouse. No lights showed at any of the windows. He altered his course a little to approach the ranchhouse on the blind side of the barn. Back of it, he dismounted, and tied his horse. Then he crouched in the barn's deep shadows at one of its front corners.

He studied the yard, and the dark and silent house. He knew the location of Myrt's room, and where to find her window. A wry grin crossed his face. Myrt, in all probability, wouldn't be too much surprised to hear a man's voice at her window. She hadn't deceived him very long. There was enough passion in her but it was too easily aroused, and it didn't go deep.

He crossed swiftly to the house, then moved along it until he came to Myrt's window. If was half open. Listening, he thought he could hear someone stirring inside.

He leaned in, pushing aside the curtain. "Myrt!"

He called again, keeping his voice low but insistent. "Myrt, wake up!" This time she heard him, answering in a startled, husky whisper, "Who is it? Who's there?"

"Joe," he replied. "Joe Edison. Myrt, I've got to talk to you."

She was at the window in less than a minute, reaching out to take his hands. Hers were warm and soft. "Joe—Joe—where have you been. I've been so worried—"

He laughed softly. "Worried, Myrt?"

She sounded hurt. "Certainly I was worried. Joe, I felt that we—"

"I know," Joe said. "But things are going to work out soon so I won't have to keep running away."

"How? What do you mean?"

"I've found the men who stampeded the herd the other night."

"But I thought—"

"That it was Tyler's men?" He shook his head. "It was Hunnicutt, Marsh, and a man named Newbold who were responsible for the stampede. Newbold was thrown from his horse and badly hurt when he was trampled on. But he's living, Myrt, and we've got him. By tomorrow we will have his full story. I mean, the name of the man who hired them."

Myrt drew back. There was a definite change in her attitude. "Are you sure, Joe?"

She leaned forward again and the coldness which seemed to have gripped her for a moment was gone. "Joe," she whispered, "I've got to hear more about it, and there's something I must tell you. Something very important. But we can't talk here. I'm afraid father will wake up. I'll put on something and meet you at the back door. We can walk down to the creek. Is that all right?"

He grinned and nodded. "Hurry, Myrt."

"It'll take me just a minute," Myrt said.

She drew back, and he could hear the rustle of her clothing as she dressed. A moment later she was at the window again. "Wait until I see if father's sleeping," she whispered. "If he knew you were here—" She hurried away without finishing the sentence.

Joe stood waiting, aware of a vague uneasiness. Myrt returned to the room. She made scarcely a sound as she crossed to the window.

"He's still sleeping," she whispered. "He hasn't heard us. I want to get a paper I must show you, then I'll meet you at the back door."

Joe started around the house, again asking himself, *Why the back door? Why hadn't Myrt climbed through the window?* He came to the rear corner of the house, and stopped, crouching there in the shadows. He heard the back door open and saw Myrt look out."

"Joe?" she called in a half whisper. "Joe?"

He still didn't move.

She came outside and looked toward the corner where

he was hiding. "Joe," she called in a louder voice. "Where are you, Joe?"

He straightened a little, but something still held him motionless. And he stared at the back door which still was open. *Had he detected a movement there?* Was someone standing there, concealed in the darkness, waiting for him to appear. He sucked in a long, haggard breath and asked himself a more challenging question. Had Myrt gone to arouse her father instead of see if he was asleep? He had his answer a moment later. The tall, gaunt figure of Ben Lindeman stepped out in the yard to join Myrt. Starlight glistened on the gun he was holding. Lindeman spoke in a low, angry voice. "You scared him away, Myrt. You should have let me come to your room."

What Myrt answered, Joe didn't wait to hear. He backed away from the corner of the house, then turned and ran for the barn and circled it to where he had left his horse.

What Myrt had told Ben Lindeman when she woke him up disturbed him more than he wanted to admit. He went out to the bunkhouse to arouse Stu Cardwell, and to see if Ed Wylie had showed up. Wylie wasn't there. This added to his uneasiness.

Lindeman swore. With Cardwell he made a search of the yard, barn, and other buildings, but Joe Edison was nowhere to be found. This didn't greatly surprise him and again he critized himself for not having gone to Myrt's room the minute she told him what was up.

He stormed back to the house where he started questioning his daughter. What was it, exactly, that Edison had said to her? What words had he used? Had he said where Newbold had been taken? Had he said definitely that Newbold had admitted his part in the stampede?

As well as she could, Myrt answered him. Then she threw a question at him, "Is it true, father? Did the three men Joe named start the stampede?"

"How should I know?" Lindeman growled.

"Don't you?" Myrt asked. She was looking directly at him, her eyes hard and unblinking.

96

Lindeman shifted uneasily. "Of course I don't. Who cares, anyhow?"

"Joe seems to think someone hired them to stampede the cattle, and that Vance Newbold can give him the man's name."

"I never heard anything crazier," Lindeman snapped.

"Then, what are you so worried about?"

"I'm not worried," Lindeman said.

He looked at her again. Her eyes were as hard and unblinking as they had been a moment before. He knew she didn't believe him, and that she had guessed at the truth.

"You're not going to pull me down with you," Myrt said suddenly. "I want you to understand that, Father. As of right now, I'll have nothing more to do with your scheming."

There was a note of finality in her voice. She turned and left the room without a backward glance.

Lindeman pulled out one of the chairs at the table and sat down. He felt suddenly very tired. He dug out his pipe and lit it, but the taste of the tobacco gave him little satisfaction. Myrt came back. She was wearing her riding skirt, jacket, and had pinned on the black, low crowned hat she so often wore.

"It's the middle of the night," he said sharply. "Where do you think you're going at this hour?"

"To town," Myrt said. "I can wake up Ellen Romney and stay with her until morning."

"And what will you gain by that?"

"I'll at least be on neutral ground, Father," Myrt said. "I told you I wouldn't let you drag me down."

Lindeman threw back his head and laughed. "Who's getting dragged down? You'll be singing a different song by this time tomorrow."

"Maybe," Myrt said. "Or maybe not."

She crossed to the door, stepped outside, and closed it behind her. A few minutes later he heard her riding away.

Joe Edison by-passed Unitah and struck off southeast toward the homesteaders' settlement on Lignite

Creek. It still was dark when he got to Houston's but he knew that morning couldn't be far away. There were no lights in Houston's cabin. He rode on, turning in under the trees near Newbold's. As he reined up, a voice challenged him.

"Hold it, mister. Git your hands in the air."

He raised his hands shoulder high, and sat waiting. A man carrying a rifle stepped out of the deep shadows close to the shack. Another man appeared from the shack's far corner. A third showed up from under the trees. Their rifles covered him. Joe thought he recognized one of the men. He called, "Dan?"

"That you, Joe?" Dan Gomez asked. He stepped closer, peered up at him, then lowered his rifle and called. "It's all right, men. It's Joe Edison."

Joe lowered his hands. He dismounted, turned his horse over to one of the men, then walked to where Gomez was standing. "Everything all right, Dan?"

"That depends on what you mean by all right," Gomez said. "We haven't run into any trouble."

"Doc Slater here?"

"He's in the shack with Newbold. He doesn't figure Newbold will last out the night."

"Did you get talk to Newbold?"

"Nope. He was unconscious when we got here. But Houston heard what he had to say—the whole story. Houston said he was conscious and talking until just a little while before we got here."

"Where's Houston?"

"Inside the shack."

Joe walked to the door, opened it, and looked inside. A lamp, turned low on a box chair, gave off a dim, yellowish glow. Two men sat on the dirt floor near the straw mattress on which Newbold was lying. One was Houston. The other man, thin, middle aged, undersized, and with sharp, irregular features and dark eyes, was Doc Slater.

Both glanced around at him as Joe stepped in. Houston nodded.

"Doc," Gomez said from the doorway, "This is Joe Edison."

"Figured it might be," Doc Slater answered.

"How is he?" Joe asked.

"Dying," Slater said in a flat, weary voice. "Ain't a thing I can do for him. Never was, since his chest got caved in. It's a mystery to me how he lived this long."

"He hasn't been conscious since you got here?"

"Nope."

"But he talked to me," Houston said. "He told me about the stampede, and about how Lindeman hired him and Marsh and Hunnicutt to file on this land, and why. They never meant to farm it. They were here to get Tyler in trouble."

Joe walked up to the mattress on which Newbold was lying. He stared down at him. Newbold's face had a gray look. His breathing was irregular. His mouth sagged open.

"There just isn't a thing to be done for him," Doc Slater said.

Houston stood up. "Edison, would it help any if I offered to repeat what Newbold said to me?"

"It might help a great deal, Houston. Thanks."

"Then just tell me what you want," Houston said. He turned to the door, looked back and added, "I'm going home now. I'll wake up Mary and we'll throw some food together for your breakfast. I reckon everyone here could do with a little breakfast."

"Thanks, Houston," Joe said. He glanced again at Newbold, then followed Houston outside. In even the little time he had been here the eastern sky had brightened. Morning wasn't far off. There was a fallen log near the shack. He walked that way and sat down.

Gomez trailed after him, rolled a cigarette, and then passed his papers and tobacco to Joe. When Joe's cigarette was ready he struck a match.

"Tough break," Gomez said bleakly. "If Newbold had lasted only one day longer—"

Joe sucked on his cigarette, and nodded. "We buried Wylie over there," Gomez said, pointing to a low mound of earth under the trees.

Joe glanced that way uneasily. There was another problem he faced—explaining to the sheriff the death of Ed Wylie.

"What next?" Dan Gomez asked.

Joe had been trying to get to that in his own thinking. He wasn't exactly sure what they ought to do next. "I've got three things in mind, Dan," he said slowly. "First, I want Houston to ride into town. I don't want him to say anything to anyone right away, but I want him to be ready with his story when we need it."

"I think we can count on him," Gomez said. "What else?"

"I want three men to ride in with me. When we get there we will find Cushing. Maybe Cushing can tell us where we can put our hands on Arthur Marsh. He can give the same evidence Newbold would have given if he had lived. We may have to beat it out of him, but the story's there. And there's one other thing Marsh can do. He can come up with the truth about the fight I had with him and Hunnicutt."

"So we got to get our hands on Marsh. And finally?"

"We've got to run a bluff—a bluff that Newbold still is living, and is ready to talk. If everything else fails, that bluff alone may frighten Lindeman into running. We know the truth, now, but how can we prove it, Dan? As things stand at the present time, Lindeman can deny the story Houston will tell. He can say we bought him."

The door to the shack opened. Doc Slater stepped out. He shook his head, and came wearily toward them.

"Is it all over?" Gomez asked.

"Yes, it's all over," Slater said. "Newbold is dead. I'd reckon we might as well head to Unitah."

Dan Gomez stood up. "Doc, you've heard enough to know what this is all about."

"I reckon I have," Slater admitted.

"Then maybe you've figured what we're up against. What Houston can say may not be enough to get Tyler out of jail. But there's another man who knows the truth. Arthur Marsh. We mean to get our hands on him. Can we borrow your house?"

"Why?"

"As a place to hold Marsh while we convince him to talk. And as a place to run a bluff with the body of Vance Newbold."

The foreman of the Wagonwheel went on talking, ex-

100

plaining what they had in mind. Doc Slater listened, and nodded. "I always sort of liked Henry Tyler," he said finally. "Sure, you can use my house."

"What now?" Gomez asked, looking at Joe.

"Why, we'll have breakfast with Houston, talk to him, borrow his wagon, and get started," Joe said.

He stood up, stretched, and stared into the sky. Morning had come, clear and bright. The day would be hot. He started walking to where his horse was tied.

CHAPTER XIV

H OUSTON started for town ahead of them, riding in alone. When he got there he had several chores to attend to. After that he would hang around and wait until called on to tell his story.

Joe, Dan Gomez, Kim Ellis, Charlie Ford, and Doc Slater followed, fifteen minutes behind him.

Houston's wagon, bearing Newbold's body, and guarded by the remainder of the Wagonwheel crew, would follow them at a slower pace. Lou Murcock was put in charge of the wagon. It would be late afternoon before the wagon could reach Unitah.

The road Joe Edison's group was following curved away from the creek, joined the main road, and from there led almost due west. This put the sun at their backs, a fact for which Joe was grateful. They didn't push their horses, nor did they talk very much.

Near the town, Slater, who had been riding with Joe, dropped back, and Dan Gomez took his place.

"What we gonna do if we run into Eli Wallace when we get to town?" Gomez asked.

This problem had been on Joe's mind. It wasn't one which could easily be answered. He still was wanted for the death of Bill Hunnicutt. If they ran into Wallace, it meant jail.

"We'll hope we don't run into him," Joe said. "I've been talking to Slater. He says we can cut south from the road, near town, and go directly to his house. That way, we won't have to ride down the main street."

"Then one of us can get in touch with Solo Cushing, and find out where Marsh is."

Joe nodded. "It may be easy to pick him up, or it may take all of us. We'll see."

"We could send for Wallace, have a talk with him."

"We may do that," Joe agreed. And then he scowled, and said, "You said you knew my father, Dan. How well did you know him?"

"Fairly well. I wasn't as close to him as Henry Tyler."

"You suggested the other morning that it was Ben Lindeman who killed him."

"And I said I was just guessing."

"A man has to have something to base a guess on."

Gomez was staring straight ahead, a tight look on his face. He said, "No, it was just a guess, Joe, and maybe a bad guess at that. I don't reckon we'll ever know who killed your father. It happened a long time ago. I'm hazy on the details of those days, but there's something you said that puzzles me."

"What?"

"You mentioned a raid on your father's ranch."

"There was such a raid, several nights after father was killed."

"Tell me about it."

"Ben Lindeman rode up to the house, just about dusk. He said Tyler and his men were coming after us. We hardly had time to pack a thing. We escaped in a hail of bullets, and until near morning were followed."

"And Lindeman?"

"He escaped with us and stayed with us until we were safe."

Gomez shook his head. "I'd like to ask him about that raid. No one from the Wagonwheel had anything to do with it. I can swear to that."

"But how could he have fooled my mother?"

"Joe, your mother hated Henry Tyler. She always hated him. She turned against him long before your father's death. It wouldn't have been hard to convince her that Tyler meant to kill her. She would have believed anything anyone told her about him. Then here's another puzzling thing, Joe. The Unitah basin never heard of the raid you described. So far as was known to anyone here, you and your mother just picked up and left without saying anything to anyone."

There wasn't even a stirring of air in the basin. The sun beat down on them from overhead. Joe mopped the

103

perspiration from his face. He shifted uneasily in the saddle. He never would forget that night ride with Lindeman and his mother, the blazing guns behind them, or the shouting voices of their pursuers.

"There's Unitah, just ahead of us," Gomez said.

The doctor's home was a block back of the main street. It was a low, square, frame structure with a lawn and a picket fence in front. There was a large barn behind it. They left their horses in the barn and went into the house. Slater talked to his wife and her mother, who lived with them, and a few minutes later the two women left.

"I sent them to my sister's place," Slater said. "If there's any trouble, they'll be safer there."

Kim Ellis had headed toward the main street, to look up Solo Cushing. The others gathered in the doctor's front room. It was a large front room, and comfortably furnished. Joe Edison stretched back in the chair he had taken. It occurred to him that he could very easily drop off to sleep. He noticed the doctor yawning, too. Charlie Ford and Dan Gomez were red eyed.

"Maybe I could stir up something to eat," the doctor said abruptly. He stood up and glanced at Charlie Ford. "Want to help me?"

"I used to be a cook once," Ford said. "No one will believe it when I tell them but I was a good cook."

"And there are graves all over the west to prove it," Gomez said.

"You've eaten my grub and liked it," Ford protested, turning to follow Slater to the kitchen.

After they were gone, Joe got up and walked to the window. He was staring toward the bank. Kim Ellis had just rounded its corner and was strolling toward them.

"I left Solo at the B & W saloon," Ellis said when he came in. "He's going to wait there until he hears from us again."

"And Marsh?" Joe asked.

"He's at the Rimrock. Lindeman and Ted Oberfelder are with him."

"What about the sheriff?"

"Off someplace probably looking for you, Joe."

"How about his deputy?" Gomez asked.

104

"He's not in town either," Ellis said.

"Did you see Houston?"

"On the hotel porch where he said he would be."

Gomez nodded, and glanced at Joe. "Well, Joe?"

"Who else did you notice on the street?" Joe asked.

"Like who, for instance?" Ellis inquired.

"Russ Vardon, Carl Ordway, Sam Russell?" He was naming the others who had been at the meeting at Lindeman's.

"I saw Vardon in front of the feed store," Ellis said. "Don't know about Ordway or Russell."

"Or Matt Brophy?"

Ellis shook his head. "Any of 'em might be in town, or might not."

"Do you think anyone noticed us ride in?"

"If they did, no one got excited about it."

Joe turned and walked again to the front window.

"Come an' get it," Ford shouted from the kitchen.

They ate, and afterwards gathered again in the parlor. Joe cleared his throat, and noticed how everyone in the room fell silent and turned to look at him. "All right, Ellis. The first step's up to you. Find Cushing again. Tell him and the two men with him to drift down to the Rimrock saloon. When they get there, if Marsh is inside they're to stay there. They are to help us cover those in the saloon if we run into an argument when we go after Marsh, but tell them no shooting unless it can't be helped. Soon as they're in the Rimrock and you are sure Marsh still is there, signal us from the back corner of the bank. Pull off your hat and put it on again. That's signal enough."

"Then what do I do?" Ellis asked.

"Head for the Rimrock. We'll get there a minute after you do. Is there a back door?"

"Yep."

"Then we'll come in the back door."

"And when you get there, we just take Marsh and walk off. Is that all?"

"I hope it is," Joe said grinning. "It might work out some other way."

"We'll find out soon enough," Ellis said. "I'm on my

way, Joe." He headed for the door, stepped outside, and angled toward the main street.

There was nothing then to do but wait. Joe walked to the window, and stood there. Gomez checked his gun, then joined him. Charlie Ford and Doc Slater came up behind them.

"Unless Lindeman's in the saloon, we won't run into much trouble," Gomez said.

"Anyone in Lindeman's crowd could cause us trouble," Joe said.

The minutes dragged by slowly. They stood watching, and in spite of the way Joe fought against it, he could feel his muscles growing tense.

A man appeared suddenly at the back corner of the bank. Kim Ellis. He pulled off his hat, ran his fingers through his hair, then put his hat on again. It was the signal Joe had asked for. It meant that Marsh still was in the Rimrock saloon, and that Solo Cushing, Jake Handler, and Will Rogell were there. The moment they had been waiting for had come. Joe glanced at the others, nodded, and turned abruptly toward the door.

"I'll trail along, just in case I'm needed," Slater said.

Joe looked around at him. "You don't have to, Doc."

Slater frowned. "Are you asking me to stay here?"

"Of course not."

"Then I'll trail along."

They headed toward the main street, cutting at an angle toward the rear of the Rimrock saloon. Joe wasn't sure which building it was but Dan Gomez pointed it out to him, mentioning he never had known the back door to be locked when the saloon was open. It wasn't locked this afternoon, but stood slightly ajar to permit a draft of air to cool the building.

They thrust it open and stepped inside. It took several seconds for Joe's eyes to adjust to the darkness of the room. The murmur of conversation faded and died out as they were recognized.

"There he is, at the side table halfway up the room," Gomez said.

Joe nodded. He had spotted Marsh seated at a table with Ted Oberfelder and two others he didn't recognize.

He raked a quick glance over the room, searching for Lindeman but didn't see him. Those at the bar and those at the tables had turned to look at them, and had fallen silent. Two at the bar had their hands near their guns.

"Kim, cover those men at the bar," Joe said sharply. "If anyone interferes, cut him down!"

He sounded as though he meant it. Kim Ellis whipped up his gun, holding it to cover the men at the bar. A man near the front door, Jake Handler, drew his, and at stations along the side wall, Will Rogell and Solo Cushing, showed their guns.

"No one will be hurt if you just stand as you are," Joe said. "Dan, come with me."

He headed for the side table at which Marsh, Oberfelder, and two other men were seated. A gray, drawn look had come into Marsh's face. His eyes had widened and in them was a glazed look of fear. He shook his bandaged head numbly from side to side. Near him, Oberfelder was wearing a tight scowl, and was breathing heavily.

Joe stopped, a foot or two from the table. "Marsh, on your feet. You're coming with us."

The homesteader gulped. He looked frantically around the room, his eyes finally centering on Oberfelder. Hoarse words came bubbling from his throat. "Ted, you can't let them do this. They'll kill me!"

"On your feet, Marsh," Joe snapped. "Do you want a chance to live, or do you want to die right here?"

Perspiration glistened on the homesteader's face. He shook his head from side to side.

Oberfelder stirred, then looked defiantly up at Joe. "You can't do this, Edison. You can't get by with it."

Dan Gomez surged forward, leaned across the table. "I'd just keep out of it if I were you, Oberfelder."

The rancher reared back. He started to get up, but Solo Cushing moved in behind him, swinging his arm up and down, the gun in his hand smashing against Oberfelder's temple. Oberfelder collapsed.

There was an uneasy stir throughout the room. This sudden touch of violence had sharpened the tension. Another instance like this, and an open fight might break out. Joe could read all the signs of it. He knew they had

107

to get Marsh out of here, and get him out in a hurry, or they might not get him out at all. He walked around the table, holstered his gun, grabbed Marsh by the shoulders of his coat and jerked him to his feet.

"Solo, Dan," he ordered, "get him out of here. I'll cover for you."

He stepped back, and drew his gun again as Dan Gomez and Solo Cushing closed in on either side of Marsh. They started him toward the back door, half carrying him. No one tried to stop them. In the matter of a few seconds they reached the back door, and were outside.

Joe breathed easier after that. He and the others weren't away from here yet, but they had taken Marsh and would get him to Slater's, and that was the important thing. He glanced from side to side, and called, "All right, we'll leave now. Handler, you and Rogell cover the front door for a few minutes, after you're outside. Ellis, Ford and I will cover the back."

He walked that way quickly. He turned and waited until Rogell and Handler were outside. Then he made one more statement, "Don't try to follow us."

No one answered him. He stood where he was while Slater, Ellis and Ford backed outside, then he followed them, pulling the door shut behind him. He felt suddenly weak, shaky. He glanced at those who had come outside with him, grinned, and said. "All right, let's go talk with Marsh." He led the way toward the doctor's home.

CHAPTER XV

LINDEMAN heard immediately of the kidnapping of Arthur Marsh. He walked to the saloon, pushed open the door, and stepped inside. Oberfelder was at the bar with Matt Brophy and Sam Russell. He was nursing a drink. He looked angry. When Lindeman approached the bar, he jerked around to face him, snarling, "You heard what happened, I suppose?"

"Yes, I heard," Lindeman said quietly.

Oberfelder shouted, "I'm not going to take this lying down! If you do, to hell with you."

"Who said anything about lying down?" Lindeman asked. "What do you want to do, Ted?"

"Cut them down to size. Smash them as we should have the other night."

"Well, we won't have to go far this time," Lindeman said. "They took Marsh to Doc Slater's."

"Then let's get a crowd together an' go after them."

"A crowd? Where will we get a crowd?"

"Right here in town," Oberfelder said. "After what happened in the Rimrock saloon there isn't a self-respecting man in Unitah who won't go with us."

"Let's find out about that," Lindeman said. "How do you feel about it, Brophy?"

"I'm with you," Brophy said. "And I've two men working for me you can count on."

"I'll go along," Sam Russell said. "Russ Vardon's in town. So is Carl Ordway."

"Find them," Lindeman said. "Get them over here. Talk to anyone you see up and down the street. We're going to have to move fast if we want to save Art Marsh."

He turned and went outside again, followed by Brophy, Russell and Oberfelder. There was a glint of satisfaction in his eyes.

He started up the walk, but in front of the next building came to an abrupt stop. A wagon, flanked by four riders was coming down the street. He recognized the riders as men from the Wagonwheel, and it struck him suddenly that Newbold would be in the wagon. What else could it mean—a wagon and guards? Edison had Newbold. This wagon, then was bringing the injured Newbold to town to offer evidence on the stampede.

He drew his gun, stepped out in the street and shouted, "Hey, you driving the wagon. Pull up!"

One of the wagon guards whipped up his sixgun and fired at him, the bullet lifting off his hat. And the man who had fired at him yelled, "Whip up the team, Tex."

Another shot from another guard skimmed past Lindeman. He fired at the first man who had fired at him, but fired too quickly, then had to jump back as the team and wagon lurched forward. He lost his balance and fell, then rolled quickly toward the walk and scrambled up.

By that time, the team and wagon and four guards were wheeling around the next corner. He fired a futile shot after them and heard others firing from the walk, Russell, Brophy and Oberfelder. But their help had come too late. They hadn't guessed what he had guessed about the wagon, hadn't acted soon enough.

Men had come out on the street everywhere. No one quite understood what had happened. Lindeman made the best story of it he could. "The Wagonwheel had Newbold in that wagon," he shouted. "They're holding him prisoner just like Marsh. They've bought his testimony to free Henry Tyler. What are we going to do about it?"

A crowd started gathering around him to hear in more detail what he had to say.

Marsh lay spread-eagled on the bed in Doc Slater's back room, his wrists and legs bound to its four brass posts. Men of the Wagonwheel stood around him. Grim, silent, angry looking men. Marsh had never been so frightened.

Joe Edison, standing at the foot of the bed, growled, "All right, Marsh. We're waiting to hear what you've got to say."

Marsh shook his head. To the men standing around the

bed he seemed stubborn. Actually, he was afraid to say anything.

He heard the sound of firing somewhere outside. The wild hope that he was about to be rescued crossed his mind, but the firing stopped. A few minutes later he heard a cavalcade ride into the yard. Most of the men who had been standing around the bed hurried from the room, Edison among them.

A few minutes later, Edison came back, calling to someone, "Carry him in here."

Two others followed, carrying a blanket-wrapped figure. Under Edison's directions, they lowered it to the floor at the side of the room, then opened up the blanket. Marsh looked that way, and caught his breath. He was staring at Vance Newbold, and Newbold was dead. He knew it from the wide, glazed eyes and from the way the mouth sagged open. He knew it from the lifeless color of Newbold's skin.

"That's the way you'll look some hours from now—if you don't talk," Edison said. "All right, cover him up."

One of those who had helped to carry Newbold's body into the room drew the blanket back over his face. The man made a grimace as he turned away. "He's already starting to smell," he muttered.

Marsh screamed. He threshed from side to side on the bed, unmindful of the way the ropes holding him cut into his wrists and legs. Exhausted and out of breath, soaked with perspiration, he now was whimpering, making noises which had no meaning.

"Throw some water on him, Kim," Joe ordered.

Kim Ellis splashed half a pitcher of water into Marsh's face, then left the room to get more. Joe stood leaning against the foot of the bed. He was silent for a time, then said, "Ready to start talking, Marsh?"

"Wh—what do you want to know?" Marsh gasped.

"Tell us first about the stampede."

"I—I didn't have anything to do with the stampede," Marsh said quickly. "I was there, but I backed out. It was Newbold and Hunnicutt who started the stampede."

"And who paid them for it? Who hired them to come into the basin?"

111

"Ben Lindeman."

"Keep talking," Joe said. "Where did you meet him?"
What did he pay you? We want all the details."

Other men came into the room. They threw question
after question at Marsh. He answered them all, some
immediately, some very carefully. For he now saw a way
out. If everything could be blamed on Hunnicutt and
Newbold, in the end, they would let him go.

Someone else came into the room and whispered something to Joe Edison.

"What's *she* doing here?" Joe asked, scowling.

"She says she wants to see you," the man answered.
"That's all I know."

Joe nodded, and turned to the door. From there he
looked back at Dan Gomez. "Who can write all this
down?"

"I can," Doc Slater offered.

"Then put down what you think is necessary," Joe
said. "We'll have Marsh sign it when the sheriff gets here
—if he ever shows up."

He left the room, and returned to the parlor where
Myrt Lindeman was waiting.

The minute Myrt saw him her face brightened and
she called out his name, then moved across the room toward him, almost as though she expected to be taken in
his arms.

He didn't do that, however. He pushed out his hand and
she had to take it, or run into it. She took it, and squeezed
it warmly, and said in a half whisper, "Joe, I just had to
come here. Please don't be angry with me."

"You had to come here?" Joe said.

"I mean that I wanted to."

"You know what may happen here in the next few
minutes?"

She nodded. "Yes, I know."

Joe released her hand. He brushed past her and walked
to the window to look out toward the main street.

She followed him, stood behind him. "I tried to talk to
father but he wouldn't listen. He's—he's like a different
person."

"Like he was last night when he waited for me at the kitchen door?" Joe asked.

She stiffened. "I didn't know he was awake, Joe. When I looked in on him he was asleep. He—he only wanted to talk to you then, anyhow."

He turned to face her. "Myrt, you said you had to come here. Why?"

She bit her lips. "Do I have to answer that question, Joe? Don't you know why I came?"

"I wonder if I do. When I first met you on the hotel porch here in town, you told me Tyler had ridden off someplace. That wasn't true. You seemed to help me get away from your ranchhouse the other night, but you really tried to keep me in your room. When I did break away, a man who seemed to know where I was took a shot at me. Last night you were going to meet me at the back door, but your father also was at the back door with a gun in his hand. Is it any wonder I'm not sure why you came here?"

She was shaking her head furiously. "Joe, you're wrong about all those things. I thought Mr. Tyler was gone. Honestly I did. And I tried to keep you in my room because I knew you'd be safe if you stayed there. Last night—"

He shook his head. "Forget it, Myrt."

"But we've got to understand each other."

"I'm sure we do," Joe said dryly.

A flush of anger showed in her face. Joe stepped suddenly forward. He took her arm, walked her to the door and opened it, then stepped back. He said:

"Good-by, Myrt. I don't know what was in your mind when you came here a few minutes ago, and I don't think I want to know. You can do one thing for me, if you will. Tell your father to play it smart. Tell him to run—while he can."

She was furious, now, so furious, she suddenly was trembling. Her hand lashed out, striking him across the cheek.

Joe said, "Thanks, Myrt. At least, that was honest."

She whirled away, stepped through the door and started back toward the main street, walking stiffly erect.

CHAPTER XVI

THREE men came around the back corner of the bank. Another group followed them. More followed those. The crowd swelled until it numbered more than thirty, and most of the thirty were armed with rifles.

Joe Edison and Dan Gomez stood at the window, watching. The sun was starting down the western sky.

"Lindeman's done pretty well," Gomez said. "I didn't think he could stir up more than a dozen men."

A man broke through the crowd. He waved a handkerchief over his head, then came forward. It was Ben Lindeman. The group behind him stood waiting.

"I'll talk to him when he gets here," Joe said. "Do you think you could find the sheriff?"

"You're going to need me here."

"No, the most important thing, now, is to reach the sheriff and get our side of the story to him. Dan, while I'm talking to Lindeman, I want you to scoot back to the barn, climb your horse, and pull out. No one will take a shot at you now. Later on, you might not be able to make it."

Gomez was scowling. "I don't want to pull out."

"Someone has to, and it has to be someone the sheriff knows well, and who is in a position of authority so far as the Wagonwheel is concerned. No one else fits that bill."

"I may not be able to locate him."

"You've got to, Dan. We can hold out here while it's light. After it gets dark we may not be so lucky."

Gomez sighed. "All right, Joe. But the next time we run into a fight, it'll be your turn to ride for the sheriff."

"Agreed," Joe said grinning.

He still was watching through the window. Lindeman had reached the front gate and was opening it. Joe turned toward the door, glancing at Gomez. "Good luck, Dan," he called.

"Same to you," Dan said, starting toward the back door.

Joe went out the front entrance and stood on the porch, facing Lindeman, who had stopped halfway up the walk to the house. Joe said, "Hello, Ben. What do you want?"

"You know what I want," Lindeman answered curtly. "Marsh and Newbold. Turn 'em over to us, and you and your men can ride away."

Joe shook his head. "We don't want to ride away, Ben. We want to settle things, once and for all. We're holding Marsh and Newbold until the sheriff gets here. We'll surrender them to the sheriff."

"You'll surrender them to us," Lindeman snapped.

"No."

"Then we'll take them, Joe."

"Maybe. But why not talk in terms of the truth, Ben. You know the story Marsh and Newbold can tell. You know who it will hurt."

Lindeman took a deep breath. He shook his head. "Any lies Marsh and Newbold come up with, I can answer. But I don't think I'll have to. We're coming after them, Joe."

"Then come ahead," Joe said.

Lindeman wheeled away. He walked to the gate and looked back. "You could have had the Wagonwheel, all of it, if you'd played this my way," he said bitterly. "You're like your father, too stubborn for your own good."

"You didn't like my father, did you?"

"I hated him!" Lindeman turned away.

Joe shouted after him, "Was there really a raid on our place the night my mother and I left the basin?"

Lindeman didn't answer him, didn't look back. He marched toward the group waiting at the rear of the bank.

"You'd better come inside, Joe," Ellis called from the parlor. "They're liable to open up on us any minute now."

He walked back inside. "Did Gomez get away?"

"Yep."

"Call the others in the parlor," Joe said. He looked back through the door. Lindeman had reached the crowd behind the bank. In a few minutes now things were going to get interesting.

The men back of the bank started forward in a massed group, as though by the force of their number to awe those who were waiting in Doc Slater's. At the windows and at each side of the open front door the men of the Wagonwheel waited.

"Let them get halfway here," Joe ordered. "Then kick dust on their boots with your bullets. If they start charging this way, cut them down—but fire low. A bullet through the leg will stop a man."

Lindeman's crowd moved on. Joe waited until they had covered almost half the distance to the house, then he called out, "Now. Spray dust on 'em."

Rifle and sixgun shots blasted from the house, aimed at the ground in front of the oncoming crowd. Those in the front ranks came to an abrupt stop. Some split to the side and dropped to the ground. A few bullets ripped back at the house. Joe could hear Lindeman shouting orders. Several of his crowd started running forward in a crazy, zig-zag fashion.

"Cut 'em down!" Joe shouted. "Fire low."

More shots screamed from the house. One of the men running forward pitched to the ground. Another dropped and lay where he had fallen, rolling from side to side, mouthing loud cries of pain. A third man fell and lay still. Behind them, the crowd broke up and started scurrying back to the protection of the buildings lining the main street. Others followed and none of Lindeman's screaming orders could stop them. In a matter of another minute the crowd which had started so boldly toward Slater's had disappeared, excepting for four figures which lay helpless on the ground.

Doc Slater got his bag and walked to the front door. "At a time like this, I always work for both sides," he said with wry humor.

He went outside, hurried to where the nearest man was lying, knelt beside him for a moment tieing on an emergency bandage, then moved on to the next man. After he had had a look at all four he stood up and shouted:

116

"Hey, Joe. Send someone out here to help me carry them inside."

"I'll go," Charlie Ford offered.

He made four trips with the doctor, helping to carry the four wounded men inside. There, Doc Slater did a more adequate job on them. One of the men was Sam Russell, who had been at the meeting at Lindeman's. He had a bullet hole through the calf of his right leg. The pain didn't stop him from blustering about how the fight would end.

"We're not finished," he declared. "We're fed up to the neck with the Wagonwheel. There'll be twice as many men in the next crowd to rush you."

"Take him into the bedroom where we've got Marsh," Joe ordered. "Let him hear what Marsh has to say. Take the others in there too, so they also can get the story."

He walked to the window where Solo Cushing and Kim Ellis were standing.

"They've got men at the back of every building along the street," Kim said. "And by this time, we're probably covered from the rear, too."

Joe went out to the kitchen. The coffee pot was on the stove. He had a cup, and sat at the table drinking it. His muscles hadn't loosened up at all. He was nervous and unsure of what lay ahead. If Lindeman's crowd closed in after dark there would be more shooting, and this time it wouldn't end up with a few superficial flesh wounds. Men would die.

The afternoon hours passed slowly. The sun went down and over the basin crept a gray twilight, its faint shadows deepening with each passing minute. Joe paced the parlor with an increasing restlessness. He took a look into the bedroom where the wounded men had been made as comfortable as possible on the floor. Russell gave him a stony look.

"Didn't you believe what Marsh had to say?" Joe asked.

"All homesteaders are liars," Russell growled. "The truth isn't in them."

"You were willing enough to believe him when he said Tyler was responsible for the stampede, and when he accused me of the murder of Bill Hunnicutt."

117

"He was a free man then."

"A free man who had been paid to lie. But we've nailed the lie down, Russell. Why not admit it."

Russell closed his eyes. "Go away. Leave me alone."

Joe shrugged and walked back to the parlor. It had grown darker while he had been in talking to Russell. It was difficult, now, to see the backs of the buildings clearly. In another few minutes the shadows would be thick enough to cover the approach of Lindeman's men.

Back in the parlor, Kim Ellis joined him. "It looks like a fight, doesn't it?"

Joe nodded. "Once they break in, we're finished."

"They'll not break in," Ellis promised.

Joe wasn't so sure of that. Then he stiffened at the sound of a voice from outside. Lindeman's voice.

"Edison!" the man shouted. "Edison, this is your last chance. We want Marsh and Newbold."

"Come in an' get 'em," Joe answered.

He stepped to the front door, then ducked, and dropped to his knees. Shots from the yard screamed past him, one searing the skin of his arm. The attack was on.

Prone on the floor inside the door, he answered the flashing shots from the yard. Others were firing from the windows, and from the back door. The din was terrific, but through it he heard someone at the window cry out then drop backwards. He thought it was Solo Cushing. He crawled that way and reaching out through the darkness touched a man's shoulder and chest. He drew his hand back, sticky with blood.

"Doc," he shouted. "Doc Slater. Someone hurt here at the window."

"Man back here has been hit, too," Slater answered. "Get there as soon as I can."

Joe took Cushing's place at the window. He emptied his gun at the flashing shots from outside, then reloaded it and emptied it again. The firing slacked off, then seemed to grow stronger, then slacked off again. He lost all sense of the passing of time. Someone in one of the back rooms was screaming. Out in the yard, close to the house, Lindeman was shouting that "they" were finished inside and was telling his men to rush the doors.

Footsteps hammered across the porch. A blurred, indistinct figure reeled inside. Joe whipped a shot at the man and saw him go down. Another man was following him. Joe fired at the second man and heard the hammer of his gun click on an empty shell. Whipping back his arm, he hurled the gun at the man, then reared up and charged after it. His shoulders caught the man in the chest. They went down, rolled against the wall, then rolled the other way, slamming blows at each other. He had no idea who the man was, but apparently he must have dropped his gun when he fell, and Joe could be thankful for that.

The man broke free. Joe caught him again, climbed on top of him and started driving his fists into his face. Half a dozen good solid blows, and the man stopped struggling.

Joe rolled off and sat up, panting for breath. He realized abruptly that the firing had stopped and that outside someone was shouting his name. Not Lindeman, this time. It was someone else. A man with a higher, twangy voice. Sheriff Eli Wallace!

"Joe Edison," came the order. "Light a lamp. We're coming in."

"Who's coming in?" Joe called.

"Eli Wallace!"

Joe got unsteadily to his feet. The relief that swept over him made him weak. He fumbled his way to the table and felt the lamp which had been there. It still was there, but in pieces.

"Wait until I find a lamp that isn't broken," he called to those outside. "Or come on in anyhow. No man was ever more welcome."

Wallace looked tired. He glanced around the parlor. Five men were down, two lying motionless, the others not so seriously hurt. Ellis had a bullet scratch across his cheek and Handler had a wounded arm around which he had tied a bandage already bloody. Doc Slater was busy moving among the injured.

"When you finish in here, there are more to look at outside, Doc," the sheriff said.

"I'll get there quickly as I can," Slater answered.

Wallace then turned to Joe Edison. His eyes hardened and his voice was crisp. "In spite of what Dan Gomez told me, this is going to take a lot of explaining."

"Suppose we go into the bedroom," Joe answered. "We'll start by letting Marsh do the talking. After that we'll hear from Houston who can tell you what Newbold said before he died." He glanced at Ellis and said, "Kim, would you mind going after Houston. He said he'd be at the hotel."

"First I want to know what happened to Lindeman," Ellis said.

"If he was with the men outside, they faded away when we rode up," the sheriff said.

"Better take someone with you," Joe advised.

Ellis nodded. "I will."

Marsh had made up his mind on the story he would stick to. He would blame everything on Hunnicutt and Newbold, and he did, admitting only that Lindeman had hired him as well as them to move into the basin. Houston arrived from the hotel and added what he had come here to say. Word of this got around and Russ Vardon and Matt Brophy, both of whom had been slightly wounded during the battle, had some bitter things to say about Lindeman. Others would add to this later on, but not Ted Oberfelder who had died in the yard in front of Slater's. Two Wagonwheel riders also had been killed, and Solo Cushing and Will Rogell were wounded.

Dan Gomez asked the sheriff, "What about Ben Lindeman?"

"If he's not in town, I'll go after him tomorrow," Wallace said. "I've been almost two days in the saddle. I'm dead tired. I couldn't ride another mile if my life depended on it."

"And Henry Tyler?" Joe asked.

"He can go home tonight. I'll set him free soon as we get to the jail."

CHAPTER XVII

THEY walked that way a little while later. The sheriff unlocked the jail, and a disturbed and anxious Henry Tyler stepped out to join them. He had heard the sounds of the battle at Slater's without knowing what all the firing was about. In the sheriff's office they brought him up to date on what had happened.

Tyler scowled as Gomez named the Wagonwheel riders who had been killed and wounded, and he had some bitter things to say about Lindeman and those who had supported him.

"Most of the men who backed him up are damned sorry about it now," the sheriff suggested. "But at the time it looked like the thing to do. It looked like the Wagonwheel meant to ride rough-shod over the rest of the basin. Joe had killed one of the men who could give evidence against you, and had kidnapped the other."

"What else could he have done?" Tyler demanded. "When Hunnicutt and Marsh jumped him, he had to defend himself. And in some way or other, he had to break down Marsh's story."

"Who's criticizing Joe?" the sheriff asked.

This mollified Tyler's attitude. A rare grin crossed his face and he asked, "Sheriff, what do you really think of the new boss of the Wagonwheel?"

"The new boss?"

"Yep. I'm about due to retire. Do you figure Joe can step into my shoes?"

"From what I've seen of him, he's equal to it," the sheriff said.

"I might be with Dan Gomez and the rest of his crew to help me," Joe said.

"We'll be around," Gomez said.

There was an unmistakable friendliness in his voice.

What Tyler had said and the way Gomez and Wallace had taken it gave him the feeling of accomplishment, made him believe he had found a place for himself here in the Unitah basin—a place to live and work and grow into.

They rode toward the ranch an hour later, and after having received encouraging reports from Doc Slater on the conditions of those who had been wounded. It was a quiet, star-filled night, warm and comfortable. Joe rode beside Henry Tyler, Gomez and Ellis just behind them; the others were following.

At Rocky Gorge, where Joe's father had been killed, they pulled up, and Tyler, recalling what had happened here long ago, turned to face Joe Edison. "Maybe you wonder why I went to jail so easily, and why I gave you the responsibility of defending the Wagonwheel. Did it puzzle you at all?"

"Yes it did," Joe admitted.

Tyler was smiling. "I wanted you on the Wagonwheel. The best way to make a man love a place is to make him fight for it."

"I came here ready to," Joe admitted. "But I thought I'd be fighting you."

"You'd been steered wrong. Your mother never liked me. She didn't like the way your father and I split up our responsibilities. She was always after your father to assert himself and to insist on a greater control of the ranch. She didn't trust me. When we had our last quarrel—"

Joe leaned forward. "What did you fight about?"

"It's something I don't like to remember, Joe. Something I don't want to talk about. Maybe it never was any of my business. Your father didn't think it was."

"What was it?" Joe insisted.

Tyler gave him an uneasy look. "I've spent hours thinking about how to tell you, but there's no easy way to do it. You're not going to like what I've got to say, Joe."

"Say it anyhow."

"All right, Joe. It was like this: Your father and mother weren't too happy. Like a good many other married folks they quarreled a good deal. Your mother disliked and feared violence, and life was a little violent here

122

in the basin years ago. I suppose you could say she drove your father to it. At any rate, he got interested in another woman."

Joe's face had tightened. He thought he knew what was coming. He made an audible guess. "Lindeman's wife?"

"Yes, Mamie Lindeman," Tyler said. "I don't know how far it went, or what might have happened. They kept it pretty well hidden. I didn't even guess at it myself until your father talked to me about it one day."

"And that was what you quarreled about?"

"Yes. I told him things never could work out for him and Mamie. I advised him to break off with her. I told him if Lindeman found out—"

"And that's what happened?"

"Yes."

"Then you've known all along that it was Lindeman who killed him?"

"I felt sure it was, but never could prove it. Lindeman had no known motive for hating your father. If I had tried to push the case against him— Well, the ones who would have been hurt would be Mamie and your mother. So I let things ride. I did go after Ed Wylie, once, but I couldn't get him to talk."

"Lindeman wasn't after the Wagonwheel in those days?"

"No. He was satisfied with the ranch he had. He didn't want more land. But the last few years have been hard ones, and Lindeman has come to realize, lately, that he's getting old, and that maybe his place will slip away from him. Starting again, when you're past middle age, isn't easy. Others were in the same boat as he was, Vardon, Ordway, Russell, and a few more. He pulled them together in a loose association, and they looked at the Wagonwheel acres and decided they wanted them."

Joe stared bleakly ahead. So there it was—an explanation of the quarrel between his father and Henry Tyler, and the key to the reason for his father's death. But it was of the past and so far as he was concerned, would be left there.

When they got to the ranch they gathered in the parlor to hash over the fight at Slater's. Tyler was interested in the full story, and each man gave his impressions of the fight.

Kathy Rogers brought in coffee while they were talking. She passed out the cups then walked from one to another pouring the coffee. Tyler watched her with a twinkle in his eye. "It's nice, Joe, to have someone anticipate what you want," he mentioned. "I wasn't sure I had been smart in hiring Kathy, but I'm beginning to feel it was one of the wisest decisions I ever made. What do you think?"

"I'm glad you hired her," Joe said. He glanced at her as he spoke and noticed the flush of color which came into her face.

Kathy said nothing, and, after pouring the coffee, she went back into the kitchen.

Joe excused himself a few minutes later and followed her, hoping his departure from the room wasn't too obvious. She still was in the kitchen when he got there, and she didn't look too surprised when he came in.

"Did you hear much of what we said?" Joe asked.

"Some—not everything," Kathy said.

"It was Marsh, Hunnicutt and Newbold who started the stampede the night your husband was killed," Joe said. "Tyler and the men at the Wagonwheel had nothing to do with it."

"I was almost sure of that," Kathy said. "But what about you and the sheriff? Does the sheriff still want to arrest you?"

"No, that's been cleared up, too," Joe said.

"What about the man who killed your father?"

"I think it was Ben Lindeman who killed him. I don't know for sure, and may never know."

"But you don't think it was Henry Tyler."

"No."

"I'm glad, Joe. I like Mr. Tyler. He seems gruff and hard, but I think he's fair. Will you be staying here from now on?"

"Here, or at my father's old ranch. I'll fix it up, anyhow. Someday, I may want to move there. You know Kathy, I've an idea?"

"What?"

"How would you like to ride out there with me some afternoon? It's not too far from here."

"I'm busy most afternoons."

"But not every afternoon."

She was looking straight at him, her eyes thoughtful, steady. A momentary smile touched her lips, but was quickly gone. "If you still feel that way in a week, ask me again," she said slowly.

"Do you think I'll feel differently in a week?" Joe asked.

Again, just as in the parlor, her face flooded with color. She shook her head. "No, I don't think you'll feel differently, but I still think we should wait. I—I'd better go now. It's quite late."

"There isn't any law says I can't walk you to your cabin," Joe declared.

He crossed to where she was standing, took her arm, and they went outside. The stars were as clear as they had been earlier in the evening. The moon was high overhead. The night was still, in its silence broken only by the rustle of the wind in the air, and the faint murmur of voices from the ranchhouse parlor.

"I feel as though a month had passed since the night of the stampede," Joe said. "It's hard to realize it's been less than a week."

"Time is a funny thing," Kathy answered. "A minute can seem like an hour, or an hour like a minute."

Joe smiled. "We're back to what's normal again. From now on the minutes and hours will behave themselves."

They had come to the door of her cabin, and there they paused briefly. Joe was reluctant to leave her. He was searching his mind for something to say, some excuse for remaining. A scraping sound at the corner of the cabin caught his attention. He glanced that way, and instantly stiffened. A man was standing there, almost hidden in its shadows. A tall, thin, vaguely familiar figure. A name jumped into his mind. *Ben Lindeman!*

He spoke to Kathy, trying to keep his voice steady. "Good night, Kathy. See you in the morning."

She nodded. "Good night, Joe. I hope—"

The man in the shadows broke in on what she was

saying, uttering a crisp command. "Stand where you are, Joe! Don't move your hand an inch nearer your gun. An' you, ma'am, not a sound out of you."

Kathy caught her breath. She wrenched around to stare toward the man who had spoken. Joe, looking that way now, could see the drawn gun Ben Lindeman was holding. Joe said:

"Ben—"

"We'll not talk here," Lindeman answered. "We'll take a walk through the night—out past the corral. And just to make sure we have no trouble, unbuckle your gun belt, Joe, and drop it. *Now!*"

There was nothing else to do. Joe couldn't risk grabbing for his gun with Kathy standing so close to him. He fumbled with the buckle, released it then dropped the gun belt at his feet.

"That's the idea, Joe," Lindeman said. "Now start walking. Take the woman's arm. She goes with us."

Joe's head came up sharply. "Why? Leave Kathy out of it, Ben."

"Can't. She might start screaming the minute we moved away. We've got a quarter of a mile to cover."

A quarter of a mile. Lindeman must have left his horse off there somewhere in the darkness. He wanted to get near it before he used his gun. He knew that the sound of a gun would bring every man boiling out of the Wagonwheel ranchhouse. He meant to take no chances on his escape.

"Hurry up, Joe," Lindeman said sharply. "We might not have much time. Take Kathy's arm and start toward the corral. I'll follow you, tell you where to go."

"And when we get off there someplace, shoot me in the back as you did my father?" Joe asked.

Lindeman made an angry motion with his gun. "Your father had it coming to him. You, too. You're no better than he was."

"Mr. Lindeman," Kathy said abruptly, "my husband was trampled to death in the stampede your men started."

"They weren't my men," Lindeman said. "They were homesteaders. I don't know what lies you've heard, but—"

"He was trampled to death," Kathy said, her voice

126

shaking. "He didn't have a chance!" She stooped over, reaching suddenly for the gun belt Joe had dropped.

"Woman, don't do that!" Lindeman shouted. Don't make me—"

Kathy paid no attention to him. She reached for the holstered weapon.

Lindeman took a step toward her, then swung the gun which he had been aiming at Joe to cover Kathy. In another instant he might have fired at her, but Joe lunged forward. The gun swung toward Joe and exploded.

A numbing blow struck Joe in the side. He stumbled. His arms, stretching out, reached Lindeman, one knocking aside the gun before it could be fired a second time. The driving weight of his body then hit Lindeman and they went down.

Lindeman tried to scramble free. He had lost his gun when they fell. His fist slammed at Joe's head. He seemed all bone and muscle.

Joe was dizzy. He hung on, clinging to Lindeman's clothing, then he wrapped his legs around the man and struck back at him. He thought he heard men shouting, somewhere far away. Kathy's screams seemed almost in his ear. And Lindeman was cursing him hoarsely with every blow he struck. Pain grew from that numb spot in his side and spread throughout his body.

He could sense that Lindeman was getting away, but quite abruptly the man stopped fighting. Joe caught a picture of Kathy kneeling near his head, a sixgun in her hand. She brought the barrel down again against Lindeman's skull. Then she looked at the gun and dropped it.

"Remind me always to have you along when I get into a fight," Joe said foolishly.

He could hear men hurrying toward them from the ranchhouse. He managed to sit up.

"I didn't mean to hit him so hard," Kathy whispered.

Joe tried to grin. "Kathy, we're lucky people. He would have marched us off through the darkness to where he had his horse tied, then he would have shot us and raced away."

"It's really over now, isn't it?" Kathy said.

"The nightmare and the fighting? Yes."

"I'm glad."

Of course it wasn't all over, Joe realized. They still faced the hangover of bitterness which was one of the by-products of every community struggle. He had a wound in the side to recover from, too, but he didn't think it serious. The men from the ranchhouse were almost here, and would take over when they arrived. He glanced at Kathy. He was sure she didn't know of his wound.

"I'm going to be a little crippled up for a few days," he mentioned. "But in a week I'll be able to take that trip to the old ranchhouse. Don't forget it."

She stood up, instantly alarmed. "Joe?"

He shook his head, grinning. "Don't worry. Don't ever worry about anything."